The EVIL WITHIN

A POSSESSIONS NOVEL

The EVIL WITHIN

A POSSESSIONS NOVEL

NANCY HOLDER

razOr
bill

An Imprint of Penguin Group (USA) Inc.

The Evil Within

RAZORBILL

Published by the Penguin Group
Penguin Young Readers Group
345 Hudson Street, New York, New York 10014, U.S.A.
Penguin Group (USA) Inc., 375 Hudson Street, New York, New York 10014, U.S.A.
Penguin Group (Canada), 90 Eglinton Avenue East, Suite 700, Toronto,
Ontario, Canada M4P 2Y3 (a division of Pearson Penguin Canada Inc.)
Penguin Books Ltd, 80 Strand, London WC2R 0RL, England
Penguin Ireland, 25 St Stephen's Green, Dublin 2, Ireland (a division of Penguin Books Ltd)
Penguin Group (Australia), 250 Camberwell Road, Camberwell, Victoria 3124, Australia
(a division of Pearson Australia Group Pty Ltd)
Penguin Books India Pvt Ltd, 11 Community Centre,
Panchsheel Park, New Delhi – 110 017, India
Penguin Group (NZ), 67 Apollo Drive, Mairangi Bay, Auckland 1311, New Zealand
(a division of Pearson New Zealand Ltd)
Penguin Books (South Africa) (Pty) Ltd, 24 Sturdee Avenue, Rosebank,
Johannesburg 2196, South Africa

Penguin Books Ltd, Registered Offices: 80 Strand, London WC2R 0RL, England

10 9 8 7 6 5 4 3 2 1

Copyright © 2010 Nancy Holder
All rights reserved

Library of Congress Cataloging-in-Publication Data is available

Printed in the United States of America

Pain and separation kill time.

—Gackt, "Dybbuk"

DEDICATION:

For John Waterhouse, who had faith in me.

THE RETURN

Battle not with monsters
lest ye become a monster
and if you gaze into the abyss
the abyss gazes into you.

—Friedrich Nietzsche

True love is like ghosts, which everybody talks about and few
have seen.

— Francois De La
Rochefoucauld

ONE

December 24

possessions: me

(as if objects, things, mattered. but they're proof that i'm a real person, in the real world)

a suitcase of the clothes i humiliated myself with at Marlwood, including:

black top from Julie

army jacket from cousin Jason

left the too-cute parka from CJ there

threw out my ruined clothes. *except* Converse high-tops (caked with mud and ash, but i will never throw them out: *proof*)

was going to leave all the textbooks, but CJ saw my homework list so i packed:

American lit

Spanish II

trig book

six half-filled regulation Marlwood Academy notebooks
embossed with crest

ditto logo pencils

ditto logo coffee cup for CJ (present, she saw it in the book-
store before we left)

ditto logo highlighters—these guys are into serious logo
usage

Tibetan prayer beads, which i am wearing down w/ prayers,
not in Tibetan

Jason's St. Christopher medal (maybe it worked!)

Dad's socks. the ones i knitted. still too big. but still his.

the digital camera Jason gave me

the memory of seeing Kiyoko Yamato dead

haunted by: what happened

listening to: myself whimpering

mood: terrified

possessions: them

everything they want, whenever they want it. proof that
their version of the real world is a different planet:

designer clothes, made just for them, with fittings in Paris,
New York, and Tokyo

family jewels: pearls from the French Revolution; Daddy's
Skull and Bones fraternity ring

techie gear like the CIA

free passes no matter what they do, including killing Kiyoko
and trying to kill me

amnesia

God, i wish i could forget just as easily. maybe they buy
    drugs for that.

haunted by: are they still possessed?
listening to: Christmas carols and Hanukah songs and
    the roar of their private jets as they fly as far away from
    Marlwood as they can, as fast as they can, *because* they
    can.
mood: if you buy it, is it still a "mood"?

———

I HAD ESCAPED. I was alive.

So why was I still shaking so hard?

Shadows stretched across the setting sun as my stepmom, CJ, drove me to Fashion Valley Mall to meet up with
Heather Sanchez, my former best friend. The radio of our
old Subaru was playing "Here Comes Santa Claus," and trim,
freckly, strawberry blonde CJ was humming along. My heart
pounded; and I couldn't stop staring at the bone-colored
clouds that stretched across the December sky like the heavy
fog far away at Marlwood Academy. That fog, so thick I
couldn't see my own hands, much less anyone stalking me
and trying to kill me.

Four days ago, I almost died, I thought, and it seemed so unbelievable. But then, my life had become unbelievable. All of it.

Last October, I had ditched my entire messed-up life in San
Diego to escape to Marlwood Academy, located in the isolated

mountains of Northern California. I had gotten a late accep-
tance on full scholarship into the super-posh private boarding
school to the rich and famous, opened again this year after being
closed for over a hundred years. It should have stayed closed,
forever, but of course I didn't know that, then. I doubt anyone
knew, not even Mandy. Especially not Mandy.

They almost killed me, I thought. *Mandy Winters and her
psycho-packmates.*

With no idea of the thoughts barreling through my head,
CJ pulled off the freeway, wound around the perimeter of busy
Fashion Valley Mall, and rolled to an idling stop beside the
escalator that trundled up three stories to the multiplex and the
food court. The elaborate Christmas lights cast colored bubbles
on our windshield. Inside, I was screaming; outside, I tried to
smile.

"You'll have fun, Linz," she said, wrinkling her slightly
turned-up nose. She was cute, in an athletic gymnast kind of
way. She knew Heather and I were making up. I thanked her
and got out, and she waved and drove away.

I stepped onto the escalator, feeling dizzy, digging my fingers into the rubber rails. It was a warm night. Christmas Eve
in San Diego wasn't about snow-covered meadows and hushed
forests; it was about surf reports and guys in Santa hats and
board shorts. Silver bells, seashells. The mall was bustling with
last-minute shoppers and kids like me, who'd managed to get
permission for a few hours out of the house.

At the top, Heather paced on the other side of the patterned
cement breezeway. The mall-bouquet of cinnamon buns, scented
candles, lattes, and popcorn wafted between us. Heather had

cut her hair about two inches short and gelled it; she used to be all long curls and pastels, but now she was more urban grunge, like me. Heather 2.0. She had on black pencil-leg jeans, nicer than my raggedy, dark-blue flares, and a black baby-doll top with silver polka dots and cap sleeves—more polished than my charcoal-gray T-shirt over a black long-underwear shirt with the sleeves rolled halfway up my forearms. I had forsaken my high-tops for flip-flops. Heather was wearing eye makeup and lip gloss, while I was bare from my madwoman hair to unpolished toes.

"Hey," Heather said, seeing me as I approached. She didn't hug me, but she did hold up two tickets. "*Feliz Navidad, Fea.*" It felt good to hear her say it. "*Fea*" meant "ugly" in Spanish. That was her nickname for me. Not Linz, like everyone else. And not because I was actually ugly or anything; I just wasn't obsessed with looks . . . or hadn't been, back in the day. Everything had changed when I'd befriended Jane.

I wasn't sure if Heather really had forgiven me for treating her like slime last year. She was definitely on her guard. If we could just get past the weirdness, maybe we'd be us again. But how did you just forget and move on? I was hoping to learn.

"How you been?" I asked her.

She semi-smiled. "Well, you know."

I didn't know. She changed the subject by opening her backpack and showing me two cans of Diet Coke. She waggled her brows. I unfastened my little boho bag and displayed my Jolly Rancher yuletide stash, stolen from the brass sled-shaped candy dish on the coffee table in our foyer.

"Sweet," she said.

We still didn't hug, which was not us, if you skipped over my season of insanity and remembered us back when. I had been so mean to her. I desperately needed to get past that.

"I like your hair," I told her, still trying to connect. She had gone through some major changes since I had left. The Heather I knew had been more bouncy and out there. This Heather kept things in close.

"Remember when you said I looked like Miley Cyrus?" she asked. There was a hint of bitterness in her voice, and I knew why, because I did remember. I had said it to dis her, to make Jane laugh, back when I'd first started hanging out with Jane. Now I swallowed, and Heather snorted in response.

"I so totally *did*. I looked like such a dork."

"No," I protested, but she smacked my shoulder, the way she used to.

"If you hadn't said it, I would still look like Miley Cyrus. So I'm actually grateful."

"You never actually—"

"They wouldn't have laughed if it wasn't true," she said, clearly remembering, as I did, when Jane and everyone else had cracked up after my comment in the cafeteria, so long ago now it seemed. I couldn't look at her. "Anyway," she went on, "it happened a long time ago. Before boarding school." She blinked at me. "What is *that* like?"

Oh, God, I want to tell you, I thought; but instead I said, "Wackier than you can imagine."

"I can't wait to hear about it," she said. "After the movie."

"Okay." I felt a little more hopeful, even though I knew the movie was a barrier as well as an icebreaker. In the old days, nothing would have stopped us from talking for hours. A movie saved us from all that. And we still didn't hug as we sailed inside and handed over our tickets. Then we half-ran into our auditorium and I finally smiled because that was how we used to be when we were best friends—rushing and running.

Four days ago, I ran for my life, I thought. *I ran even faster than this.*

As the screen loomed before us, our eyes adjusted to the light, and we turned and studied the banked rows of chairs. There were maybe twenty people in the theater.

Then I spotted Riley, and I froze.

"Oh . . . kay," Heather whispered, and she half-turned to leave, casting me a look that said, *We're gone, if you want*. By then, Riley had seen us, and he half-rose from his seat. Grossmont blue-and-gold letter jacket, black T-shirt, ripped jeans. My favorite combination on him.

Riley. Riley, my cliché ex-crush—captain of the football team, homecoming king, super-nice, tender, lying, creepy jerk. My ribs squeezed hard as he got up and started loping down the stairs toward us, as if he couldn't wait to grind me into dust all over again. He reached us in less than ten seconds.

"Hey," he said, blinking his long, chick-magnet lashes at me. "Lindsay. You look good."

In all my post-breakup crying sessions, I had made a million silent bargains with the universe, if only I could see regret on the sharply sculpted face of the guy who had broken my heart. And in the darkness of the theater, I saw that it was *there*.

I nodded at him. My throat was tight and my lips were

prickling. He smelled like shampoo and Gummi Bears. I remembered that mixture very well.

"Do you . . . want to sit together?" he asked. I wondered how he had the courage to ask, and I wished I was like that. Brave. A bit audacious.

You are, I reminded myself. *You are so far past that it's not even funny.*

Heather looked at me, and I didn't look at anyone. Riley took silence for agreement, turned, and led the way back to his otherwise empty row. Dead center. I don't know how it happened but Heather sat down between us, and I was so grateful my toes curled against the rubbery edges of my flip-flops.

"This movie is supposed to really suck." Heather pulled our DC's from her bag and I got out the Jolly Rancher assortment from mine, wrapped baubles of sugary mania. We moved in rapid unison, like soldiers on a special mission unpacking our weapons.

"God, I hope so," Riley said, and I smiled, faintly. I didn't ask him why he wasn't with Jane or any of his jock friends. Why he was alone. He was one of the most popular boys in school. I suddenly got the suspicion that Heather had set up this whole running-into-my-ex-boyfriend-accidentally thing. Maybe Riley wanted to get back together. Maybe Heather figured I would want that under my Christmas tree.

I felt some butterflies, and my cheeks warmed up—plus a few other things—at the exact same time that Troy Minear's face blossomed in my mind. Troy was not just a crush. Troy was something more, far more. And he was still missing in the woods around Marlwood. And so far, there was nothing I could to do help find him.

My heartbeat picked up and I started to fuzz out. Oh no, was this a panic attack? Dr. Yaeger, my therapist, had explained about the symptoms of my post-traumatic stress disorder, which he believed had been caused by the death of my mother, and triggered by "the stresses of adolescence." He had *no* idea. There was stress, there was massive betrayal followed by heartbreaking loss, oh yeah, and then there was nearly getting *killed*.

You are safe, you are safe, you are safe. You will NEVER go back to Marlwood. It will all seem like a bad dream, I told myself. *And the searchers will find Troy. He will be okay, too.*

Zombielike, I sat through the commercials and the previews, just trying to breathe calmly while Heather texted a bit before she put away her phone. Riley offered us some popcorn and Heather paid him back with sour apple, his favorite. I didn't move, didn't talk to them. I thought about asking Heather if we could leave. But our friendship was already on shaky ground, and so I kept taking slow, deep breaths to ease myself through my freak-out. *Be normal,* I silently commanded myself.

The movie started. We settled in. On the screen, lowering himself down a chimney with a winch, the jolly old psychopath in the Santa suit was filling the Christmas stockings as the little girl's disbelieving father crept up on him. Without warning, Santa grabbed a fireplace poker, shrieked like a ninja, and stabbed the man through the heart. Blood gushed everywhere; as the man died in agony, Santa showed him the letter his daughter had written: *Dear Santa, please make Daddy stop hurting me.*

"Yeah, that's the kind of Christmas cheer we're talkin' about," Heather said, and Riley snickered. Then he snaked his arm around her shoulders and tousled my hair. I tossed my head to show him that I was not about to be won back easily, if at all. I started to laugh along with them . . . when all of a sudden, an intense rush of grief and horror gushed through the center of my being like icy mud. Troy was *missing*.

I stared at the fire poker on the screen; something about it was familiar. A strange buzzing vibrated against my ears and I blinked hard and bit my lower lip between my teeth, tasting copper, or was it something citrusy, acidic . . . and then clouds spilled across the screen, moving from right to left, superimposing themselves over the movie. I gripped the armrests as I glanced at Heather and Riley, who were joking about Santa's sack, now filled with Daddy's corpse. But what I saw was Searle Lake, back at Marlwood, with its shoreline of rushes and large boulders, and the stretch of loamy earth where fellow sophomore Kiyoko Yamato's body had washed up.

Where I had discovered her. Less than three weeks ago. Her hair had been so frozen that it broke off when they moved her.

Above the movie-lake loomed a huge, heavy moon, and grainy, gray clouds. The clouds riveted my attention; I couldn't stop staring at them, and my heart pounded. Heather dug into Riley's popcorn. Riley slurped his theater fountain drink.

The clouds blossomed in strange, muted colors—sepia, shades of gray, and amber, growing and spreading across the screen; and in the next second, they flooded over the surface, completely blotting out the movie.

"Attaboy, Rudolph," Heather said, and Riley groaned.

It's all right, I told myself. *The clouds are not really there.*

The buzzing in my ears got louder. Chills like fingertips skittered across my shoulder blades and ran down my spine. I tried to look away, or close my eyes, as I began to realize that the clouds weren't clouds at all. What I was seeing were billows of smoke.

"You put too much butter on this stuff," Heather grumbled at Riley.

"No such thing," Riley shot back.

"Guys?" I murmured. Now I smelled the smoke, and something else I couldn't place, like oil, something for camping. It was so strong my eyes watered.

"*Guys?*" I said again. I heard the shrillness in my voice.

"What?" Heather asked.

Heat rose around me, like a bad sunburn—then hotter, too hot. Flames shot to the ceiling of the theater; I saw through them, yellow, red, and orange, crackling around me, and the black smoke, pouring into my lungs. I started choking. My hands began to blister; my face—

"Oh my God, the door is locked!" the scream tore through my parched throat as I dizzily tried to stand, waving smoke from my face. Oh God. I was suffocating. "We're going to die!"

TWO

COUGHING AND SCREAMING, I bolted, falling over Heather's legs as she grabbed hold of me. Diet Coke and Jolly Ranchers flew everywhere as I seized her wrists, panicking.

"Fire, there's a fire!" I shrieked. "We have to get out of here!"

"God, calm down!" Heather shouted into my face. She dug her fingers into me as I tried to crawl over her. "What the hell is wrong with you?"

As abruptly as it had happened, it was over. The fire was gone . . . and I was left with no way to explain. As people hooted and two ushers with flashlights darted up the stairs, I clutched my elbows and blinked back tears. The bright yellow beams blazed into my eyes from two directions, and a voice said, "Please come with us. You too."

Heather jerked, completely freaked. "*I* didn't do anything." The light didn't get any dimmer, so she grabbed her purse, slipping on hard candy and soda, and followed them down the aisle.

I trailed after, mutely, too mortified to look back over my shoulder at Riley. The ushers led us down the stairs like prisoners while the other moviegoers applauded and laughed—this was more entertaining than the movie—and out the auditorium into the foyer.

A man in a suit glowered down at me—I'm only five-two—while Heather took two steps away from me. My knees were sopping wet.

"I didn't do anything," Heather said again, shaking her newly chopped head. "I didn't know she was going to do that."

The ushers and the man in the suit—his name tag announced him as R. TELLENHEUSEN, MANAGER—stared stonily at me, as if they were waiting for me to explain myself. How could I? What could I possibly say? I shuffled my feet. There was a Jolly Rancher smashed against the sole of my right flip-flop.

"Do you know that there's a law against shouting 'fire' in a public theater?" Mr. Tellenheusen asked me. "Shall I call the police?"

Shaking my head, which began to throb, I felt like I was going to throw up. Then I let his stern voice and Heather's protests rush over me as we were taken to the exit and booted out the airlock, into the warm night and canned Christmas carols blaring too merry and bright.

Riley hadn't come out of the theater. Somehow he'd been granted a reprieve, not been associated with me and my OOC behavior. What was he thinking now? Would he tell Jane?

"Why did you do that?" Heather's voice was shrill; she was smoothing back her hair, over and over, staring at me as if she had never seen such a freak in her life.

I swallowed. "I'm sorry."

"Sorry? *God*. Are you having another breakdown?"

She didn't sound sympathetic. She was pissed off and embarrassed, and . . . *afraid*. She was afraid of me.

"No," I said quickly. But was that it? Should I say that it was?

"No," I said again. "I thought . . . I was trying to be funny." If she was still my best friend, she'd know that I was lying. I didn't want her to be afraid of me; I wanted to let her know how terribly afraid *I* was. But from the way she was looking at me, I knew it wasn't going to happen. Her mouth dropped and her eyes narrowed, as if she couldn't believe what a jerk I was.

The Christmas music was past ironic. I thought about taking it back, but honestly, it had been so left field . . . couldn't she see that there was no way I meant it to be a joke?

"Heather . . ." I took a deep breath. "Heather, listen . . ."

She waited.

"I fell asleep in the theater. I was having a nightmare."

She made a show of widening her eyes. "Oh my God! Jane taught you how to lie better than that."

"No—"

"I was supposed to drive home. Come on." She turned to go without even checking to see if I was following her. Without another word, she took the breezeway to the parking structure.

Her silver Corolla was on the topmost level, and I climbed in. I felt sick, humiliated. My face was hot. She punched in Tori Amos and the singer's goth-drama voice reverberated off the windshield as she backed out of the space and drove too quickly toward the exit. Heather and I had never listened to Tori Amos together in our lives. Gripping the armrest, I heard my heart beating too fast as we merged onto the 8. The terrifying clouds gathered above the freeway, smothering the moon. Not super-natural smoke, just stupid clouds, real ones this time.

"Did you do it to get attention?" she finally asked. "Because Riley was there?"

When I was with Jane, we did insane things to get attention. We demanded it. Sometimes Jane would count to three and then we would shriek at the top of our lungs. It had seemed so funny, because it was *us* doing it. We all got makeovers at Macy's, and then no one bought anything; we just skipped away in hysterics. We were awful. We were bitches. I didn't care. I was with Jane.

Heather never was with Jane, never could be; and maybe that was why I had been mean to her when Jane wanted me to be. When it first started happening, Heather would text me, or call me, and say, "This isn't you. I know it's not."

But she didn't know me anymore.

I shook my head again, unable to speak. Anything I said would just sound like more craziness. More attention-getting.

We got home fast; it was Christmas Eve, and the streets were clearing.

Heather jerked to a stop at the curb in front of my house. She didn't say a word.

"I want . . . " I began, but I knew what that must sound like to her. Me, wanting. Like Jane, always wanting. Like Mandy and nearly every other girl at Marlwood. Endlessly needing more—so much so that they were willing to conspire with the dead to get it.

"Listen," I said, but that was about me again, me talking. So I reached over and touched her hand. "I'm sorry."

Her face broke, and her eyes welled. She exhaled, took another breath and started to say something. I swallowed hard, waiting; I could tell she was making a decision.

"You aren't the old Lindsay I used to know," she said, giving her head a shake. I was stabbed through the heart: she was breaking off our friendship.

"I am sorry," I insisted.

"I have to go." She sounded defeated; she'd had hopes for our friendship, too, and she was letting go of them. Of *us*.

I got out and watched her Corolla peel away. Panic rose inside me, as if she was taking my last chance of a normal life away with her. I had blown it. Badly.

I opened the front door to darkness and immediately flicked on the lights in the foyer. There was the candy dish I had raided for the movie, half-empty now. Trudging down the hall, I made it to the family room and turned on those lights, too. The house was deserted; there was a note on the breakfast bar:

Hi Baby,
Gone to see Santa. Back by ten. Hope the movie was fun!
Love,
Daddy

With my bag still over my shoulder, I crossed to the sliding glass door that led to the yard, stepped outside and turned on the porch light. I saw Casals, our tortoiseshell cat, named for the famous cellist Pablo Casals. He was slinking through the grass, stalking something, in a trajectory toward our black-bottom pool.

Something white glittered on the water.

No, I silently begged. *Please, no.*

I thought it was over. I thought I was free.

I thought she was gone.

A deep, dark, soul-piercing iciness washed over my entire body, as if someone had just dropped me into the same frozen lake where Kiyoko Yamato had died; and I shuddered, hard. I staggered to the left, bumping one of our aluminum chaise lounges with my leg. It made a scraping noise that seemed to echo in my head, as if it were a far distance away, as if I weren't standing right beside it.

I lurched forward and confirmed the whiteness floating on the water. I gasped and went deadly still; and then I peered over the edge of the pool.

I saw her. White oval, hollows in her cheeks, black, eyeless sockets. More a skull than a face.

"Celia," I croaked. Celia Reaves, who had died in a fire at Marlwood in 1889. The ghost who had possessed me at Marlwood, and who possessed me still. The reflection was proof. I could actually *feel* her shifting restlessly inside me, like layers of ice coating my bones, cracking and refreezing as I trembled. Just as I had experienced the fire that had killed her.

"*I'm so sorry, Lindsay,*" she said, through my voice but not quite my voice, speaking aloud, through me. I couldn't feel my lips moving, but the sound was definitely coming out of my mouth.

"What have you done to me?" I demanded, bursting into tears.

Her face rippled, as if someone had dropped something into the pool. "*I thought I could leave you in peace.*"

"Why—why can't you?" I was trying, very hard, not to scream.

Moonbeams highlighted the black water as Casals slunk back and forth against my ankles like a caressing, comforting hand. Sparkles danced beneath Celia's hollow eyes. Were they tears?

"*Because we have to go back,*" she said. "*To Marlwood.*"

Then my cell phone rang. I plunged my hand into my bag, too panicky to remember where I'd stashed it. Sucking in my breath, I tipped my bag upside down; my wallet and pens and keys and wadded up receipts and notes and sticks of gum tumbled to the ground and where the hell was my phone—

"Heather?" I cried, as I grabbed it and I accepted the call. "I'm so sorry—"

"No," said a low, raspy voice. "It's me, Lindsay. Troy."

Troy. Who had gone missing after that horrible night. Lost, in the woods, in the snow. I sank to the ground.

"Julie gave me your new number. She said you can't find your old cell and—"

"Oh, God, oh my God," I yelled, gripping the phone with both hands. "Where are you?"

"I'm okay. Okay *now*," he said. "I've been in the hospital. I had a concussion. They found me in the woods. By the lake."

"A *concussion*?"

"I don't remember what happened. I guess I fell."

"Fell," I echoed.

"Yeah, they said I was lucky. I could've died. It was so cold that night."

I closed my eyes. I tried to swallow but my throat was closed. I didn't realize until that moment that I thought he *had* died.

"Listen, we're staying in La Jolla. I want to see you," he went on.

I could barely keep myself from shrieking with joy. *He was in San Diego*. La Jolla was only a forty-minute drive from my house.

"Yes," I managed.

"Is tomorrow okay? I know it's Christmas, but—"

"Yes." I wanted him here. Now. "It's okay." More than okay.

"Great." His voice was warm. He was *alive*. "So. Merry Christmas, Lindsay."

We disconnected and I was so happy that for a moment I forgot about the dead girl inside me, whose white face floated on our swimming pool. I forgot I had lost my mind in the movie theater, and that I was afraid for my life.

"*He didn't fall,*" Celia said, her voice echoing inside my head as I collected all the things I had dumped out of my purse. "*He was pushed.*"

Shaking, I got to my feet; moving stiff-legged, I walked closer to the edge of the pool and looked down. Her white face, her black, eyeless sockets, her mouth an endless scream. Bubbles popped on the surface of the water, and I stiffened. Was she coming *out*?

More bubbles dotted the surface, like something rising from somewhere very deep. Very cold. As they churned, I screamed and raced back into the house. I slammed the sliding glass door shut, turned on every light, and huddled on the couch with my knees beneath my chin, trembling, until everyone came back from visiting Santa. *Hah,* I thought. *I wasn't going to get what I wanted this year.*

"I have to go back," I said to myself, over and over again, making it real, forcing myself to accept it. If I wanted this over, if I wanted to live a normal life—if I wanted to stay alive—I had to go back.

THREE

I DIDN'T SLEEP all night. I sat in my bed, breathing too hard, avoiding the dresser mirror. And the bathroom mirror. And any shiny object in our house that might cast a reflection. I didn't want to see Celia. I didn't know how the possession worked—if that cold feeling on the back of my neck meant she was taking me over, or if she was somehow inside me all the time. I didn't know if there were other times she possessed me that I was unaware of. I wondered if other people who got labeled as crazy were actually possessed, like back in the Middle Ages—possessed by ghosts.

The next day I went through the motions of Christmas—the presents, the dinner—forcing myself to stay calm, even though I was becoming more and more afraid that I would do or say something crazy, the way I had in the theater. No one seemed to notice how exhausted and edgy I was. Over the summer, I had knitted CJ and my father matching Aran sweaters—nubby Aran wool, one very petite for CJ, and the other long, with long arms, for my gangly dad—and it struck me how much I used to love to knit, and how I never did it anymore. My redheaded seven-year-old stepbrother Sam was over the moon with the vast additions to his Lego empire. My parents heaved a sigh of relief that Tom, who was nine, very tall, very thin, was content with more games for his Wii—they had been afraid he was going to ask Santa for a new game system.

They're just things, I wanted to tell them. *Things won't keep the monsters away.*

Exactly at seven, just as we'd cleared dinner, Troy pulled up in his vintage T-bird. My Dad and CJ had given permission for him to come over; maybe they sensed that my reunion with Heather had not gone very well, and they wanted me to have someone my own age to spend Christmas with.

He must have driven the car down from Lakewood, his private boys' prep school across the lake from my all-girl school, and it was clean and shiny, like a Christmas ornament; my dad couldn't keep away from it. CJ was startled by how great-looking Troy was, turning to me when Troy was out of the room, raising her brows and fluttering her lashes. He was tall, with soft, chestnut-brown hair that curled around his ears, and the darkest, deepest blue eyes I had ever seen. He wore a navy blue hoodie, a San Diego Padres T-shirt, and jeans, but even in his regular-person clothes there was something about him, some kind of polish, that revealed just how wealthy he was.

"So you live in La Jolla," CJ said.

"We have a house there," Troy replied, and I wondered if CJ understood what he was really saying. How many months out of the year did you have to stay in a house to qualify as "living" in it? How many houses did the Minears own?

"Look at the sweaters Lindsay made for us," she added, posing a little.

"Nice," Troy said sincerely. "My mom knits."

I wasn't sure if I liked having the same hobby as his mother, but he was so charming when he said it that I decided I didn't care. I'd thought I would be embarrassed when he saw our little house, but he seemed so happy to see me that I let it go.

"So, that T-bird," my dad piped up, leaning his elbows on the fake wood counter of our breakfast bar. The overhead lights gleamed on his semi-bald head. Troy's brown hair was thick and shiny. "Sixty-eight?"

"Yup," Troy said.

"Floating Caliper brakes?"

Troy nodded, and my dad whistled. "*And* a 390 Special V-8," Troy added.

"Oh, *man*." My dad groaned and looked at CJ and me. "Sixty-eight was the last year for the 390."

"Dang," I said.

"They were right to stop using it," Troy said. "My car's really heavy. My gas mileage is a joke."

My dad's face softened, as if he were looking at a younger version of himself. Or at his younger self's dreams, maybe. "I had big plans for a '70 Mustang. Got too busy, though."

Too busy taking care of my mom. I remembered when he'd had the Mustang towed home and he had begun work on it. A year into her illness, he'd sold it to some guy who knew our next-door neighbors, the Hansens.

"Well, I'm sure you two want to catch up," CJ said, giving

my dad a pat. He got the hint and they headed for the living room.

I took Troy to the backyard for some privacy. We bounded into the darkness, me avoiding the pool, and threw our arms around each other. We kissed, hard, and it was like body surfing at high tide—shocking and wonderful, thrilling, a little scary. My knees gave way but he held me so tightly he wouldn't have been able to tell. He was alive. And he was here. I rode the waves of joy and relief, pressing myself against him. We clung to each other, fingers moving tentatively, exploring, believing. I wanted to kiss him for years.

"Oh, Troy," I said, and then I was sobbing, hard, and he reached around the back of my head and eased my face against his chest. He leaned his chin on the crown of my head and stroked my hair, soothing me, letting me finally get it out. I'd had no one to talk to, no one to hold me while I cried until I couldn't cry anymore.

Finally, I shuddered against his chest, and pulled away slightly. He tipped back my head and studied my face.

"Sorry," I gritted. "I actually *am* glad to see you."

"I've had nightmares, too," he said, smiling sadly.

I widened my swollen eyes. "You *have*?"

He nodded. "I keep seeing Kiyoko. The way we found her." He had found me wandering in my pajamas on the shore; I had lost time, and I still wondered if I had seen Kiyoko die.

He took my hand and led me to the chaise lounge beside the pool. I glanced in, but Celia wasn't there. Maybe she was gone. Or just dormant, like a volcano. Maybe I would survive all this—at least it was a good sign that my snarky side seemed to be rising from the dead.

"You must be a wreck," he said, as we both sat down. "First semester at boarding school, and seeing her like that . . . " He trailed off. "Julie said you were going through some tough times."

From the way he said it, I was pretty sure he knew I'd had a nervous breakdown before I'd gone to Marlwood. But I wasn't positive, so I didn't respond, just let the warmth of his body heat seep into my fear. He began playing with my fingers, pushing against the tips of them with the tips of his, and I smiled a little.

"Your dad's a car freak. Like me."

"Cars are cars," I retorted.

"Not my T-bird." He pushed harder on my fingers. "You should know. You've ridden in it." The way he said it sounded very sexy. A bunch of us had crammed into his car after Julie hurt herself during one of Mandy Winters' stupid pranks. Troy had offered to get us back to our dorm in the same car.

I was *not* going to think about Mandy tonight.

"Maybe I was a little distracted," I allowed.

"You need to give it another shot." He blinked, and grinned. "Drive back with me to Marlwood."

Whoa. I couldn't even breathe now.

"We deserve it," he said, "after what we've been through." He leaned toward me and raised his brows. His smile was sweet, cute.

The porch light flicked on and the sliding glass door opened. My dad poked out his head. "Hey, kids, we're going to play Monopoly. Want to join us?"

I knew that was my dad's subtle way of asking me to be with the family again. Troy moved his shoulders *what the heck?* and nodded.

"I'm in," Troy said.

"Sure," I called to my father. Then to Troy, I said, "My parents would probably say no." To driving back to Marlwood with him, I meant.

"We have some time to convince them," Troy replied, smiling his model-charming smile.

TROY CAME OVER the next day, and he made himself at home. Everyone liked him. It was as if he'd been around for a long time, as if he had absorbed our daily routine by osmosis— he got CJ a cup of coffee and he watched cartoons with my little stepbrothers. CJ told him a little bit about her divorce—things I'd never heard—and my dad yakked on about his computer engineering job until I got embarrassed by his obsessiveness and tried to change the subject. But Troy wanted to hear more, as if Java applets were his life.

Everyone started teasing me as soon as he left. Tom started doing the K-I-S-S-I-N-G chant and Sam mimicked him, screeching with demonic glee because at seven, you think anything that rhymes and makes your stepsister blush is hysterical. My father kept calling Troy "Linz's beau." CJ told me Troy had great manners.

The day after that, Troy came much earlier, bearing late Christmas gifts for us—some homemade peanut brittle and the San Diego version of Monopoly. When we were alone, he handed me a beautiful card of a full moon trimming the waves of the ocean with silver.

Dear Lindsay,

A donation has been made in your honor to the Surfrider Foundation.

"Thanks," I said. "This is amazing. No one's ever done anything like that for me."

"And . . ." He reached into his pocket and handed me a small box. Jewelry, I knew. I opened it. It was a black crocheted silk necklace decorated with a silver crescent moon.

"Oh, it's so beautiful," I murmured. My cheeks went hot. Jewelry from a guy was so special and personal. Jewelry from Troy was beyond anything I had ever received. I hadn't bought him anything. I would make it up to him some other way.

"I hope it's not too goth," he said.

"No, I love it." And I did. It was different, kind of edgy. I wondered if he had picked it out because the crocheted silk reminded him of my knitting.

"Let me put it on you. Lift your hair."

I put the silk chain up to my neck, then lowered my head and closed my eyes as he fastened the clasp. His fingertips lingered on the nape of my neck and then he bent down and kissed me there, once; and then he kissed my earlobe.

"It looks good on you," he said. "Really good. Merry Christmas, Lindsay."

"Merry Christmas, Troy." And I kissed him to show him that I meant it.

By ten at night, my parents had agreed to let us drive back to school together. They were actually relieved; our Subaru was in need of major repairs and CJ's old pre-marriage Camry was in even worse shape. They told me that they trusted Troy and me. It would take eight to ten hours straight to drive depending on traffic, then at least two more up the winding road to my school. Alone all that time . . . were they nuts?

I was amazed, but Troy wasn't. "Parents like me," he said. He wasn't bragging or being devious. It was a statement of fact. Some people have charisma like that. Jane had it. Mandy Winters had it too.

I promised myself I wasn't going to think about Mandy anymore for the rest of the break. I touched my necklace to remind myself that Troy had spent Christmas with me, not her. She was his ex. I was his current . . . or so I hoped.

The fourth day after Christmas, my true love's family left to spend New Year's in Cabo San Lucas, down in Mexico, and I was by myself with my family again, and my loneliness . . . and Celia.

It was almost as if as soon as Troy was gone, Celia got back to the business of making my life miserable. The next eight nights were filled with a mind-crushing mash-up of her nightmares and my own night terrors: I was sharing the bad dreams of a ghost. And I would keep sharing them unless I went to Marlwood, and got rid of her. How, I didn't know. Yet. In these nightmares it was never clear what I had to do exactly in order to help Celia, to free her, but I knew I had to put her to rest somehow. As soon as I figured it out, I'd make sure my Marlwood friends were safe, too; and then leave again, and never go back to Marlwood, ever. That was the promise I made to myself, to stop from completely losing my mind.

I talked to Julie on my cell a couple of times, and texted a few more. It was obvious that she didn't remember a thing about the night I had almost died. She thought all the bruises and scratches she'd found on her arms and legs the morning after were from getting way too drunk—a blackout binge she had no memory of. In her fifteen-year-old world, blackout drinking should have been cause for significantly more alarm than I heard in her voice. Marlwood had changed her, too, and not for the better.

I was so sleep-deprived by the end of vacation that I slogged through each hour as if I were dragging Celia's body around, like she was part of the jumble of things I was cramming into my luggage. I cried silently as I packed, holding back a confession as my stepmother got another suitcase out of the garage to hold all my new loot. *It was crazy there. It was evil*, I wanted to tell her. *I tried to stop it, but I failed.*

Heather didn't call. Neither did Riley.

I wanted to hate Celia for possessing me. But I had pulled her into myself by accident, on my very first day at Marlwood; and now that she was here, she couldn't leave, not until she was at peace. Not until we had returned to Marlwood, and put her to rest.

On the last evening of break, I finished packing all my Christmas clothes, pretending to my family that I couldn't wait to leave. But watching the clock the next morning, I felt like a condemned criminal, counting off the minutes and seconds until it was seven thirty, and time to go. I played with my crescent moon as if it were a magic amulet that could ward off evil. It was a reminder that good things could happen.

"Here's something for the road," my big, tall dad said, slipping about six twenty-dollar bills into my sweaty palm as he kissed my cheek. I kissed him back. With a sharp pang, I remembered when I was little and I used to give him "butterfly" kisses on his cheeks with my eyelashes. I wanted to be his little girl again, let him fight the monsters for me.

"We're going to miss you so much," CJ said, sweetly wearing her sweater, her blonde hair pulled up and held in place with the snowman clay-on-hair-clip Tom had made for her in art. Her delicate, gentle fingers brushed curlicues of hair off my forehead. I knew she was conflicted about the way I was dressed. I had on my usual tattered jeans combined with the new soft-as-sin black cashmere sweater she'd given me for Christmas. And my new Doc Martens.

Troy was wearing his brown bomber jacket, a plain white T-shirt, jeans, and Cons. I still couldn't figure out what it was that proclaimed that he was a rich kid. Was it his subtly perfect haircut? My dad had wanted one of those vacuum-haircutters he'd seen in an infomercial. My stepmom had refused to let him bring one in the house. Go, CJ.

"Are you going to get married?" Sam asked Troy.

"Not today," Troy said easily.

"You shouldn't marry her. She farts in the car," Tom added helpfully.

"Boys," CJ warned them while I silently rolled my eyes. It would take more than fart jokes to embarrass me.

Troy just smiled as my dad passed him my cheap chocolate-brown-and-turquoise polka dotted suitcases and equally cheesy matching backpack, tagged for delivery to my dorm.

My luggage was years out of date. My mom's medical bills still haunted us, too.

In the immaculate trunk of the T-bird, Troy's single suitcase was leather the color of a good tan, no brand name anywhere, definitely not from Target like mine was. It featured a discrete brass plate with TAM engraved in bold capital letters. Troy's last name was Minear. I didn't know what the A stood for. Maybe the clue that revealed his wealth was his perfect, short fingernails or the simple ID bracelet he wore on his left wrist. It said TAM, too. Troy was heavily personalized.

"Here's a couple six-packs of sodas and some snacks," CJ said, hefting me a soft picnic container. She kissed my cheek. "Let us know you got there okay."

"I will." I kissed her back, closing my eyes and remembering my mom. I'd gotten used to this cognitive dissonance—missing my mom while at the same time being glad for the presence of CJ in my life. It was a minor version of my other seismic conflict—spending the day with Troy (yay!), going back to Marlwood (oh God, *why?*).

"Drive safe," my dad said to Prince Charming. They shook hands. Troy was taller than my father.

We climbed in. I had hoped Heather would show up at the last minute, but apparently she and I really were done. She'd probably texted everyone she knew that Lindsay Cavanaugh was still as insane as ever. Maybe after I left Marlwood for good, I could bypass the San Diego experience by living with my Aunt Doreen in Hick-Sticks, Georgia. That's what we called it, anyway. She loved bingo night at the Catholic church. I could learn to love bingo, too.

With me beside him, Troy backed his T-bird out of our grease-stained driveway. I waved again at my family, my throat tight as they smiled and waved back, the two boys hopping up and down and wiggling their butts. *I might die*, I told them in my mind. *I might never see you again.*

"Your family's nice," Troy said, waving too as we drove away and my little green house on the corner got smaller and smaller.

"Thanks. You should unroll your window. I feel an awesome fart coming on."

He cracked up and slid a glance at me. "You're funny. I missed you in Cabo."

"I missed you, too," I said honestly. "What did you do there?"

"Surfed, swam, hung out. You?"

"Pretty much the same. *Farted* around," I joked. It wasn't exactly lying. Except that I hadn't gone anywhere near our pool. And as for surfing, I had surfed the net for information on the history of Marlwood Academy and all my rich new schoolmates.

"Partied with old friends?" he said, raising his brows above his hypnotizing eyes.

Was that *jealousy* in his voice? Was he really asking about old *boy*friends? I felt a little smug, and very thrilled. Presents, jealousy—I was on a roll.

"Some." Okay, that *was* a lie.

"Let's go up the coast," he suggested. "We'll take the 5. It'll morph into Pacific Coast Highway." PCH was a Southern California historical landmark. The ocean views were the best to be had, and that was saying something.

"Sounds good."

I studied his profile. Long, straight nose, cleft in the chin, dimple at the side of his mouth. Troy had modeled, as a lark. Friends of the family in the movie industry begged him to be in their films and TV shows.

There is a dead girl living inside me, I thought as he took his ocean-blue eyes off the road and glanced at me. His easy smile warmed me; if an amazing, hot guy like Troy could like me, I could throw Celia out of my life.

"What are you thinking about?" he asked me, a little lilt in his voice—as if he already knew.

"Not much," I said.

He grinned. "Me neither."

I tingled. Of course it had occurred to me that we could stop the car anywhere we wanted. We could look for a secluded spot. Or Troy could rent us a hotel room. Jane had rented lots of rooms; like her, he looked older and he had lots of money. What would it be like? I'd made out with guys, sure, but I had never gone further than second base. Everyone assumed I had, but it was my one big secret, back in the day.

He glanced at the road, then leaned sideways and kissed me, quickly, brushing his lips over mine. He smelled so good. His skin was warm and golden from the sun.

"I really did miss you," he said, and then he leaned in, and kissed me again.

We made out in the car. A lot. We went pretty far, parked at various ocean vista stops along the way north. It was incredible—like flying: all these amazing sensations pulsating through me, far more intense than it had ever been with Riley. I tried to catch my breath and stay in control; but his skin smelled so good and his hair was so soft, and his lips were warm and he was gentle. . . . It felt like he was respecting me, in a way Riley never had. Riley had always pushed; when he and Jane had snuck into my parents' room that night—she'd later asked me, "What did you expect? You teased him. What were you waiting for, an engagement ring?"

Troy and I ate all CJ's snacks—tangerines, cookies, sandwiches, Christmas turkey, guacamole, and cheese—and drank most of the sodas. Then around three or four in the afternoon, Troy insisted on stopping at a French bakery for an enormous pink box of all kinds of pastries, which we scarfed. And later, as we got closer to the mountainous northern region of the state, there was a spiffy sit-down steak dinner in a cozy, dark restaurant called La Vie En France—me in my raggedy jeans, gazing at Troy across a candlelit table, the light catching my necklace. He'd loaded an iPod with great songs, which we listened to through his car speakers, then tore up the freeway laughing and singing.

The seaside town of San Covino was the last outpost of civilization before we began the slow climb into the mountains on a one-lane road. It would take about two hours to travel from San Covino to Marlwood. As we prepared for launch, it was almost eight o'clock, and I had to physically check in with Ms. Krige, my housemother, by ten. As we drove down Main Street in search of gas, shadows stretched across the mirrored storefronts, making the town seemed deserted . . . dead. We stopped at a Chevron station, and I called my parents, reminding them that I probably wouldn't be able to reach them again until I got to the landline in my dorm. We had terrible cell phone coverage at Marlwood.

Then we were back in the car in the Chevron lot when Troy got a text message on his wafer-thin phone, so new you couldn't get it in the States yet, and his face fell. He was quiet for a moment, and then instead of pulling out of the station, he took my hand.

"I need to tell you something," he said.

As soon as he said that, my heart dropped and the whole day of fun—the views, the salt spray, tossing tangerine peels at each other in the car . . . it all fell away like background noise, like a carousel winding down until the music warps, slows, and stops. Let's face it. There's never anything good coming when someone says, "I need to tell you something."

Troy hesitated, tossing his thick dark hair out of his blue eyes. "I don't want to seem like a player . . . " Then he trailed off, and loosened his grip on my fingers.

A sickening dread rushed through me. I waited.

He gave his head a little shake. "I told you I would break up with Mandy. But she came to the hospital and . . . "

I wasn't stupid. I could fill in the blanks: he hadn't done it. As I worked to keep the pain out of my expression, I was suddenly very grateful for my year as a Jane-bitch—because she had taught us never to show weakness in front of boys. Never to confirm that we liked or wanted them. *They* had to work to deserve *us*.

"She didn't used to be so . . . so bad," he said, wrinkling his forehead. Just . . . it's so weird. She's so *bad*." And I wondered if he *knew*. About the hauntings. "She was . . . "

He sighed hard and tsked his teeth, as if it was too baffling for him. "It's her brother. Miles is crazy. He's ruined their whole family."

Before I could say anything, he looked up at me. "She was crying when she came to see me. She said she was afraid."

"Of what?" I asked.

"My guess is Miles. But she wouldn't say. She told me I wouldn't understand."

Of all the things that Mandy might fear, her brother Miles did not seem to be one of them. Word all over campus was that she and her brother had slept in the Lincoln Bedroom at the White House. Together. And that was why she got sent to Marlwood—late, although not as late as me. She had been going to boarding school in London, but Marlwood was much closer to San Francisco, where the Winters lived, and her parents could keep better tabs on her. I half-believed the gossip; she talked about Miles all the time.

"She was *terrified*," he continued, and I listened hard. Could it be that Mandy and I both wanted to be free of the ghosts that were haunting us?

"I know what you're thinking," he went on. "That *she's* playing *me*."

You didn't really want Riley, Jane had told me after she stole him, *or you would have done anything to get him back*. I knew she was wrong. Guys weren't possessions to be fought over. And I wasn't going to fight over Troy. If he liked girls with issues . . .

. . . *Then I am the girl for him. Haha.*

Just as with Heather, I had no idea how to respond. He kept gazing at me, then down at his hands, then back at me, and I knew he was expecting something. I just didn't know what. How did rich girls deal with things like this? Should I give him back the necklace? Tear up my donation card from the Surfrider Foundation? Hitchhike to Marlwood?

"Lindsay," he said. "I really like you. A *lot*."

But let's just be friends, I mentally filled in, and I wondered what form of insanity I had, that I had actually agreed to riding back to Marlwood with another guy bent on breaking my heart.

"Whatever," I muttered, trying to keep my voice steady. I hadn't *asked* him, specifically, to break up with Mandy.

For a moment I thought I saw Celia's face staring back at me in the windshield; I shifted my gaze and had a terrible thought, and not for the first time: that maybe she really wasn't there. Maybe it was stress that made me see her. Maybe back at Marlwood, none of that had really happened. I had awakened on the porch, bruised and sopping wet, so maybe it had all been a terrible dream. Or part of a blackout. Or some kind of hallucination . . .

It did happen.

"I just . . . " he persisted, "I feel like I have a duty toward her. We've been together since we were little kids, and Kiyoko was one of her best friends. It is over between her and me, Lindsay. It really is. But . . . she was so upset. And I didn't want to do it at Christmas . . . "

"I'm tired," I said. It was the truth. "Can we not talk?"

"But we should talk." He reached out to touch my hair, just like Riley in the theater. I pulled my head back slightly, just like in the theater. "I'm going to do it. I promise. But I haven't done it yet. I'm just trying . . . " He fumbled, his blue eyes searching mine for understanding.

I melted a little. He was trying hard to be honorable.

"I can't help you with that," was all I said.

"She won't be there until tomorrow," he added, and I stopped melting. What was he trying to say? That we were still in the clear to cheat on his girlfriend for another twenty-four hours? Did he think I *would*? "She has permission to show up late."

"I know," I snapped. "Julie's coming up with her."

"Oh." A beat. "So you've been talking to Julie."

"Not really. Just a couple of calls," I said. "I didn't tell Julie that you came over, if that's what you're worrying about."

He drew back. "I didn't mean to imply—"

"I have to go to the bathroom," I told him, and practically jumped out of the car.

And he didn't stop me. Which was good, because I couldn't have held the tears back another second.

FOUR

I HID IN THE CHEVRON bathroom, which was incredibly gross, splashing water on my face to wash away the tears I could not hold back. Then I took several deep breaths, and worked to make my face a mask, so Troy wouldn't see my misery.

He didn't break up with her. Stupid—I was so stupid for believing there was a chance this was real.

As I walked across the breezeway, fog washed over my ankles like a low tide, trailing in wisps across the concrete expanse between the mini-mart and the pumps. I studied the mountains, and my stomach clenched as thick waves of fog crept down the tops of the pine trees like wild animals searching for prey. Crossing my arms over my chest, I shuddered, hard. I knew what really lived in that fog . . . crazy, angry dead girls obsessed with revenge.

"Hey," Troy said behind me, and I jumped. "Whoa, sorry. I thought you saw me at the register." He held up two Red Bulls and some trail mix. "I just got a couple of things to keep us going."

Peace offerings.

"Thanks," I said, as we walked back to the car. The fog billowed with our strides as we climbed in and he turned the engine key; the motor purred to life and the car idled eagerly. I clenched my Red Bull so hard my fingertips went numb.

"Last chance," he reminded me, gesturing to my phone. I texted Julie, but there was no answer. I pictured her riding up with Mandy, probably in a convertible, talking about Troy and Spider, laughing like BFFs.

I'm going back to that, I thought. *All of that.* My heartbeat jackhammered; beads of sweat tickled my forehead. I began to breathe too shallowly, and I could feel myself pulling away. I was on the verge of a full-blown panic attack. *No,* I thought. *Not in front of Troy.*

Unaware, Troy plugged his phone into a charger connected to the cigarette lighter and put the car in reverse. He looked left into the side mirror, and then up to the rearview mirror. And then, he looked at me.

"I'm sorry," he murmured, and the soft sadness of his voice seeped into my silent freakout. I held onto those three syllables as if my sanity depended on them.

Then he brushed my cheek with his lips, and then he kissed me on the side of my mouth. The warm, smooth sensation of contact startled me—tempted me—but I didn't turn my head toward him, which might—or might not have—led to a full, deep kiss. I wanted him to kiss me like that again, even if it was the last time, even if—

—No. I was *not* like that.

"Okay, on our way," he said, guiding the T-bird out of the

gas station. Then we headed off for Marlwood, and I let the sound of his voice and the touch of his lips warm me like a candle flame.

The higher we drove on the bumpy road, the more fog tumbled down on Troy's car, until we were inching along and he was swearing under his breath. It was way after nine. We tried calling Marlwood on both our cell phones to check in, but as we expected, there was no reception. We talked about turning around; we talked about just stopping. But there was a good chance we'd drive off the road into the deep ravine on Troy's left; the other side hugged the mountain face. Since it was the night before classes, other cars would be trailing behind us. If we stopped, we might get hit.

COME TO ME, come to me, come to me, come to me. Get the ice pick. Push it into her brain. She will become biddable, and gentle. A lady. An asset to the name of Marl—

"We're here," Troy said to me, jostling me, and I exhaled as I woke up, as if I had had to hold my breath for a long time.

"Don't worry about being late," he said. "They'll understand."

He didn't know that my headmistress, Dr. Ehrlenbach, had protested my admission into Marlwood. I had no doubt she was looking for any excuse to boot me.

The fog had thinned very slightly, and I could make out my surroundings. We were in the parking lot next to the creepy three-story Victorian mansion that was the admin building, complete with stone columns and dim lights in a few of the windows. Limos and luxury cars scattered the lot. Golf carts driven by Marlwood staff collected luggage as tired parents and their students walked to their dorms. There were two hundred of us now; there had been two hundred and one last semester. But Kiyoko was dead.

With dark shiny hair fluffing out over her puffy silver jacket, jeans, and boots rimmed with fur, Shayna Maisel was walking down the incline with a heavily bearded man in a yarmulke. Her dad the rabbi, I supposed. Shayna had once been Kiyoko's best friend. First her BFF, then her ex-BFF. I had met her in my lit class on my first day at Marlwood, when she'd been trying to get Kiyoko to eat a protein bar. But that was before Kiyoko had crossed over to the dark side and hung with Mandy. Before Kiyoko died.

Shayna had stuck up for Kiyoko when Mandy had humiliated her with one of her stupid pranks—forcing Kiyoko to skinny-dip in Searle Lake. Shayna had wrapped her freezing, anorexic friend in a blanket down at the shore while Mandy laughed uncontrollably. But Kiyoko had dumped her anyway. Shayna had been Kiyoko's Heather. There were dark rings under her chocolate brown eyes. Part of me wanted to say something to her—but I didn't.

Trailing slightly behind Shayna, Charlotte Davidson, our closest thing to a goth, tapped each of the white horse heads that held oversized white painted chain links in their mouths with the brass tip of an old-fashioned black umbrella. Her blue-black hair streaked with red, Charlotte had on a long steampunk black coat with a high collar and black gloves with scarlet lace on them. The man and woman walking with her were bland rich parents in London Fog raincoats and boots.

Shayna glanced my way and gave me a wave. I waved back. Troy hadn't actually believed that our ride together would remain a secret, had he?

"So, thanks," I said to him now. "For driving me."

He stepped closer. "I-I . . . you're welcome." He searched my face and started to say something else. Closed his mouth. I nodded, and turned away, even though I was hurt that he didn't kiss me goodbye or say anything about meeting up later. Jane would have been proud of me for keeping my issues to myself.

"Lindsay," he said.

I stopped without turning around. "Yes?"

"I thought I saw something. In the fog."

Oh, God.

Now I did turn around. His hands were in his pockets, and his head was lowered slightly as he gazed down at me. He was grinning. "You were asleep. I almost woke you but it happened so fast. Just a split-second—"

I kept my voice neutral. "What did you see?"

He waggled his brows. "I was tired. I was thinking about that old story about the ghost that runs down the bypass. The girl who's on fire. And . . . I thought I saw her."

I felt as if someone had pushed me into the lake; that I was so frozen my hair might break off—

"I think it was just some light bouncing off the fog, but it was freaky," he finished, looking a little abashed.

"Do you think she was really there?" I asked him.

He laughed. "Naw. But it would have been cool if she had been."

"You're wrong," I blurted.

He blinked. "Excuse me?" He slung his thumbs in his jacket pockets and tilted his head. "You don't really believe in all that stuff, do you?"

"Of course not," I said stiffly. "Thanks again for the ride. Bye."

"Wait," he said, but I knew it was time to go. "Thanks for not farting in the car—you know, like your brother said . . . " he added, searching, I knew, for a way to make me laugh, to recapture the magic.

I grunted sadly to myself, and headed for Grose, my dorm and one of the oldest buildings on campus, staring down at Jessel, where Mandy lived, on the hill below us. With its four turrets tiled in slate and its hunchbacked shape, Jessel was far more interesting than Grose—and said to be the most haunted. I knew for a fact that that was true.

The curtains of Jessel were open, but all the windows were dark, except for one—the large, arched window of the turret room that was Mandy's single. Candlelight flickered dimly, and someone was standing in the window, head bent, staring straight at me. My blood ran cold.

Mandy Winters was already here.

Behind Jessel, the inky blackness of Searle Lake winked through the fog. The thick promotional booklet about Marlwood (eighty-four pages) showed glossy pictures of pine trees and wildflowers, extolling the virtues of the campus:

three hundred acres of forested land, hiking and biking trails, seventeen dorms, the quaint bell tower of Founder's Hall, and excellence in education. It failed to mention the nearly thirty condemned buildings where students held all-night parties and occult planning sessions about whom to murder next.

"Hey." Shayna came up beside me now, and I nearly leaped out of my skin.

"God, Shayna," I said, trying to force out a laugh instead of a scream. "You scared me half to death."

"Sorry." Shayna was gaunt, her cheekbones too prominent, her eyes deep in their sockets. She toyed with a large abstract pendant dotted with diamonds—I had no cause to believe they were anything but real—as she began to walk toward my dorm, then stopped when I didn't immediately follow.

"How have you been?" I asked, catching up to her. There were lines of tension around her mouth. I realized that in the two weeks between Kiyoko's death and our winter break, I had never said a word to Shayna, never comforted her. I had been lost in my own angst. And too busy trying to stay alive.

"Well, you know." She looked at her dad, who had stopped to wait for her about twenty yards ahead of us. She lowered her voice. "There's a welcome-back party," she said. "At that creepy lake house. You know the one?"

I nodded. "Who's going?" I looked over at Jessel. The figure in the turret room hadn't moved.

"Whoever can sneak out." She smiled cynically. "It's the Marlwood way."

"Are you going?" I asked her.

She gave me a long, measured look, as if trying to decide

something about me. Her expression didn't change as she stopped playing with her necklace and dropped her hands to her side.

"Oh, yeah, I'm going," she told me. "Wouldn't miss it."

I had the sense that she was trying to tell me more than I was hearing, but I just flashed her a quick smile as we reached the door to Grose. The Marlwood Academy crest, a carved M surrounded by leaves, jutted from the center. *Like a stop sign*, I thought. But I opened the door, wondering if Shayna wanted me to invite her in. Shayna had never hung out with me before. Maybe none of her friends had arrived yet. The fog had messed up everyone's schedule.

"Okay, so, I'll see you there," I said. The sooner I got to the business of getting rid of Celia, the better. And maybe seeing all the girls again would give me *some* idea how.

Just then, the little golf cart with my luggage pulled up on the walk. I wished I didn't care that Shayna would see my low-rent luggage, but it still embarrassed me.

"I need to call my parents," I said gently. "Check in. And . . . recharge."

Her cheeks reddened.

"I won't tell her," Shayna said. "That you were talking to Troy in the parking lot."

So that's how it looked, I thought. *People will assume he and I ran into each other here at school. No one else will know he drove me up here . . . unless he tells them.*

"Thanks," I said. Then I opened the door and went inside the second-most-haunted dorm on campus.

Judging by the beautiful burnished luggage placed beside

antique canopy beds, and iPods and cashmere scarves dangling from half-opened cherry wood and ebony dresser drawers, some of my dorm mates had arrived. But there was no one else actually in Grose except for my housemother, Ms. Krige, who greeted me in her bathrobe and told me with a yawn that everyone else had gone to bed. I couldn't believe she was so naïve; or maybe it just made her life easier to look the other way.

"Be very careful," she added. "There were some mountain lion attacks over break. They lost a dog at Lakewood."

She went back into her room and shut the door. I heard the TV go on. She really *didn't* want to know what was going on.

I faced the hallway. The overhead chandeliers cast pools of light on the waxed hardwood floor, which I disturbed as I walked toward my room. The walls were covered with offerings from the art classes—a lot of them fairly bad—and the overly large eyes of a poorly painted portrait of a girl with an enormous forehead followed my every move.

I reluctantly changed out of my dad's socks but I did put my Doc Martens back on. They were a Christmas present from my cousin Jason and his boyfriend Andreas. I also put on the army jacket Jason had given me earlier in the year. I had to choose between it and my mom's ratty UCSD sweater, which was one of my most treasured objects. After the long day, it was time to switch out the beautiful cashmere sweater for something else. I put on my black long-underwear top—which was kind of sexy-sheer, not that it mattered—and stuck with my old, ripped jeans.

And I took off the silk crocheted necklace, and put it in the topmost drawer of my dresser.

My Tibetan prayer beads, wrapped around my left wrist, completed mademoiselle's ensemble. I couldn't compete with the ultra-high-end designer clothes of the other girls, and I had renewed my commitment to rebellious non-conformity. During my free time, at least. I would never let Dr. Ehrlenbach catch me in jeans like these.

It began to snow as I quietly climbed out the bathroom window. I clicked on my flashlight and took one last look at the figure in the turret room. It still hadn't moved.

Anxious, I headed for Searle Lake. My breath was a ghost climbing out of my chest. My stomach tightened as my boots crunched on the snow mixed with the mushy, grainy soil of the shore. I walked past the large boulders and the NO TRESPASSING sign, which the Lakewood boys used as a tie-up when they snuck over to our side in rowboats.

Fresh bouquets of store-bought flowers marked the spot where I had found Kiyoko's body. Roses, chrysanthemums, daisies. My mind flashed to the wreaths and bouquets at my mother's funeral. Kiyoko's parents had held a memorial for her in San Francisco, asking for donations to the Physicians Committee for Responsible Medicine in lieu of flowers. Kiyoko's eating disorder was public knowledge.

Memmy, I thought, my pet name for my mom. *I wish you were here. I wish I could tell you what is going on. I'm haunted, Mem. I need to get free of Celia Reaves, or I'll never be safe or normal again. I'll do anything . . .*

But would I really? My stomach clenched and my throat tightened. *Could* I get free of her?

I picked up my pace.

There it was, as before: a ramshackle hodgepodge of gables and tarps. I climbed gingerly onto the porch and swept the darkness with my flashlight, hesitating before I crossed the threshold into the deserted room. Reggae music provided an ironic backdrop to my high anxiety as I scanned the moldy couch spewing rotten stuffing, the shapes covered with shredded drop cloths. On the walls, shattered glass frames slashed the sepia faces of unsmiling girls in constricted, high-necked blouses from a century ago. Not Celia, or Belle, but other girls, long dead.

What am I doing?

The music grew louder, and I heard girls laughing and then a guy half-yelling. Three things were forbidden at Marlwood: cheating, drugs and alcohol, and guys. I had come to understand that rich girls didn't break rules. They didn't even ignore them. The concept was so foreign to them that they didn't perceive their existence.

Into the belly of the beast, I thought, as I clomped down the stairs. The music provided a perky counterpoint to my clunky rhythm. Susi Maitland and Gretchen Cabot stood at the bottom, sharing a flashlight, waiting for me to come down so they could go up. They were totally glammed in new big-hairdos, and I swear Susi had on false eyelashes. Their jeans had probably cost in the hundreds if not thousands of dollars, and were topped with silky gem-toned camisoles beneath wool coats with wide elaborate belts. Susi had a pack of cigarettes in her hand and Gretchen was carrying two plastic glasses of red wine. I thought everyone knew smoking was repellant. I had never seen Susi with a cigarette before.

"Hey, Lindsay," Susi said, blinking up at me. She swayed, already a little tipsy. "You came back."

Had they assumed I wouldn't?

"Who's here?" I asked.

"Oh, you know, the usual," Gretchen replied, and they scooted around me to go upstairs.

The crowded basement flickered with candlelight—another Marlwood tragedy waiting to happen—and at first I couldn't make out any details, just silhouettes. Shadows stretched on the walls and I hesitated to enter—I was the one who had never belonged, and who still didn't.

As my eyes adjusted to the light, the first person I saw was Mandy Winters. Of course. She was standing sideways, so that I saw her profile, and she was laughing. It was bizarre, knowing what I knew about her—that she had allowed a murdering, insane spirit to possess her—but I still felt a warm glow as I stood in her orbit. Mandy had more charisma than anyone I had ever met. So did Satan, I supposed.

And she was beautiful. She was wearing her white-blonde hair in a bouffant, with opal earrings the size of Jolly Ranchers. A black wool Edwardian maxicoat brushed the tips of her pointy city boots. I couldn't imagine she'd walked through the snow in them. The coat hung open, revealing tight black leather pants and a cream-colored sweater, a belt loosely circling her hips.

The world telescoped for a moment, and I shivered, hard.

I can't do this, I thought, and began to hang a U.

"Linz," Mandy said to my back. "How was your drive?"

I turned around, to find a taller, slightly older-looking male clone of Mandy approaching her with two shot glasses. Wearing a nubby, loosely knit gray sweater over a white T-shirt and a pair of jeans, he raised his arms high into the air, then settled them over her shoulders, twining himself around her like a serpent. A retro fifties ducktail of platinum hair, darker scruffy five o'clock shadow, the same icy eyes, staring at me as if he were a rattlesnake and I was the juiciest chipmunk that had ever lived. I had only seen pictures of him, but I knew who he was—Miles, Mandy's partner in kinky crime, who until recently, had been in rehab, again. The brother Troy blamed for ruining the sweet girl he'd grown up with. The guy who looked strung out, and shaky, but far more muscular than I had anticipated. His shoulders were massive.

Mandy gave me an eye-sweep, quirking half her mouth as if she had to keep from laughing at my lame outfit. She opened her mouth and Miles poured in the hooch.

She licked her lips, then said to me, "Up to your old tricks, I see."

"What tricks would those be, hmmm?" Miles asked. Although he was smiling, his eyes were flat, dead. Here was a guy to stay clear of. Definitely.

I didn't say anything. I just looked at her, trying to stare her down. She gave as good as I did. We were back on her territory again—Marlwood—and she had friends. It occurred to me that if she was here, then my roomie Julie had to be, too, since they'd been planning to drive up together.

Alis DeChancey and Sangeeta Shankhar slunk over, in to-die-for wool and leather jackets and striped Italian scarves, facing me head-on as if to make it clear that they were on Mandy's side. Next came Lara, Mandy's second-in-command, her short red hair glimmering with gold glitter that matched the gold sparkles on her cheeks. She still wore her signature preppy-boy plaid jacket, white blouse and tie, and short skirt. Over that, a heavy car coat. She rested her chin on Miles's shoulder.

"No tricks, just treats," I replied, ticking my glance toward Miles. He blinked, and then he grinned, and it changed him completely. He became a friendly, handsome guy, as if he'd just taken off a mask and revealed his true self. Or vice versa.

"I'm Miles," he said.

"Lindsay."

"Got that. I like your look." He sounded sincere.

"She dresses like that to dis us," Mandy said. "Too bad we don't care."

"No, because she knows grunge works and Walmart doesn't," Lara said.

Bingo. Most mean girls are also really smart.

Miles just smiled.

"Where's Julie?" I asked, ignoring Lara's backhanded remark, and Mandy shrugged.

"Dunno." She worked her arm under Miles's chin and cupped the side of his head. "We went skiing. Julie stayed home." She rubbed her cheek against his, like a cat. "Thermal hot springs. Much communal skinny-dipping. It was fabulous."

"She's around here someplace," Lara said.

"Lara, get Linz something to drink. She needs it," Mandy said.

Lara flushed. Mandy cleared her throat and Lara huffed and broke from the pack, off to do her liege's bidding.

"Pass," I said. Trying to hide how hard I was trembling, I edged away, into the crush of girls, and looked for Julie. I began to see more boys, all of whom I recognized as Lakewood Prep students. A little tingle tickled the based of my spine. Was Troy here? Wouldn't he have mentioned it?

Not if he was going to hook up with Mandy, I thought.

Of the rest of the crowd, more people were nicer to me than not. I saw my dormies—Claire, Ida, Marica, and Elvis. We caught up with what we'd been doing over the break. I lied. Claire was a bronze Maui goddess, Ida had gone home to Iran, and Marica did some modeling in Brazil. She was still wearing her big-ass emerald earrings. Elvis had attended an opera intensive at Julliard. They confirmed that Julie had come to the party, too, but they couldn't tell me where she was at the moment.

After we swore to cover for one another if Ms. Krige checked on us, I resumed circulating. Shayna was in a corner with some girls from Stewart—her dorm—drinking red wine. She didn't see me, and I kept my distance in case she slipped up and said something about seeing me with Troy in the parking lot. I felt a little weird, since she'd essentially invited me to the party, and it really dawned on me that in the eyes of Marlwood, Troy was Mandy's boyfriend.

Julie was nowhere to be seen, and I figured she had probably gone back to our room. I looked for Rose Hyde-Smith, who'd been my partner in spying on Mandy . . . until she, too, had become possessed. She wasn't there, either. Having made the rounds, I decided to leave. It was past time for me to unpack and get ready for the first day back, and if Mrs. Krige decided to do a bed-check (although she hadn't done a single one during the first semester), we would be way busted. As the only scholarship student in Grose, I couldn't afford to get in trouble. By sneaking out, I was already playing with fire.

I worked my way back out of the basement to the stairs, through the upper room and out on the rickety porch. It had stopped snowing, and the wind was still. There was no denying the beauty of my surroundings, and my heart ached for the ability to simply enjoy life again. I hadn't stopped bracing myself for the next bad thing since my mom's death. And it seemed that life kept handing them out.

I heard a familiar giggle on the opposite side of the building, on the porch overlooking the lake. Cautiously, I avoided the rotted planks and gaping holes of the floor and walked around the corner. Julie was sitting with Spider, her boyfriend, on a fuzzy yellow blanket and they were bundled up together in another one, of Marlwood hunter green. Julie had cut her hair to a chin-length geometric bob, very Katie Holmes in her Beckham phase. Spider looked like Corbin Bleu, from his mocha-gold skin to his tight ringlets, his hair even crazier than mine. He was rubbing noses with her, and I smiled, cheered up.

Excellent timing, universe, I thought. *Thank you for this moment of goodness.*

"Hey," I said.

They turned their heads in unison. Julie let out a happy yelp and jumped up to hug me. She towered over me—she was at least five inches taller than my five-two—smelling of vanilla and a whiff of vodka.

"Linz, Linz!" she cried. "You made it!"

I hugged her back, teary and relieved. Spider got to his feet, too, and gave me a quick hug once Julie was done. I was among *my* friends.

"How did you get here?" I asked her, as she and Spider laced fingers. They really were an adorable couple.

"My parents," she said, pulling a little face. "Not the original plan, as you know." I could see that there was Mandy-related gossip in my future. "You?"

I ticked my glance toward Spider, to see if Troy had told him our little secret. They were close friends. It was hard to tell, since he was staring at Julie. "Drove," I told her vaguely. "By the way? It's mucho late."

Julie grabbed Spider's arm to check his watch, which was a simple gold-rimmed rectangle with a worn leather band that had probably belonged to his great-grandfather, who had gotten it from Albert Einstein, or Abraham Lincoln. All Lakewood boys had history, and connections.

"Oh my God, I totally lost track of time," Julie said, aghast. "We should go back to the dorm."

"I'll row you both back," Spider offered, slipping his hand around her waist as she let go of his wrist. "We came over in some boats."

"Thanks, but you guys go ahead," I replied. "I'll walk."

Julie looked dubious. I gave her a little nod and she said, "*Oh*," as if she realized that I didn't want to go on a boat in the lake where Kiyoko had died. "If you're sure . . . "

"I am," I told her.

"'Kay." Julie bent forward, her wheat-colored bob swaying as she kissed my cheek. "And everything's . . . okay?"

"Yes." She'd thought I'd lost my mind last semester, and had begged me to see my old therapist during the break. "All checked out," I added, even though that bordered on a lie. Actually, it *was* a lie. Dr. Yaeger had retired.

We walked down the broken stairs together and they peeled off toward a trio of rowboats pulled up on shore. The boats were painted white with LAKEWOOD added in large green letters. I watched as they pushed the boat into the water, Julie stepping in at the last moment, Spider balancing on a rock jutting out of the water, then hopping in, too. I gave them a wave and Spider took up the oars. Julie waved. She looked so much older with her haircut; having a boyfriend had matured her, it seemed. I reminded myself that she could swim; so could Spider. But the lake was half-frozen, and if something happened . . .

I hate this place, I thought, as they disappeared into the darkness. I exhaled, watching my breath, feeling my eyes well. I imagined my tears freezing to my cheeks.

I remembered Kiyoko's blue-white face again, and her shiny eyes. Lurching forward, I felt my stomach clench, hard, and I coughed slightly, trying to keep everything down. The day had been long and stressful; the party was a bust. But I had seen Julie, and there was peace between us, and Spider adored her. Good things happened to good people.

Lowering my head against the chill, I stuffed my bare hands in my pockets and started walking. Two weeks gone by, and I had forgotten how to dress for Northern California. Yesterday it was shorts and a tank top; tonight, I needed mittens. It was cold, and I was tired. And scared. I wished with all my heart that there was a route back to Grose that didn't involve walking along the lakeshore.

After a few minutes, I heard a sharp crack, like a breaking branch. A chill scurried up and down my spine and I cocked my head, listening. Maybe it wasn't such a good idea, going back alone. Maybe Marica and the other Grose girls were ready to go, and we could walk together. Or maybe they were behind me, hurrying to catch up.

I turned around—

—And I nearly ran straight into Mandy. And Lara. And Alis, lined up beside her, three abreast. They stood in shadow; I could only make out their silhouettes, standing very still.

"*Come to me, come to me, come to me, come to me,*" Mandy whispered. Then her head snapped back, and she exhaled slowly, almost as if she were dying. She straightened, and took a step toward me, into the moonlight. Her eyes were completely black, and the smile on her face was terrifying—crazy. Cruel.

And I knew she was Mandy no longer.

"Hello, *Celia,*" she said, in a voice that was not hers. Syrupy-sweet, with a Southern accent, and filled with deadly menace. I knew that voice—it was Belle Johnson, the ghost who blamed Celia for her death and the deaths of her five friends, in the fire of December 20, 1889. The same fire that had cut Celia's life short. The fire that haunted me.

Nausea clenched my stomach. Acrid smoke seared my eyes. Flames crackled in my ears. I took a step back, into a stand of pine trees, and knocked the back of my head against a low-hanging limb. The impact rattled my skull and I grabbed onto a couple of branches to keep my balance.

"Julie," I groaned, trying to call for help.

Hidden by the darkness, Lara . . . or whoever was possessing

Lara . . . snorted. "No one's coming this time, sweet bee. It's just us." Her new accent was pure New York.

"No," I whispered fiercely. "Spider," I called again, just a little louder, but far too softly for anyone but us to hear.

They began to walk toward me. I ducked underneath the pine branch, keeping my eyes on Mandy—on Belle. *Help me, Celia*, I thought, but if she was there, she was hiding. That was how she had come to me in the first place—to hide from Belle. It was all so crazy—how could a ghost hope to kill a ghost? But Mandy, when she was possessed, wanted to kill me.

My mouth moved but no more sound came out. I stepped backward and my foot slid into a hole. I lurched, grabbing the branch.

They came closer. I remembered that Troy had told me Mandy was afraid. Maybe she would help me here, now.

"Mandy," I said. "Mandy listen to me. Make her leave."

"Mandy, Mandy, Mandy," Belle chanted in a singsong voice. "Oh, she's a little whore, that one."

"Lara, Alis," I begged. "Please, help me."

One of them laughed. The other was silent. Both of them moved toward me, slowly, like zombies.

I began to pant. I couldn't make a sound, couldn't run, couldn't save myself. Then freezing cold swept though me hard, shocking me, like a jolt of electricity.

"Julie!" I screamed. My voice—*mine*—echoed off the lake. The flapping of wings buffeted the echo as startled birds took flight. "Julie! Spider!"

Mandy, Lara, and Alis kept coming.

For a moment, I stood rooted to the spot. Maybe they

expected me to run away. It was my first impulse. Instead, something made me stand my ground; then, before I realized what I was doing, I ran hard into Mandy, barreling into her like a linebacker, and knocked her down. She fell hard on her back with a grunt.

Hit her, said a voice inside me. *With your flashlight.*

I bent at the waist, arced back my arm, and sucked in air through my teeth. And in that moment, the blackness in Mandy's eyes vanished. And I knew I couldn't do it.

I jumped away from her and crashed into Lara. Her eyes were normal. I pushed passed her to the shoreline, running so fast I couldn't stop in time and sloshed into the freezing water. I gasped from the icy pain, swaying as I waved my hands. I remembered my flashlight and turned it on.

"Julie!" I yelled. I splashed backward onto the shoreline, aiming my flashlight at the lake as I half-ran, half-staggered back toward the lake house. "Julie! Spider!"

Soon a circle of light blossomed on the water. "Lindsay?" Julie bellowed behind the light.

"Please, come get me!" I shouted, looking over my shoulder as I ran. Alis and Lara were helping Mandy to her feet.

"No problem." That was Spider.

My feet sizzled with cold. I fell and pushed myself back up. I couldn't see Mandy, Alis, or Lara; the darkness had swallowed them. Run-walking, staggering along the curving shore, I reached the other two Lakewood rowboats, and squinted out at the lake, shifting my weight from one throbbing foot to the other as I watched for Julie's flashlight, for their little boat. The cheery reggae had been replaced with a dark, ambient gothy drone. Shivering, I tried to ignore it as I listened for other, more dangerous sounds—the footfalls of Mandy, Lara, and Alis.

Suddenly, I had the sense that I was being watched—a prickling sensation between my shoulder blades—and I whirled around, passing my flashlight over the jagged porch. Shadows moved across the exterior wall. A board creaked.

"Hurry, Julie, hurry," I whispered, even though I reminded myself that the lake house was crammed with partying students. There was safety in numbers—witnesses. Mandy wouldn't try anything now.

"Lindsay," Julie called. I saw her flashlight. "Here we come."

I opened my mouth to answer as a figure stepped from the blackness of the porch. It was Miles Winters. *How long had he been standing there? Had he seen Mandy and the others go after me? There was no way he could have seen me push his sister . . . could he?* The burning tip of a cigarette flared orange as he inhaled, angling light into the hollows of his faintly-stubbled cheeks. He saw me and slowly took the cigarette from his mouth, exhaling, lowering his hand to his side. Smoke and breath mingled and rose around his angular face. His bleach blond hair almost glowed against the night. He didn't speak. Neither did I.

Then he dropped the cigarette off the porch into the snow, turned, and walked back into the darkness.

FIVE

January 8

I am drowning, they are holding me down, they are killing me. The ice pick burrows in; stop them if you love me, stop them.

My love is like a red, red rose. I love you, of course I do. Let me prove it to you:

The door is locked!

My hair is on fire!

———

IN MY antique Marlwood bed, I jerked awake and covered my mouth with both hands to stop my scream. Across the room, in the blessed, soft gray of early morning, Julie sighed gently and turned over. Panda, her little stuffed Corgi puppy—a Christmas present—fell off the mattress and landed with a soft *poof* on the cabbage-rose carpet that separated our beds.

I took a deep breath and exhaled slowly, forcing all the air out of my lungs, down into my abdomen, the way Dr. Yaeger had taught me. I was vibrating all over. Horrible, horrible dream ... or was it a memory of Celia's? Some of both? What had happened to her? What had really happened here, at Marlwood, that had caused so much rage and pain?

I had to know, and I wished I could ask Julie to help me find out. When Spider had rowed back for me, Julie had assumed I was afraid to walk back by myself, which was, in essence, true. And my sweet friend had wrapped me in her green Marlwood blanket and given me a hug. She didn't know how afraid I really was, and I didn't tell her. She was anxious about the lateness of the hour, and distracted by Spider; she didn't know I was watching the shoreline, waiting to see if Mandy and the others would reappear.

After Spider had guided the boat to the NO TRESPASSING sign in the inlet behind Jessel, he tied it up and helped us both out. Then he and Julie lingered, and I knew he wanted to say good night to her in privacy. So I began the walk back to the dorm by myself, all my senses alert in case I was being watched ... or stalked.

Julie hadn't caught up until I was on Grose's porch with my hand on the doorknob. She scooted up quietly behind me, startling me; and as I turned my head, I saw the figure in Mandy's window again. As though it had never moved.

We had crept into our room and got ready for bed in record time. Julie giggled and whispered about how cute and sweet Spider was, while I remained silent. Then as we climbed in our respective beds, she added, "So, Mandy ditched me halfway through vacation. She and Miles went skiing. I'm not even sure if their parents went with them."

I'd crossed my fingers that this meant Julie was no longer part of Mandy's inner circle. That she was free. I'd envied her.

I still envied her, asleep with her mouth partly open, looking rosy and childlike and happy. I got out of bed and reached down to pick up her stuffed animal, and I felt icy coldness on the back of my neck. Celia. I whimpered in protest, imagining the ghost actually crawling into me, wearing me like a costume. I straightened, trying to sense if I was still just me, but I really couldn't tell.

I nestled Panda on Julie's pillow. Above Julie's head, on the windowsill, the white ceramic head she had found last semester stared blankly at me. The brain was marked in sections with faded black paint, the way old butcher-shop prints used to delineate pieces of meat—leg of lamb, baby back ribs. Cerebellum, amygdala. The center for processing sensory perceptions, the seat of emotions.

The head watched me pace; I was overwhelmed with everything that had happened in the handful of hours I'd been back. I fought the impulse to grab it and throw it across the room.

I was going to die at Marlwood.

Tears welled, and I gave my head a stern shake. I couldn't think like that. I was a survivor.

You had a nervous breakdown, the head seemed to say. *Life . . . broke you. The weak perish*

"Wrong," I whispered. "I'm not weak. And I'm still standing."

I tore off my rust-and-navy plaid pajama bottoms and maroon camisole and dressed in sweats, threw on my army jacket and high-tops, and blasted outside, into the dawn. I began to jog past the empty Academy Quad, watching my breath, trying to dilute the adrenaline in my system, picking up speed, pulling off the army jacket as I began to sweat. Without breaking stride, I wrapped the jacket around my waist. I didn't know exactly what Celia had hoped to accomplish by dragging me back to the school. But whatever she'd assumed, we weren't going to be able to pull it off. There were too many of them.

The wind buffeted against my chest, whispering in my ears. *Wrong*, it seemed to say. *You're wrong.* Or maybe it was, *You're gone.*

Fog churned around my knees like ocean breakers, the white-water fringes of the tsunami of thick, wet mist tumbling from the mountaintops into the valley of our campus. Its coldness smeared my face like iced oil. I pulled my cell from the pocket of my jacket. No bars, but I could read the time. It was only 5:00 a.m. Technically, I was still breaking curfew.

It had been five in the morning the first time I saw Mandy standing at the edge of the lake, talking to herself—or so I'd thought. She'd been talking to Belle, the evil ghost who possessed her. Now I jogged there on purpose, as fast as I could, my teeth chattering from the cold, standing beside the No Trespassing sign, gazing into the water at the white, eyeless face of Celia. Anyone passing by would assume I was staring at my own reflection. I experimentally touched my face, to make sure I still had skin, eyes. In the water, Celia did not touch hers.

"Make it stop. Tell me what to do. *Now*," I ordered her. "I'm here. So let's get it over with."

"*Very well*," Celia told me, in a voice that came out of my mouth, but was not mine. "*You must set a troubled spirit free.*"

Celia's spirit, I filled in. I knew this part.

"Okay," I said, hearing myself talking to myself in two different voices. This was exactly what schizophrenia was, hearing voices, talking back. "Fine. But you have to tell me how."

Her face drifted with the current . . . except that Searle Lake had no current. What made it move? The wind?

"*I know this will be shocking*," she replied. "*But it's the only way. If there were another . . .* " She went silent.

"Well, what is it?" I leaned farther over, and almost lost my balance.

"*I'm sorry. I'm so sorry. I didn't mean to . . .* "

"Celia," I said. "Come *on*. What is it?"

"*Can't you guess?*" she asked me. "*You have to kill her.*"

My lips parted in shock. "Kill—"

"*Mandy Winters. Before she kills you.*"

SIX

I RAN.

As fast and as far as I could go, I fled the lake and lost myself on a tree-lined path. Kill Mandy? Kill another living human being?

"No," I breathed. "No."

But the coldness in me turned my blood to ice as I kept running. I could almost hear Celia hissing "*yes*," in a voice like fire hitting the water.

"It won't stop Belle," I argued. "She's a ghost. She's dead. She'll just find someone else to take over."

Or was there something special about Mandy that Belle wouldn't be able to find in another person? Was I that way, for Celia? If I died while she was possessing me, would *she* "die" for good?

I kept running, aware that I was going deeper into the forest and farther away from the dorms and the dining commons— the populated buildings. Still I ran, as if I could run away, even though the blacktop path seemed like just one more dead-end passageway in a maze, and I was a stupid, insignificant nobody who would never find her way out.

"Let me go, leave me alone," I shouted, as I crashed through the bushes.

I flew until my side hurt, and my lungs burned, and my legs refused to go any further. I staggered sideways, catching my balance against a tree trunk, and tried to catch my breath. My surroundings were so dense with trees it still felt like night. It was freezing, and silent. Tears slid down my cheeks.

I won't do it. I won't.

I cried forever. I cried a lake full of tears, it seemed like. Then, when I thought I was done, I cried some more.

I turned around, gazing at the thick criss-crosses of branches barely visible in the gloom. One looked the same as the next. I started forward, nearly tripping over a huge rock that hadn't been in my path before. Stepping to the right, I pushed against a branch, to find it lashed together with another branch, from another tree. Not the way I'd come through, either.

I moved to the left. Another rock I hadn't encountered, and then a deep gulley. I made a quarter turn and took a few steps, but it didn't feel right, either.

I was lost. Like Troy, who fell last semester in the woods . . . or was pushed.

"He was found, he was fine," I said aloud, over the jackhammer of my heartbeat. Snow sprinkled down like icy powdered sugar.

I hadn't run very far. I would be found, too.

The woods are lovely, dark and deep. The words sprang into my head, like an echo of my mother's voice. Memmy and I had loved the poetry of Robert Frost, and we'd memorized many of his poems. We played duets together, me on cello, her on the piano. We did so much. Oh, God, I wouldn't even be here at Marlwood if she had lived. If she had lived. If my life had not fallen apart; if she had been there . . .

Lovely, dark and deep.

"Memmy?" I whispered, crossing my arms and sliding my hands into my pits for warmth. If ghosts were people who hadn't left, why not my mother? "Mom? Memmy?" I called.

Run.

I jerked as adrenaline gushed into my system. Then, in my path, there was a small, dark shape. It was like a bundle of shadow and I had almost stepped on it before I realized it was a little bird, dead, its left wing oddly angled. My stomach lurched.

Run.

I bolted forward, not even seeing where I was going. A root caught the toe of my shoe and I fell forward, into a net of branches. One of the branches bowed back, then snapped into place, scratching me across the cheek. I shouted in surprise and pressed my hand over the wound, feeling wetness on my fingertips. I swayed for a second, then dropped to my knees and fell forward on my hands. Pine scent and wet earth rose around me like a sack closing over my head. But there was a light stream of sunshine shining onto the icy ground in front of me.

I took a deep breath and pushed up to get to my feet. I heard something moving through the underbrush. Something big. And stealthy. I remembered that Ms. Krige had warned me about mountain lions, and hysterical laughter threatened to bubble out. I imagined my obituary: *Lindsay Anne Cavanaugh, surrounded by evil ghosts, was eaten by a mountain lion.*

I heard more rustling. Closer. My heart shot into overdrive. I was trembling. Without moving my head, I ticked my gaze left, right, searching for a weapon. Next to my right knee, weak sunlight glinted off a rock the size of my fist. About a yard in front of it was a broken branch with a sharp, pointy end. If I could stun it with the rock, then stab it with the branch . . .

What if I missed? What if all I did was enrage it?

I looked up at the nearest tree, a pine at least twenty feet tall. Could mountain lions climb trees? But the trunk wasn't very thick, and I wasn't sure if the branches would hold me.

I reached out my hand and grabbed the rock. Then I froze, wondering if I had made any noise; if I had just betrayed myself. I pushed against the ground with the rock, using it as leverage, while I stretched out to pick up the stick with my left hand. I closed my fist around it and yanked. It came free with a snap.

There was more rustling in the bushes. Very close, maybe three feet away. If a mountain lion sprang . . .

I caught my breath and held it. Contracting my stomach and pressing my chin to my chest, I pushed back until I was sitting back on my haunches. My sweatpants were soaked through with snow, and I was shaking so hard I wasn't sure I'd be able to throw the rock, much less hit anything with it.

I licked my lips and brought my fist with the branch against my chest. The rock seemed the better weapon; I couldn't imagine getting close enough to a wild animal to stab it.

I swayed, dizzy. I thought of my dad, and CJ and her little boys; I thought of Julie and Troy; and then, my mom. *Are you here, Memmy? Am I going to die now, and be with you?* I didn't want to die. I would do anything . . .

Anything?

Directly to my right, the leaves on some bushes jittered. It smelled like Thanksgiving; the bushes were sage. I squeezed the rock and brought up my hand, silently weeping; no, I was wheezing. I sounded like I was dying.

I got ready to throw it—

—And from behind the trees, Miles Winters slowly rose to a standing position. He was wearing a pair of black sweatpants and a black hoodie sweatshirt with a plain gray T-shirt, and his white-blond hair hung loose around his chin, damp with sweat.

"You asshole!" I screamed. And I probably would have thrown the rock at him, if he hadn't darted forward, grabbed my hand, and plucked it out of my fist, as he stared at me.

"What the hell is wrong with you?" he asked. I scrabbled to my feet, brandishing the stick. He blinked at it, and at me. "I heard shouting," he said. "I came to help."

I started to back away, stumbling on a low-lying bush; as I began to fall backward, he caught my forearm. His grip was very tight.

"Easy, princess."

"Let go of me." I jerked on my arm, and when he didn't let go, I poked his hand with the stick, lightly.

"Ow," he protested, but he didn't release me. "What are you doing out here so early, little Red Riding Hood?" He touched my hair. Then his fingertip grazed my cheek. "That might leave a scar," he said. "It'll make you look edgy. Edgi*er*," he added, checking me out, stem to stern. He smiled faintly. "Marlwood. How *did* they let you in?"

"What are *you* doing out here?" I was stung by his insinuation that I didn't belong, even though I didn't. "Detoxing?" It was stupid to bait him, but I couldn't help it. That was one of my flaws, going for the sarcasm in times of stress.

"Detoxing? I suppose so. In my own special way. I'm shedding my skin, like a snake." He examined my blood on his finger. "Listen, Lindsay Anne Cavanaugh," he said. All the warmth and amusement vanished, and he glared at me with his cold, hard eyes. His grip on my arm tightened.

"I'm very protective of my family. I'm sure you look out for yours." He narrowed his eyes. "Your dad. And stepmom. And your stepbrothers, Tom and Sam."

So he knew the names of my stepbrothers, so what? I knew Julie had spent part of her vacation horseback riding with Mandy. I also knew that Miles had been released from rehab so he could spend Christmas at home. Julie probably talked about me. Maybe she even told them that I lived on the corner of wacko and high-strung.

"Don't try to hurt one of us," he said. "Don't even think about it."

I had a crazy moment where I thought he had overheard me talking to Celia at the lake. About killing Mandy. But if he had, I doubted he would have stood there in relative calm, trying to intimidate me . . . and succeeding so well.

"No worries," I retorted.

His eyes narrowed. The hair on the back of my neck rose

as he jutted his face toward mine. I could smell sour wine and cigarettes on his breath.

"You already *have* hurt her," he said. "I'll give you a chance to back off. Now."

My cheek burned as if he had slapped me. "What are you talking about?" But I knew he was talking about Troy. About me being a boyfriend stealer.

"On your mark," he said.

"*What?*"

"Get set."

"Go to hell." I jerked hard on my arm. To my surprise—and intense relief—he let go. With as much dignity as I could muster, I walked away from him, all senses on alert in the event that he decided to come after me after all. What if *he* had killed that bird? It didn't look like an animal had gone after it. Its wing had looked . . . bent.

I kept walking, waiting for a parting shot, or some more patronizing laughter, or proof of his craziness, but there was silence. And I when I looked back over my shoulder . . .

. . . He had vanished.

REPOSSESSION

He who does not punish evil commands it to be done.
　　　　　　　　　　　　　　　　—Leonardo da Vinci

Cursed is the man who dies, but the evil done by him survives.
　　　　　　　　　　　　　　　　—Abu Bakr

SEVEN

January 8
possessions: me
(there is no me. there's only free-floating high anxiety. no way,
no way, no way, no way . . .)

> *haunted by:* Celia's dead voice
> *listening to:* the same
> *mood:* if a fire was coming, would you stand still and wait
>   for it?

possessions: them
> luck
> good fortune
> the lottery

> *haunted by*: they do the haunting
> *listening to:* the world, promising them more, now
> *mood:* blissfully unaware

possessions: mandy
>   my future
>   my life?

>   *haunted by:* me?
>   *listening to*: Belle
>   *mood:* terrified, if she's smart

I DON'T know how I found my way out of the forest. But as I raced away from Miles, suddenly I recognized the path I'd taken and within a few minutes, I had jogged back to the blacktop path. The white horse heads stared straight ahead, each dusted with snow. If they knew my secrets, they were keeping them to themselves.

Shaking, I went back to Grose, where my dorm mates were starting to wake up. Julie was still in bed, groaning about a hangover; I grabbed my bathrobe, towel, and toiletries and hurried to take a shower.

I passed the long row of mirrors over the sinks without looking into them, and the five strangely huge ceramic bathtubs, which no one could use because there were no faucets attached to them—and stripped off my sweaty clothes.

I went into one of the showers. The walls were slick and white; I turned on the water and let the heat sluice down on me. I thought I would never be warm again.

I burst into tears, and slid to the bottom of the stall. I couldn't kill Mandy. I wouldn't. I . . .

There was a dim impression of a face on the blinding white tile floor. I covered my mouth with both hands to hold in the scream. Celia had followed me in. I violently shook my head as water dripped off my hair in hard, heavy, unnatural droplets. My spine seemed to melt; and then I was falling somewhere, struggling and screaming and falling and wet and . . .

"HOLD HER DOWN until she swears," Belle told Pearl and Martha. Belle's blonde braid had come uncoiled from the top of her head and hung over her shoulder like a snake. Her ruffled blouse was undone to the top of her corset; her sleeves were folded back. "She will never go near him again."

Celia was kneeling in her white gown in one of the hydrotherapy tubs, filled to the brim with icy water. Headmaster Marlwood would order the treatment for the most willful girls—first into the tub, then the wooden lid locked tight in place, so that only their heads were visible. They had to rest quietly or they might drown. But the lid was off now, and there were no matrons or doctors to see what was being done.

"For the love of God, Belle," Celia pleaded, up to her breasts in the water.

"She will never go near him again," Belle shouted, as Pearl clutched Celia's right arm, and Martha dug her fingers into the left. Their clothes were disheveled; there were spatters of blood on Pearl's pinafore. Belle darted forward and grabbed Celia's hair in her fist, pushing on the back of her neck with her other hand and forcing Celia's face under the water.

Bubbles escaped her mouth; her lungs began to ache. She wasn't afraid, not yet. Belle was mean and vindictive, but she wasn't insane. She wouldn't murder a fellow student; if she did, she would suffer for it, as surely as Edwin Marlwood held all their lives in his hands. For others had paid horribly, and for lesser crimes. . . .

. . . The ice pick . . . the ice pick . . .

Celia was out of air. She'll let me back up now, *Celia thought.*

But Belle didn't.

Celia's strained body was beginning to convulse. She pushed against the hand that restrained her head, and moaned; and bucked. She couldn't move. She couldn't breathe.

She panicked. She had to inhale, had to—

—And just as she was about to draw in a fatal breath of ice water—

—Belle yanked up her head. Celia drew in air, her aching lungs searing, her back arching. Pearl had backed away, sobbing, while Martha was hitting Belle's shoulders, shouting, "Let her go, Belle! You're killing her!"

"She will not love him!" Belle screamed, her voice echoing on the tile walls of the hydrotherapy room. "She will not!"

"Let her go," Pearl shouted.

"She will not!" Belle shrieked.

"Belle, I'm here," Celia said, dazed. Why was Belle speaking of her as if she were not there? "Belle, please, listen, I—"

Belle's face went white. Her dark eyes burned in her face, like bottomless pits. For the first time, Celia saw the pure hatred there. The madness. "Back down, back under," she decreed.

"No, Belle, no, please," Celia cried. "Someone, help me!"

Down she went, into the ice water . . .

. . . Longer this time—

———

"GOD," I gasped. As I panted, Celia's face, barely visible, stared up at me from the shiny white floor of the shower stall.

"So you see. It's happened before. Two girls, in love with the same young man. Belle, and me. You, and Amanda Winters. And she'll kill you for him. Like she killed me."

The words were in my head, in my own mouth, but it was Celia talking.

"No," I whispered, but Celia was right: Mandy Winters was every bit as vindictive as Belle. She would kill me rather than give up Troy. She'd *already* tried to kill me.

"You have to fight fire . . . with fire," Celia said. *"You have to strike first. Or it will be too late."*

I covered my mouth. I didn't know if I was going to be sick, or to scream. I was losing it. Panic attack. I could feel my mind shutting down.

"Kill or be killed."

I started to hyperventilate.

"Lindsay? Are you still in there?" It was Elvis, pounding on the stall door. "I forgot my conditioner. Can I borrow yours?"

Oh my God. Heaving, I fell onto my side; I gathered up my thick dark hair and wiped my face with my hands several times before I connected that it was still wet because the shower was on. Disoriented, I swallowed hard and awkwardly crawled up the wall with my fingertips until I was upright. Then I leaned against the wall, numb.

"Lindsay?" Elvis called. "Are you okay?"

"Yeah," I said quickly. "Conditioner. Hold on."

Hold on. Hold on. Hold on.

——————

I MOVED as if I were underwater, floating as I got dressed and brushed my teeth—without looking in the mirror. I swam upstream to our room, to find Julie showered and dressed in fashionable new clothes, even less tweeny and more grown-up. She'd unpacked a few things from her suitcases, and she was holding a scarf in both hands. I had the sudden uncontrollable terror that she was going to strangle me with it. I knew that was crazy . . . unless she was possessed. But her eyes were their usual hazel. Her smile, pleasant and sweet.

"So," she said, as we left our dorm and joined the dozens of other girls heading for the commons, "how did you sleep?"

There was an edge to her voice, and I knew I couldn't tell her anything. She obviously still didn't remember any of the terrors of last semester, including the fact that she herself had been possessed. As before, she thought I had either made up everything, or imagined it, in some twisted attempt to paint Mandy as a villain so that she, Julie, would remain my best friend. Maybe Jane would have been able to pull something like that off, but she wouldn't have bothered—it was dumb. And ridiculous. And too much work.

I was the proof of that.

As we reached the opened door of the commons, I smelled coffee. And oatmeal. And a hundred different exotic perfumes on the polished, coifed girls who swirled around us.

"Bleah," Julie said. "I'm a little hung over. Maybe I shouldn't drink on school nights."

"Maybe we shouldn't drink on any nights," I said. "You know, cut back for a while. Until we're settled back in."

She squinted at me. "Who are you and what have you done with Lindsay?"

"My grandmother says that alcohol robs you of your wits," Shayna said, as she came up behind us. "And you should always keep your wits about you. In case a *dybbuk* tries to possess you. Then you can talk him out of it."

"What's a *dybbuk*?" Julie asked. Already seated at our table— dorms usually sat together—Marica and Ida waved at us. Julie waved back, but I just stared at Shayna.

"Look at Marica's sweater. Isn't it amazing?" Julie chirruped, distracted. Then she hurried over to greet them as if she hadn't seen them less than seven hours ago.

Shayna gave me a long, measured look. She was so perfect, with her dark, glossy hair, beautifully shaped thick eyebrows, and perfect skin. "A *dybbuk* is the dislocated soul of a dead person," she said quietly. "At least, that's what my grandmother used to say."

I caught my breath. Felt the blood drain from my face. *Shayna?* I thought. *Shayna knows?*

"What do you think?" she asked me.

"Hello? Blocking the door?" Lara snarled, bumping Shayna's

shoulder as she and Mandy sauntered into the room. Mandy was dressed all in black, and Lara wore a red-and-black argyle sweater over black trousers. The red clashed with her hair. It was clear to me that they hadn't heard our conversation.

"Some people," Mandy said, sighing melodramatically.

Shayna frowned, then went neutral, and headed for the food lines. I started to follow, but she gave her head a shake.

"What you just said . . . " I began.

"Shouldn't be discussed in public," she finished.

She looked over at Mandy, then at me. She gave me a nod that I couldn't interpret precisely, but I was pretty sure I had the gist.

"Come after classes. I'm in Stewart."

Right. I'd seen her in Stewart, when I went there to plot strategy with last semester's ally—Rose Hyde-Smith. Rose, who had broken into Jessel with me, and discovered so many secrets . . . and whose eyes had eventually turned black, and who had tried to help Mandy kill me. And who didn't remember any of it, either.

Rose was seated at the Stewart table, in a wacky outfit that was a combination of Amy Winehouse and *I Love Lucy*—bouffant hair, red-and-yellow paisley scarf and red hoop earrings, and a black sweater with big red buttons. Spotting me, she waved with both hands, and then blew me kisses.

"You okay?" Ida asked me, approaching me with her tray of practically nothing—just scrambled egg whites and tomato slices—for breakfast. Tea.

"Yeah," I said. "It's just hard to get back into the swing."

Ida pulled a sad face. "No kidding." Then she brightened.

"But I have a total jewel of gossip, speaking of swinging. Gretchen Cabot has a thing for Mandy's brother."

"That *is* scary," I opined. *In ways you cannot begin to comprehend.*

"Well, he is kind of hot, in a savagely mad King Henry VIII kind of way." When I obviously didn't connect, she said, "English history? First he boffs them, then he cuts off their heads?"

"You find that attractive?" I jibed.

"Well, actually, Miles Winters is a bit too Aryan for my taste. My parents are modern Iranians, but I wouldn't push them past their limits." Her grin turned mischievous. "I mean, I might boff him, but I wouldn't bring him home."

"Oh, eeew," I protested, working overtime to sound only mildly disgusted.

"I'm just kidding. He's Mandy's brother." When I didn't say anything, she said, "I am not a fan of Mandy's *anything*, not since Kiyoko . . . " She trailed off. "Mandy wasn't nice to her."

"No, she wasn't." She was so not-nice to her that she killed her.

She *killed* her. This wasn't about dead birds and gossip. This was about a frozen body in a lake, and me nearly dying, and Mandy just sitting over there, laughing while she pushed food around her plate. Who knowingly started all this by inviting Belle to possess her. It hadn't happened to her by accident, as it had with me. She had *made* it happen.

I clenched my jaw. God, I really did hate Mandy Winters. I hated her down to my soul. And I hated Belle just as much. They were two evil bitches who deserved to die.

But did I hate them enough to kill them?

EIGHT

CLASSES ENDED at three thirty; then there were extracurriculars, which included all the sports teams. So while Julie was busy kicking soccer balls in the powdered-sugar snow, I was at Stewart at three thirty-five, ready to talk about dislocated souls. If Shayna knew about the possessions, maybe she knew some way to get rid of Celia without killing Mandy. I would give *anything*, everything I had, if that were true.

I was shaking as I rapped on the front door. Stewart was a new dorm, with brick faces and lots of windows trimmed in white, very airy. Very not vintage Marlwood, which was Victorian and dark.

The door opened, and Rose, not Shayna stood on the threshold. Her hair pulled back into a ponytail, she was wearing purple sweats shot through with cheesecloth and a black cashmere dove wrap sweater with the ends dangling around her knees. She had on black socks with white peace signs on them. She threw her arms around me and kissed my cheek. My anxiety skyrocketed. I was desperate to talk to Shayna, and I had to do it alone.

"Oh my God, Linz, come in, you're frozen," Rose said. "Don't you remember how to dress for these climes?" She reached forward and shut the door as she urged me inside. "Did you get my Christmas card?"

"No," I said.

"The one with the puppy in the stocking? No? Maybe I got your address wrong. My parents turned Christmas into the OK Corral. They're getting divorced. It's in the tabloids. I'm glad you don't read them."

She quickly shook her head. "Don't say you're sorry. It's completely irrelevant to my real life. But how've you been? You look tired."

She walked me into the common room, where three of the other Stewart girls were studying. Shayna was not among them.

"We're making hot chocolate," Rose said. "Shayna," she bellowed, "Linz is here."

"Coming," Shayna announced.

"So." Rose led me down the hall to her bedroom. I looked at her autographed poster from Cirque du Soleil in the red frame and a tie-dyed goose down comforter practically floating on her bed. Matching pillows were squashed into a nest and a book in French lay beside a dirty plate—looked like hummus—and a can of Red Bull on its side. New items were a poster of the rocker David Bowie as Ziggy Stardust, very glam and metro, and a vintage yellow rocking chair. She'd threaded strings of yellow and red beads through the arms of her *de rigueur* Marlwood chandelier. "We're in my room," she yelled.

She plopped cross-legged onto her bed and folded her arms over her chest. I perched on the edge. I was very nervous.

"Mandy's already throwing down," she said. "You should have heard her rip Gretchen Cabot for talking about Miles. Like no one is even allowed to say the hallowed name of incest boy."

Troy's dimpled face popped into my mind. I wonder what he would think of his poor, terrified girlfriend if he'd been there. My heart registered further insult.

"I'm surprised *Gretchen* didn't end up dead in the lake this morning," Rose went on.

I stared at her. She waved her hands.

"I know, sorry, that was tacky. Rest in peace, Kiyoko."

"Hey," Shayna said from the door. Stewart girls favored after-class warm-up clothes; she had on beige cashmere and gold hoops that glittered against her perfectly shaped long cut. Her dark eyes took in the scene—me on Rose's bed, Rose sitting up semi-possessively, angled toward me. She was holding two steaming coffee cups. "The cocoa's ready."

"Cool," Rose said, smiling at Shayna. "Thanks."

"C'mon, Lindsay." She looked at Rose. "We're studying."

"Oh." Rose's face fell. She looked from Shayna to me and back again. "I . . . see."

Awkwardly, I got up off her bed. Shayna handed me a cup and I passed it to Rose, as if that had been Shayna's intention. Rose took it, slurping noisily, then smiled at me.

"When you guys are done, we can walk to dinner together," she announced. "Us three."

"That'd be great," I said. "Shayna's totally helping me catch up in trig." I sounded like a moron, but I was uncomfortable.

Shayna led me out, down to a room at the end of the hall. She opened the door and I went in, to a room furnished more cheerfully than I had anticipated. She had an abstract oil painting on the wall beside a poster of a gorgeous girl who bore a resemblance to her. The girl was lying on her side, on what appeared to be a sheet of Lucite lit from underneath with blue lights, holding out a shiny red apple. Suggestive shadowing implied that she was naked.

Shayna's bedspread was white decorated with purple and red tulips. She had covered her chandelier with a large purple paper star decorated with silver wires. On her desk were several plastic containers of silver, black, and green beads, a pair of pliers, and a spool of stringing wire.

And on her nightstand was a five-by-seven picture of Kiyoko and her, wearing matching pink feather boas and cheap rhinestone tiaras over what appeared to be baggy peasant-style dresses. They were blowing kisses at the camera.

She handed me the other hot chocolate and gestured for me to take a beanbag. She was wearing what looked like red thread on her left wrist. I remembered reading an article about all the Hollywood celebs who were wearing them, but I didn't remember why.

She saw me looking at it and said, "My stepsister got this in Israel. It's for protection."

I sank down, flashing for a brief moment on the horrible vision I'd had in the shower. My hands shook, and I silently cleared my throat, struggling to reboot.

"My parents didn't want me to come back. I'm here for Kiyoko." She swallowed hard. "They murdered her."

I closed my eyes for a few seconds, struggling to keep it

together. Wondering if I could trust Shayna. "They . . . they tried to . . ." *Kill me too*, I added silently. I couldn't say it. I just couldn't.

She leaned forward and gave me a long, penetrating look. Beneath her perfectly applied makeup, there were deeper, darker circles around her eyes. And I saw that she'd gone heavy on the blush. The actual Shayna was washed out and pale. "Why did you come back?"

I felt Celia's icy presence flooding through me. Was she warning me not to tell?

"Tell me about the *dybbuk*," I said.

"I never really listened to all my grandmother's old stories. Until . . . now." She gave me another look. "It's usually the ghost of a dead person, someone who's not done here. Earth, I mean."

"Not done," I ventured. "Like they have a grudge?"

She smiled her cynical smile, pulling up the left side of her face, her lips pursed tightly together. "I guess you could say that."

"And . . . they're evil?"

"Not always. But yeah." She ran her hands through her hair. "The *dybbuk* that's possessing Mandy Winters is most definitely evil."

The dybbuk that's possessing Mandy Winters.

"Take it easy," Shayna said, leaning forward and easing my hot chocolate to my lips. It was an intimate gesture, and it made me more uncomfortable instead of less. I didn't know Shayna. But who *did* I know anymore?

"What about the ones that aren't evil?" I asked.

"They're usually spirit guides. Helping you to complete a task." She appraised me. "Are you okay?"

"Define your terms."

"They possess people who have the same kind of psychic makeup as them," Shayna said. "So, say you're a vindictive, insane *bitch*, like Mandy . . . "

"No, helping you. How do they help you complete a task?"

She thought a moment. "Well, say you've been bullied all your life. Like Kiyoko was. You need to stand up to people. So a *dybbuk* might come into you to give you courage, and help you. Help you so no one can hurt . . . " Her voice caught. She picked up her pliers and played with them. "But that didn't happen to Kiyoko."

I tried to get Kiyoko to talk to me about Mandy, I thought. *She was scared to. And then . . . she died. I could have tried harder. Maybe I could have saved her.*

Silence grew between us. I struggled not to see Kiyoko's frozen face. Her eyes had been unnaturally shiny, as if someone had sprayed silver over her corneas. According to the autopsy results, that shininess was proof that she had drowned, not frozen to death. I didn't remember how I'd found that out, but it had terrified me.

Now I thought I knew why it scared me so badly. Either Mandy had succeeded in drowning Celia in one of those huge tubs in our bathroom, or had threatened to so many times that Celia's terror of drowning had become part of our shared nightmare. Then why was I so afraid of fire?

Shayna pulled out the top drawer of her desk and brought out a little white candle in a lavender votive holder and a pack of matches. She lit the candle and we watched the flame for a few moments. The orange flicker made me uneasy for some reason, and I finally broke the silence.

"What *do* you think happened to Kiyoko?"

"Mandy happened." Shayna hunched her shoulders. "Mandy's possessed, that's for sure. And she's got some way to convince her little ass-kissers to let themselves be possessed, too."

Bingo. Shayna knew exactly what was going on.

She looked hard at me, as if daring me to contradict her. I didn't.

"So," she said. "You know, too. I thought so."

"Why?" Had I given myself away?

"You really stood up to Mandy the night of Kiyoko's prank. I liked you so much for that. So I started watching you. And you were watching Mandy, because you were so protective of Julie. You *knew* Mandy was dangerous. And you didn't let her hurt your friend...."

That was all true. It hadn't even occurred to me that someone outside Mandy's cabal would be watching me. Like all the other girls at Marlwood, I'd centered my attention on Mandy and never looked anywhere else.

She reached out her left hand, the one with the red string. I took it, startled by how thin it was. It was like encircling a small bundle of sticks.

She began to cry. "I couldn't help Kiyoko."

"I couldn't, either," I reminded her, welling up. We shared a moment of silence, and as I tried very hard not to see Kiyoko's blue-white face and frozen hair, I began to feel very panicky.

"I'm not crazy," she said between sobs. "I'm not." Her mascara started to smudge and I handed her a tissue from the silver box on her nightstand.

I squeezed her hand just a little harder. "You're not." *Or else, we both are.*

Taking a deep, ragged breath, she forced herself to stop crying almost as quickly as she had begun. Shayna was strong. I could be, too. I *would* be, too.

"So, how do you get rid of them?" I stared down at the steam rising from my chocolate. "D-do you have to kill the person they're possessing?"

"*What?*" Her voice was shrill. She looked at me as if I *were* crazy.

I didn't return her gaze. I was afraid that if I did, she would know what I was thinking. So I took a sip of cocoa. "Kiyoko died," I pointed out.

"No. No, that's not it at all." Then she jerked. She got up off her bed and walked quietly to her door, signaling me to be quiet as she pressed her ear up against the door and listened for a second. I watched her. She half-turned her head, and pressed her finger to her lips. Then she put her hand around the knob. As she began to turn it, she looked at me and grimaced, the color draining from her face.

She came back to the bed. "Someone was in the hall," she whispered. "Maybe Rose. If they know that *we* know—"

I began to tremble harder.

"You can't tell Rose about this," she said. "Swear to me."

"How do you get rid of it?" I whispered, my voice rising. I had to know if what Celia wanted . . . *no.*

No.

"Swear to me," Shayna insisted. "Don't tell Rose."

"Okay. I swear." I waited.

Shayna beckoned me over as she picked up a pen. She grabbed a piece of notebook paper and wrote.

An exorcism.

I blinked at her.

"That's how you get rid of . . . *them*." She let that sink in, nodding faintly as I processed. I wanted to jump up and down. I wanted to make her promise me she was right. If we could do *that*, then we wouldn't have to kill Mandy. *I* could get exorcised. Whatever that meant.

"We need to find out more about this place. About what was going on here when the *dybbuks* were still living people." Shayna fell silent and looked at me as if to say, *Your turn.*

I hesitated. Could I trust her? Could I really?

She narrowed her eyes, her forehead wrinkling, pursing her lips. I gripped my cup; the warmth seeped into my palms, but the rest of me went cold. Very cold.

Can you help with that? she wrote.

Before I could answer—not sure what I would say, how much I would reveal—someone knocked hard on her door.

"Yo," Rose bellowed. "Chow time."

Shayna didn't move, only kept looking at me, and my face prickled. I took the pen from her.

Yes, I wrote. *I can help with that.*

Shayna took the piece of paper and folded it in half, then half again. Then she dipped one corner in the candle flame. It ignited. I watched the flame and began to lose myself in my fear of fire. I felt the heat, smelled that awful gas odor . . . *kerosene*, I thought.

I leaped out of the beanbag and staggered backward to the door. I hit it with my back.

"Put it out," I begged. "*Put it out.*"

She dumped it into my cup of cocoa. Stared at me.

"What happened to *you*?" she asked.

"Guys, c'mon," Rose yelled.

"Lindsay, tell me," Shayna said.

The knob on her door turned. Rose was on the other side. Shayna stared at me with wide eyes.

"Coming," she yelled back.

"I have these terrible nightmares," I whispered. That was the truth. Not all of it, but it was something. "About fires. And drowning."

"Maybe you're psychic," she whispered. "Or maybe . . . you have a spirit guide."

"Maybe." It was all I could tell her for the moment. I just couldn't go there. I wasn't ready.

"Yo, yo ho." Rose pounded on the door.

Sighing, Shayna dipped her thumb and forefinger into the chocolate and then pinched the candle flame, extinguishing it. Then she pulled a red string out of the same drawer, pushed my Tibetan prayer beads out of the way, and began wrapping it around my wrist.

"We'll find out," she promised.

NINE

THE SNOW TURNED TO ICY RAIN as Shayna, Rose, and I shuffled our way to the commons. Last semester, Julie had taught me about black ice, which wasn't really black, but transparent. It was also especially slippery; combine the two—invisibility and danger—and I thought it should be called ghost ice.

The commons smelled of perfume and wet wool; noisy chatter bounced off the hardwood floors and copper pots dripping with ivy. Our first dinner back. Dressed like Icelandic fashion models, girls were standing in the food lines; parents had been complaining that, at forty grand a year, they did not expect their daughters to fetch their own meals. They didn't care that the menu had been developed by some world-famous chef I had never heard of. They cared that their girls had to get the food themselves.

"That was fun," Rose declared, as we three surveyed the room. I was flanked by her and Shayna, feeling a bit like a possession they were each trying to claim. "We should do it more often."

She peered through her lashes and made a show of frowning at me. "Haven't seen you much since we got back."

"What are you doing?" I heard Mandy shout.

We turned to look. Seated at the Jessel table, Mandy was staring over her shoulder at Charlotte Davidson, who stood slightly behind her. Charlotte was clutching a hunter-green backpack against her chest, her arms through the straps; and a bottle of what appeared to be vodka was sticking out of the top.

"But I thought . . . you said . . . " Charlotte stammered. Beneath her multi-colored streaked hair, her face was turning purple. " . . . To bring . . . "

"Not into the commons, tea leaf." Mandy made a show of plunking her elbows on the table and burying her face in her hands. "Charlotte, Charlotte, Charlotte, what *am* I going to do with you?"

"I smell a prank in progress," Rose muttered.

"Run, Charlotte," I replied. "You'd think Mandy wouldn't do that anymore, considering."

"She's got to replenish her supply of mindless Mandy-bots," Rose said. "Kiyoko's gone, and hey, howdy, you've brought Julie back to the light side of the force. So she's low on worshippers." She gestured to Julie, who was sitting at Grose's table, tacitly ignoring the drama at Mandy's table. "How did you manage Julie's conversion, by the way? She was totally Mandy's poodle last semester."

"Mandy ditched her at break," I told her. "They were supposed to drive back together, but Julie came up with her parents instead."

"It never gets old, demeaning the less fortunate," Rose

muttered, as Mandy continued to berate Charlotte for bringing forbidden alcohol into the commons.

Rose was right, though. Mandy did need to replenish her followers. Last semester, she—or Belle—had worked hard to find six girls for her and her dead friends to possess. They had been: Mandy, Lara, Kiyoko, Sangeeta, Alis, and Rose. And after Kiyoko died . . . Julie.

Seven girls had died in that fire. Celia was the seventh. And Celia was . . . me. If Julie was out, Belle would need another. If Rose was free, she'd need two. There was something about having all of the spirits back—Belle wanted to recreate the past, to change it maybe . . . to get her revenge on Celia. She blamed Celia for the fire. She was jealous that the guy she loved had loved Celia instead. So she had tortured Celia. And now she was back from the dead, trying to torture Celia—to torture *me*—all over again.

And along the way, that meant Mandy also got to torture as many other girls as she wanted. It was sick. And now Charlotte was the next target.

I knew that a few intriguing details of the prank would spread through the room during dinner. That was how Mandy maintained interest—our own Marlwood version of Twitter. Girls got status by being in the know and sharing what they knew . . . selectively. By dessert, even the outer rings of the least cool would have learned the nature of Mandy's challenge to gauge Charlotte's willingness to suffer for the privilege of being considered for entry into Mandyland. And even if Charlotte passed her ordeal, it was still no guarantee that she was in. It seemed unlikely. Charlotte was a *goth*, after all. Plus, chubby. Mandy was far too wise in the ways of the world to put out the welcome mat for someone who was so blatantly an outcast. Even if she *did* need more followers for Belle's secret cabal.

Fashionably possessed, I thought. I hoped Charlotte would fail. I hoped I could restrain myself from leaping onto a table and yelling out everything I knew.

Weighed down by too much to deal with, I went to the food line and got the pasta with vegetables, and some milk, and approached my table. Julie scooted over, making sure I knew she wanted me to sit beside her. She was so sweet.

As I put down my tray, Elvis said, "You are not going to believe this. The prank is going to involve swimming. *Au naturel.*"

My mouth dropped. "Mandy wants Charlotte to skinny-dip? After Kiyoko drowned?"

"Yeppers," Ida confirmed. It was the *exact* same thing she'd made Kiyoko do last semester.

"Oh my God, that is unbelievable." I couldn't fathom it. Not even Mandy could be so callous. It had to be Belle's idea.

"You going?" Julie asked me, taking a bite of chicken. She turned to the group. "Linz is a lifeguard."

"Then you should go," Claire said.

Images, sensations of the vision in the shower stall swirled around me. Drowning. That frigid body floating on the surface of the lake . . . I couldn't stop the visual of Kiyoko's ghastly blue-white face from blossoming in my mind, so like Celia's. It was the first time I had connected those dots—Celia's face looked like a victim of drowning's.

I tried to force myself to speak, but I couldn't. I stared down at my plate.

"I think someone should tell Dr. Ehrlenbach about this prank," Marica declared.

Elvis snorted. "Like *she'd* do anything. Did you read the newsletter Marlwood sent out over break? Mandy's parents are donating a new sports center."

"They've already had one dead student," Marica countered.

I clenched my jaw and gripped my hands together in my lap. Did I really live in a world where girls like Mandy could do things like this to girls like Charlotte because they were rich? Yes, I did. My hands shook. I was livid. Watching the gossip spread, sensing the eagerness in the room. The thrill of the danger and drama, provided by Mandy and her victim.

Jackals, I thought. And I'd been one of them, back home. I would have been laughing and murmuring right along with them.

So who was I madder at: Mandy or the old me? I didn't know, but I felt as if I might pop right out of my skin.

"Lindsay? Are you okay?" Julie whispered.

I looked up into her hazel eyes, filled with concern for me. She put her hand over mine and patted me. It brought me back down. Calmed my inner beast. What if I'd lost it the way I had in the movie theater? Stood up and starting yelling craziness about possessions and victims?

I glanced over at Shayna; true to her word, she was watching me. She dipped her head and looked steadily at me, as if to remind me that I wasn't in this all alone.

"Yeah, I'm good," I told Julie. Then I couldn't help myself; I ticked my glance over to Mandy's table, where she serenely sipped from her water glass, a little smile playing on her face. The center of our universe. Sleek, blonde, beautiful, vicious, evil. A tremor shook me. She had to be stopped.

Yes, Celia agreed. *Exactly.*

TEN

SHAYNA CAUGHT UP WITH ME as I left the commons with the rest of Grose. I slowed and let my dorm mates go ahead; they didn't notice because they were too busy discussing whether or not we should attend the prank. Last semester no one would have thought twice.

"Remember that old abandoned library?" Shayna asked under her breath. We'd gone there first semester for another of Mandy's pranks, when she'd transformed the whole thing into a haunted house. "You 'got' to go inside." She made air quotes. "And you told the rest of us that there were a lot of books still on the shelves. About brain surgeries and reforming bad girls and stuff."

I thought of the forbidding library, a cavernous room bulging with bookcases that reached into the gloom. The shelves were clogged with moldy books. Some of the titles were still visible. Female Behavioral Reformation. Neurological Science. Psychology of Hysterics.

"At least half of them were rotten," I replied, but I nodded as I spoke. "Which leaves the other half."

"Which leaves the other half. Let's skip Charlotte's mortification and check them out," she suggested. "Everyone else will be busy watching. It'll be the perfect time to start researching the unfinished business of the *dybbuks* of Marlwood."

I considered it. "Maybe I should watch out for Charlotte. Mandy forced Kiyoko to skinny-dip in the lake, and look what happened."

"She died much later," Shayna countered. "Not because of the prank. And anyway if we can do something to stop Mandy, *everyone* will be safe."

I knew that at least twenty or thirty girls would sneak out to watch Mandy's cruel hazing ritual. If Charlotte got in trouble, surely someone would have the sense to jump in and rescue her. And if Shayna and I were going to do this thing, we should do it. If I could find some way to placate Celia, to free her and Mandy, too . . . if *I* could be free of her, forever . . .

Free of all this. It sounded like a wonderful dream.

"Okay," I said. "What time is the prank?"

"One would assume it'll be the same as usual. Elevenish. When all the trusting housemothers will be fast asleep."

When all the housemothers could *say* they'd been asleep, to deny knowledge that their charges were breaking curfew and risking hypothermia in a pitch-black lake.

"Then we'll meet in front of the library at eleven," I said.

We nodded, and parted. I caught up with my dormies, who were complaining about homework—no fair, we were just back—catching up on what they'd done over break, and expressing their disbelief that Charlotte Davidson would actually agree to swim naked in Searle Lake in January.

"Mandy's just doing it to be mean," Ida said, and we all nodded, even Julie.

"Charlotte has to know she doesn't really have a shot at becoming one of Mandy's elect," Claire said.

"But why else would she do it?" Marica argued.

"Because no one else has made her the center of attention?" Julie said. "You know she wants to be. She wouldn't dress like Countess Dracula if she didn't."

"How very sad," Marica said. And then she ticked a quick glance toward me; I realized maybe she thought *I* dressed like an orphan just to get attention. It was a little embarrassing; she was so rich and exquisitely put together that she truly couldn't fathom that someone might just opt out of the fashion race because it could not be won, not for someone like me.

The icy rain returned that night, so the prank would have to be delayed. I watched as the word spread, as people got more and more excited as suspense grew. Charlotte basked in the attention for the next two days straight: noticed, selected by Mandy—the kiss of popularity burning like a brand on her forehead. Even if Charlotte didn't make it to the winner's circle, she was being given a chance to run the race, and few Marlwood girls had gotten that far. No matter that she might get shot down (probably), humiliated (definitely), or even . . . killed. For a few brief shining moments, she could see paradise.

"Someone should clue her in that she's just the sideshow," Julie told me as we looked on over those two days. "She's not Cinderella. Not to be mean, but it just doesn't seem like

Charlotte is going to turn cool overnight. I guess it wouldn't matter if we said anything, though. Right?"

It hadn't mattered last semester to the girls who had vied for spots on Mandy's team. In fact, I had come to Mandy's attention—lucky me—specifically because I had made it so clear that I didn't want to play. My uniqueness made me attractive. A challenge. Not to mention that I was possessed by Celia, and Mandy by Belle. But neither of us had known that when I first arrived at Marlwood.

As the tension mounted, Shayna and I planned our excursion to the old library in more detail. Shayna had a sense of mission, of purpose: avenging her former best friend, Kiyoko. I felt as if I were standing in front of an open grave, a shovel in my hand and a choice to be made—either I handed the shovel to Mandy and lay down in the dirt . . . or I hit her over the head with it and buried the evidence.

Please, please help me find a way out of this, I silently begged Shayna, at meals, between classes. Walking through the snow, staring at the white horse heads holding the thick white chain links in their mouths. Sitting in my room as Julie chattered obliviously on, while I watched the light shift on the ceramic head—*or was it moving?*—and the frozen figure in Mandy's window.

Fog swirled, covering our faces, hiding us from one another. Girls started playing tricks on each other, sneaking up, jumping out and saying, "Boo!" Screaming "Marco! Polo!" and talking about ghosts. Marlwood was known to be haunted. Everyone said so. Many, if not most of us, of course, believed it.

THEN THE RAIN FINALLY CLEARED, and it was Prank Night.

That evening, after dinner, Ms. Krige shared some gingerbread she'd made with her grandnieces in Portland, Oregon, and we brewed some spiced cider. As the evening stretched into Ms. Krige's bedtime, eyes gleamed and girls grinned secretively to each other. A death-defying Mandy Winters prankapalooza was about to begin!

I had my excuse prepared: I was on probation. So I told Julie I wasn't going.

"But Charlotte may need a lifeguard," she argued.

"*You'll* be there. You'll watch out for her."

So as was our habit, Julie went to bed fully dressed, while I put on my camisole and plaid pajama bottoms, pretending to really go to sleep. I was exhausted, but I lay with my eyes wide open, trying to fake being asleep, trying even harder not to stare at the white head, which Julie had transferred to our nightstand because she was afraid it might fall off the windowsill and break. It was angled slightly toward me, and the moonlight glinted off its forehead as Julie quietly slipped out of bed and tested her flashlight.

I heard Ida and Claire giggling and whispering in the hall; someone was creeping down the stairs. Julie mentioned my name. Then silence. They were in the bathroom by then, easing up the sash of the wooden window frame. There was a boulder outside the window, very convenient for climbing down.

I checked the digital alarm clock. It was 10:45 p.m. I got up, dressed in tights and jeans, a long-underwear T-shirt, and my mom's UCSD sweatshirt over that. Then I grabbed my army jacket, mittens, and a black knitted cap; also my flashlight and cell phone, even though there would probably be no reception. I just felt better having it with me.

I had to walk through the bathroom in the dark in order to get out the window. The five large tubs sat in the center of the large, white-tiled room, between the bank of sinks and the bathroom stalls. The showers were on the far wall, the single window above the large white wicker hamper for our towels. The window was cracked slightly open, making it easier to climb back into the dorm. I crawled onto the hamper, slid open the window, and slung my legs over onto the boulder. Then I dropped into the snow.

I gazed over at Jessel. The figure in Mandy's window was still there, and chills washed over me as I looked away. I didn't think that it was Celia's reflection, but I didn't know who—or what—it was. And I wasn't about to investigate just then.

I hurried through Academy Quad toward the buildings with our classrooms. There was the commons, and behind it, our old gym, with its frieze of naked Grecian male athletes, scheduled for demolition during the summer, when it would transform into the Winters Sports Complex. I'd seen the watercolor sketches in Dr. Ehrlenbach's office. Very lavish, very modern, looking nothing like the rest of the campus. I wondered if they'd keep the old Greek statues in the sculpture garden behind the gym. I hoped not; they creeped me out.

You won't be here next year, I reminded myself. And I shivered, hard; because what if I *was* here next year? What if I still wasn't free by the end of the term?

It began to snow again lightly, big, powdery flakes that at least weren't a repeat of the earlier icy rain. I felt awful for Charlotte but also annoyed—she'd asked for her own torture, after all. I gritted my teeth and zipped up my army jacket, still unused to the cold weather. If it ever snowed in San Diego, it made the national news.

I skidded along another path, remembering to slow down because of the black ice. The blank, staring horse heads observed me as I turned left, moving into the edge of the forest, tracing the route to the library from memory. I thought of Charlotte, who was slightly overweight, a major infraction among our skinny, toned student population. Mandy had probably targeted her because of it. Undressing in front of so many size zeros and twos would just add to Charlotte's humiliation, and Mandy would like that. A lot.

Troy, you're such an idiot for dating her, I thought. But when I even thought of his name, I went warm inside. Maybe that was proof that *I* was an idiot, too.

Or recreating a love triangle so powerful it had lived beyond the grave? Belle had tried to kill Celia over a guy. And Celia wanted *me* to kill Belle—but in self-defense, right? Because Mandy, possessed by Belle, was stuck in the same pattern?

Finally, I reached the old library—it reeked of dirt and decay. There was a light glowing in one of the upstairs windows. Shayna had nerves of steel, I thought, if she was brave enough to go upstairs alone. I reached the threshold of the front entrance, to find the splintered, moldy door canted against the rotting wood, leading to a pitch-black entryway. My Doc Martens sank into a pile of dust and trash, and I aimed my flashlight, sweeping up, down, seeing spiderwebs overhead, and dusty, broken beer bottles strewn across the floor. Last semester, Mandy and friends—and I, so very much not a friend—had tromped up and down the same hallway; it hadn't taken long for it to revert back to its abandoned appearance.

Above my head, I heard a hollow, knocking sound, like a very loud footfall, or, more likely, someone moving furniture. I wondered if Shayna had found something interesting. Images of operating tables and scalpels flashed in my mind; goosebumps rose over my skin, as if someone had just walked over my grave.

I had decided to tell her everything that had happened, and everything I knew: about the fire, and Belle, and my visions and/or nightmares. I would trust her, and she would help exorcise not only Mandy and company, but me as well. No murders, no more deaths, just . . . life.

And maybe, Troy.

"Hey?" I called. "It's me." My voice seemed to echo around me, too noisily. I winced; we needed to keep our mission on the downlow.

Another hollow sound. I shone my flashlight into the dark, deciding to wait for her to come to me. As a cold gust of wind blew behind me, I jumped and checked over my shoulder. It wasn't the same cold hand-like pressure that was Celia's trademark, I assured myself. Just . . . wind, making the spiderwebs dance.

I shifted my weight; I was cold and my nerves were starting to fray. I thought of Charlotte. I hoped she had come to her senses and told Mandy to go to hell. Or better yet, that Charlotte had pushed Mandy into the lake. Or best yet . . . just walked away. You did not want to be a target for Mandy Winters. You didn't want to be on her radar at all.

Another footfall. What was Shayna *doing*? I pulled out my cell to check the time, and I was shocked to discover that it was nearly eleven thirty—we were supposed to meet at eleven. How long had I been standing in the dark waiting for her to appear? Had she already come and gone?

There was a creak on the floorboard directly behind me, and I jerked my finger, accidentally taking a picture. The flash went off, blinding me; I blinked rapidly and whirled around, expecting to see Shayna.

But there was no one there.

"Hey, can you hurry up?" I said loudly—too loudly; actually, I shouted—and then I was so freaked out I scooted out of the library and onto the snow, turning to look up at the upstairs window where I had seen the light . . .

. . . But all the windows were dark.

"Shayna?" I whispered. It was the loudest sound I could make. Because suddenly, I was more than afraid. Something was wrong. I could feel it. Fear chilled me; or maybe it was Celia, serving as my spirit guide, warning me, as she had in the woods. I was in danger; I knew it.

I cleared my throat. Twice. "Shayna, come on. We have to get out of here."

There was no answer except for whooshing of the wind. My

mind raced. I had heard her upstairs. I had seen the light. She couldn't be pranking *me*. She'd been serious about the *dybbuk*, and Kiyoko's murder. Mandy was the sadistic hazer, not someone like Shayna, who had suffered at Mandy's hands.

"Come on, this isn't funny," I croaked. I sounded a hundred years old. I ran my flashlight over the front of the house, the gaping holes in the walls and the blackness. My heart sped into overdrive. I started backing away, squinting at the darkened windows, shivering in the snow. I pushed the button to check the time again . . . and instead, I opened up the picture I had taken a minute before.

The picture was a white blur, vaguely human-shaped. Maybe the bright flash had washed out the person's features. Maybe it was just Shayna teasing me, or someone spying on us . . . or . . .

. . . Or . . .

Someone else had been in there with me.

Terrified, I turned and ran.

ELEVEN

I RACED AWAY from the ruined old library, past beams of light flashing off the windows of the gym. It was coming from the statue garden, where eerie white marble figures of Greek gods and goddesses posed below the boughs of overhanging trees laden with snow. I avoided looking at them whenever I crossed from the dining commons to the gym. Despite their blank stares, they were eerily lifelike—and just one more thing about Marlwood that gave me the creeps.

So maybe that was it, I told myself. *It was somebody behind you with a flashlight. Or they dragged a statue out to the library somehow. That was the noise upstairs—them moving it around. Shayna's probably yukking it up with them right now, having a laugh at your expense.*

I had trouble believing that, accepting it. Shayna had seemed so sincere. But I'd misjudged people before. Riley had been sincere.

Troy, too.

"Go, Charlotte, go!" someone shouted. There was laughter,

some hoots, then a lot of shushing. I skidded on ice, nearly face-planting, not wanting to face them, to be the butt of a joke. I had to pull myself together. I was scared. And if Shayna had played me for a fool . . .

"*You know this is Mandy's doing.*" Celia's voice filled my head.

I jerked, hard. I was inside the pool area, standing on the low diving board, and staring down at her reflection three feet below me in the black water. Chlorine-laced mist rose from the surface, revealing her white face and her black eyes staring up at me; I could see them clearly even in the darkness. I was so startled I nearly tumbled off the board. Flailing my arms, for balance, I gave my head a shake. I didn't remember pushing on the door that led inside the pool area, or climbing onto the board. But here I was, and the door was hanging open, blowing in the icy wind, revealing the falling snow in the moonlight.

"*You have to stop her,*" Celia added.

Then the wind slammed the door shut, hard. I yelled, but footsteps and laughter drowned out the noise I made . . . jostling and shushing and someone crying, hard.

They were coming in here.

I turned and ran-walked the length of the board, unsteady and anxious, jumping down and crouching behind the board, then scooting backward, into the shadows thrown by the dark green wood equipment locker where kickboards, noodles, and weights were kept. I crouched beside it, shaking.

They came through the same door that I had, whispering and laughing. A single flashlight blinked on, revealing Mandy, dressed all in black, wearing a black knitted cap, and drinking from what looked to be a bottle of champagne. Mandy was holding the flashlight, and Lara walked beside her, bundled up against the cold.

Then the pool lights flicked on—both below the surface, one at the far end of the pool and the other beneath the diving board. Otherwise it was still dark in the gym. Mandy walked toward the edge of the pool and looked down, the light giving her face a bluish cast that reminded me of Kiyoko's face after she had drowned. A strange little smile flashed over her face and I glanced at the water. Had she seen Belle?

Next came Gretchen and Sangeeta, bundled in beautiful leather jackets trimmed in fur, and then Charlotte, flanked by Susi and Alis. Charlotte was wearing her steampunk coat and she was crying. Her red-streaked black hair was covered with snow. Julie walked behind her wearing a cute blue knitted cap, brushing the melting flakes off the shoulders of Charlotte's coat like Charlotte's valet. Julie's face was ruddy with cold.

Then more girls pushed their way into the room, giggling and snickering. Their breath mingled with the steam rising from the pool. Someone bellowed, "Be quiet, you guys," and there was more laughter and stumbling.

The door slammed shut. I was still hidden in the shadows, and I pressed my back against the wall. The snow on my clothes began to melt and I shivered.

"Oh God, that was so awesome," Rose declared, swooping down in front of Mandy. Her profile was to me and alcohol fumes wafted off her. She bowed with her arms extended, making *I am not worthy* motions. Sucking up. I was shocked. "A work of art, lady. *How* did you do that?"

"It's totally obvious. She replaced the statue," someone called out.

"Ssh, whisper," Lara commanded.

"Well, duh," Rose retorted, whispering. "But it was so *perfect*. It looked just like the original, with the perky chi-chis and all. I can't even figure out when you made the switcheroo."

"Did anyone else think Athena looked like Ehrlenbach?" Alis murmured.

"I've always thought that," Sangeeta replied. "Those statues are creepy even without turning them into robots."

Mandy grinned, in her element as the center of attention, when it was Charlotte who was crying. Ida and Claire pushed through the crowd and gave her little hugs. Then Julie handed her some tissues and Charlotte wiped her face with them.

"So how did you do it?" Rose persisted.

"If I told you, I'd have to kill you." Mandy waved her flashlight at the water in the pool as if she were drawing a picture, or writing words. Then she handed the flashlight to Lara. Lara played with it, holding it beneath her chin so that the light beamed upward, making her look demonic. Her eyes were hidden in their sockets; I couldn't tell what color they were.

Mandy yawned. "Now, let's finish this up so we can get *some* sleep before breakfast." She smiled at Charlotte. "Mademoiselle, onward?"

"She's totally traumatized," Ida snapped, stepping in front of Charlotte and raising her chin, squaring off. I remembered when Shayna had done the same for Kiyoko. She wasn't in the crowd, at least among the girls I could see from my hiding place. So where was she?

"Is that true?" Mandy asked Charlotte. "You want to bail?"

Sniffling, Charlotte shook her head. Then after another beat, she started unbuckling her coat.

"Take it off," Lara murmured.

"Take it off," Susi whispered. She nudged Sangeeta, who grinned, and echoed the words back to her.

More girls joined in. "*Take it off, take it off, take it off.*" The whispers rose like steam, like mean-girl energy made visible in the cold.

What possessed girls to do things like this to other girls, to themselves? Before I became a Jane-bot, I had been stunned by some of the really cruel things she and her friends had done, but at the same time I admired them because they were so subtle and effective. She'd drop a word here, make a suggestion there, and people's worlds collided. She wasn't a bully so much as an imp of the perverse. And she made it seem effortless, and even kind of classy. But what she did added to the chaos of making it through school, and wasn't that already hard enough?

But then, once I became one of her followers, all that stuff we did had seemed not mean but funny. Figuring out what to do next—what prank, what hilarious "practical joke"—and who to do it to was like learning a new language. I got better and better at it, and I reveled in my bizarre sense of accomplishment. It stopped being about my victims and became all about me. About power. That was Mandy in a nutshell.

Charlotte was still crying as she took off her coat. Julie took it from her. Beneath, she was wearing black boots, black trousers, and a black sweater with a bronze clockwork design on it.

Steampunk. She pulled off her boots and then her pants, which Julie also took, and stood in her black boy-short underwear and her sweater.

"*Take it off.*"

Charlotte hesitated, then pulled her sweater off over her head. She stood in her bra and underwear, looking miserable and determined, and climbed onto the diving board—where I had been standing ten minutes before.

"Wait. First, give me back the locket," Mandy said, reaching out her hand. Charlotte climbed back off the diving board and went back to Julie, who held out her coat. Shivering, Charlotte dug into the side pocket. She frowned slightly, and looked in the other one. She looked at Mandy.

"Um, it's not . . . let me look again . . . "

I looked over at Mandy. Her eyes narrowed and she pulled her lips back from her perfect white teeth. She looked a little crazy.

"You'd better have it," she said tightly.

"Let me check," Julie murmured to Charlotte. "Maybe in your pants . . . "

"Charlotte?" Mandy walked toward her. "*Where's my locket?*"

Charlotte felt in her jacket, checking the sleeves. She was shaking with cold. "I don't know! I had it . . . I thought it was in my pocket."

Now Ida joined in, searching through Charlotte's clothes. Mandy yanked the coat from them and turned it upside down, shaking it. Julie put Charlotte's sweater over Charlotte's shoulders. Charlotte barely noticed.

"If you lost it . . . " Mandy said, and she looked back over at the pool.

A terrible icy feeling washed over me and my mind filled with the memory of Belle pushing me—correction, pushing *Celia*—under the water in the huge tub in the bathroom. Forcing Celia's head down, on the verge of drowning her.

I looked at Charlotte, and at Mandy. My heart skipped a beat. Mandy . . . Charlotte . . . the pool . . .

I was about to step from the shadows and yell at them to stop when the door slammed open. Snowy wind rushed in. There were a few gasps; someone said, "Oh God." I heard Sangeeta whisper, "Is it Dr. Ehrlenbach?"

Then Julie said, "Shayna?"

I left my hiding spot and quietly joined the group. At five-two, I couldn't see over Julie, so I gave her a nudge. She glanced at me, looking surprised, then made some room for me.

Lara aimed the flashlight at a figure in the doorway. It was Shayna, dressed in jeans and striped legwarmers, her silver puffy jacket, and a fur hat. She had on black gloves. Her eyes were bulging; her mouth was a huge O and she stared straight ahead, as if none of us were there.

"Hey, good one," Rose said. A couple of the girls clapped.

Shayna kept staring.

"Oh, I'm so scared," Claire drawled.

"Shayna," I said, pushing through the crowd. There was a ripple of comments—no one had seen me, of course. I didn't care. Something was very wrong.

Something in her face made me stop, dead. I was about two

feet away from her, and I was afraid to get any closer. She stared at me; then she gasped.

"*Dybbuk*," she said. Or at least that was what I thought she said. I wasn't sure.

I yanked off my gloves and put my hands on her face. She was freezing. Her lips worked and her shoulders rose. She began to mumble.

"Shayna," I whispered, aware that everyone was staring at us, not sure what else to do. I tried to ease her back outside, but she remained rooted to the spot. "Shayna, what's wrong? Tell me." I pressed my ear against her lips.

"He . . . he . . . " she whispered. "He . . . "

She made a strangling sound. I jerked my head, and she didn't move hers back; we stood nose to nose staring into each other's eyes. Now she stumbled backward, and shifted her attention over my shoulder, and exhaled in a ragged way, as if someone were repeatedly punching her in the stomach.

I turned. Mandy stood in Shayna's line of vision. Lara, Susi, and Gretchen stood on her left, and Sangeeta and Alis were on her right. Their eyes were normal, but they were still scary. They looked like a glammed-out gang, the rich bitches of school.

Then suddenly, without warning, Shayna threw back her head and started screaming. That set off a chain reaction, girls shrieking, the tile walls echoing and magnifying the sounds.

"God!" Mandy shouted. She raced forward, knocking me out of the way, and clamped her hand over Shayna's mouth. "What the hell is wrong with you?"

Shayna flailed wildly, batting and kicking at Mandy. Mandy held on.

She's smothering her, I thought. I raced forward and tried to pry Mandy's hand away from Shayna's mouth. Then Shayna staggered backward and landed on her butt on the concrete floor. She heaved, whispering, panting. Tears rolled down her face. She saw me, grabbed at me, chattering at me in what sounded like nonsense. I bent down and she clung to me, jibbering.

"Tell me," I whispered, "in English."

"Call someone," Julie said. "Get help!"

"No one's phone will work," Mandy snapped, sounding both frightened and irritated, and I wasn't sure if she was reminding us or giving an order. Mandy squatted beside me and Shayna clung harder to my hands, gazing up at me with huge, pleading eyes.

"Don't touch her," I told Mandy. "She's scared of you."

"Oh, *right*," Mandy sneered. "Get up, Shayna. Knock it off."

"She's having a breakdown," Ida said. "She needs help!"

"We'll take her to the infirmary." Mandy looked over her shoulder. "C'mon, Lara."

"No." I said. "No way." I eased Shayna to her feet, forcing Mandy to break contact. All expression left Shayna's face and she stared straight ahead—not at me, not at anything. Her hands were icy. I squeezed them. "Shayna, it's me."

She didn't respond.

Mandy raised a brow at me. "We need to get her some help. What do you think I'm going to do, eat her?"

"Oh, God, we're going to get in trouble." That was Gina Troyes, who was in Hanover Hall.

"We aren't," Mandy said, facing the group. "Not if we stick to a story. Lindsay, Lara, and I heard Shayna screaming and we came running into the quad. The *quad. No one else was there.* Right?"

The other girls shifted and looked at each other. A few were crying. Julie mouthed, *What is going on?* And I just shook my head.

Mandy glared at the group. "If you stick to the story, you'll be okay. But if one person blows it, just one . . . "

Then she frowned at me. "Let's go."

Lara held the door open and we crossed the threshold. The snow was coming down hard and I shivered. The door shut, leaving Shayna and me with Mandy and Lara, and the snow. There was no way I wanted to be alone with them, but I wasn't going to leave Shayna with them, either. I turned to get someone who was on my side, but Shayna stumbled forward like a zombie and I had to hurry to catch up. Maybe as long as their eyes were normal, we would be okay. Or maybe I should yell for help, wake up an adult. But maybe that would escalate the situation faster than anyone would be able to get to us . . .

"Hurry up," Mandy said to Lara and me. She wrapped both hands around Shayna's slack face. "She's half-frozen."

I let that simple act of kindness reassure me—or rather, I clung to it like a life ring, hoping that Mandy would stay Mandy and Lara, Lara, as we rushed to the main road, leaving the gym in our wake. I was trembling all over, afraid my knees were going to give way. That was the thing about Mandy—as mean as she was, as thoughtless and cruel, she could also be very charming and sweet. Queen bees didn't gather loyal followers if the only emotional depth they had consisted of various layers of cruelty. At some point, meanness outweighed any advantages they offered, even for someone as rich and exotic as Mandy.

But there's Belle, I reminded myself. Mandy had deliberately let Belle come into her life. Maybe she hadn't known how dangerous Belle was. Maybe her fear had been real when she'd visited Troy in the hospital.

"What the hell *is* wrong with her?" Lara asked, peering at Shayna.

Dybbuk, I thought. Had she really said that? I checked her eyes. Not normal, but not completely black. Her lush dark hair, usually straightened, was now frizzed out, almost like she'd been electrocuted. I couldn't reconcile the person I saw in front of me with the girl who had whispered her worst fears to me. I slipped my hand through hers, lacing gloved fingers, squeezing, trying to get a reaction. There was nothing. It was as if she were . . . empty. After all the screaming, she was left with nothing.

"What did you do to her?" I demanded.

"Oh, no, you don't," Mandy said. "You're not blaming this on me. You blame me for everything."

"What did you do?" My voice rose.

"Jesus, keep your voice down," Lara snapped.

I pulled Shayna away and wrapped my arm around her waist.

"I didn't do anything to her. Why would I?" Mandy asked. Her lip curled. "Why would I even bother?"

"You can drop the act," I said. "There's no one here but us."

"Don't start with me," Mandy said. "Just shut up and let's go."

"Where?" I demanded. "Where are we *really* going?"

Mandy rolled her eyes. "To the infirmary, tea leaf." She pointed. "Right there."

Not fifty feet from us, the old Victorian brick building stood like a stalwart guardian beneath the snow. Mandy rang the buzzer beside the green door and Ms. Simonet, our nurse, answered. Her brown hair shot with silver, she was wearing a bathrobe over plaid pajama bottoms, socks, and nurse's clogs. As I held onto Shayna, Mandy gave an Oscar-winning performance: worried friend, good deed, scared and cold.

"Shayna, did you take anything?" Ms. Simonet asked her. She meant drugs. Shayna was mute. Ms. Simonet got out a penlight and checked her pupils. "Thank you, girls," she said. "Go back to your dorms."

"Okay, Ms. Simonet," Mandy said. She and Lara took off. Resolute, I remained behind.

"Please let me stay," I begged.

"Sorry." She gestured for the door. "You've done all you could. Go back to bed."

I touched Shayna's cheek.

"She's so cold," I murmured.

"Say goodnight," Ms. Simonet ordered me.

"Goodnight, Shayna. I'll come see you in the morning." I tried to smile. I felt horrible. I hadn't done all I could. I should have . . . what? What could I have done?

"*Kill her,*" Celia said aloud, in my voice. I coughed to cover it and left, running as fast as I could.

TWELVE

I FELT THE COLD creeping through my head and down through my body as I headed back to Grose: Celia, making me aware of her presence. I shook harder. I thought Shayna and I were going to pull it off—find a way for me to get rid of Celia that didn't involve killing. But right now, as I was forced to abandon her, I felt such incredible anger rise inside me—that if Mandy had been there—

Yes, Celia said.

I stomped back down the main path staring into every shadow, half-expecting Mandy and Lara to jump me. I listened to my overcranked heartbeat roaring in my ears as I reached the door of my dorm, hoping it was unlocked.

As I touched the handle, I heard whispering behind me. I darted into the bushes at the corner, in the darkness, watching as Julie, Marica, and Ida crept anxiously along the path, like enemy soldiers about to launch a surprise attack. Julie was a pale face surrounded by dark fabric; Marica's long black hair waved in the wind beneath a fur hat. Ida had on a fur-trimmed hoodie and all I could see of her face were her large, dark eyes.

"Oh my God, that was so weird," Julie whispered. "I've never seen anything like that."

"I have. When my *abuelo* went crazy," Marica said. "He was like a, how do you say it, a zombie."

"Ssh," Ida murmured. "Someone's here."

I stepped from the shadows, and Julie ran to me and threw her arms around me.

"Linz!" she cried. "What happened? Where is Shayna?"

"We walked her to the infirmary." I took a deep breath. "I didn't want to leave her."

"I wouldn't have wanted to either," Julie said. She studied my face, silently asking questions I had no answers for.

"Well, what are they doing with her?" Ida demanded.

"*Guys,*" Ida remonstrated. "Don't wake up Mrs. Krige."

"What were you guys doing before you came in the gym?" I asked, trying to make some sense of it all. "Did Mandy move the skinny-dipping from the lake?"

"Yeah, because it's so cold," Julie said. The others nodded. "It started in the statue garden—"

Just then, a light went on in our bathroom, illuminating the window I had left open.

"Shit," Ida said. "Is that Krige?"

We all crouched down, watching as a head poked out. It was Claire, who'd come back ahead of everyone else. We stood and dashed over, Julie in the lead, and Claire leaned out, gesturing for us to climb in.

"You guys, get in here," Claire said. "Ms. Krige is up."

We clambered in, even me, and sped through the bathroom. Julie and I flew into our room, where we stripped off our clothes and put on our pajamas, hopped into our beds. I was shaking so hard my head began to throb.

"I'm scared," Julie whispered. "It was awful." Then, after a beat, "Were you ever like that? Like Shayna was? Um, when you had your . . . breakdown?"

"No," I told her, and it was true. "I just cried a lot, and I couldn't sleep." I tried to breathe, but my chest was too tight. Shayna. What had they done to her?

What were they doing to her now?

The hall light came on; I could see the light beneath our door, and then there was a soft rap on our door.

"Come in," Julie said.

It was Ms. Krige, in a long belted apricot bathrobe and a pair of fluffy slippers. She was wearing foam curlers. I didn't even know you could still buy them. She stood in the doorway for a moment, as if letting her eyes adjust.

"I just wanted to make sure you were all right," she said. "Sorry to disturb you, girls."

She shut the door. It was the first time she had ever checked on us. Ever.

Julie turned on the spindly ebony lamp on the nightstand between our beds; the white head gleamed. Julie was clutching Panda to her chest, and she looked like she was ten years old at the most.

"What is going on?" she said.

I got up and went into the hall. Ms. Krige was heading toward her own room by now, and I caught up with her.

"What's the matter?" I asked. "Is it Shayna? I was one of the girls who found her wandering around. I know I should have gotten you, but . . . "

"Her parents have been called. She'll be going home."

"No," I breathed.

"Dr. Ehrlenbach is with her in the infirmary." She cupped my cheek. "She's in good hands."

No, I wanted to shout, *she's not. No one here is in good hands.*

"Go back to bed." Her voice was kind. Ms. Krige liked me; I wasn't a rich, spoiled girl who treated her like hired help. At least, that was what she told me when we had parted for winter break. "Try to get some sleep."

She left me there, and I headed back into our room. Julie was sitting cross-legged, Panda in her lap. The white head was gazing at me. I ignored it and walked to the window. The figure I had seen in Mandy's window was gone.

"Shayna's been locked up before," Julie said, quietly.

"Who told you that?"

"She . . . she sees things." Her voice was strained.

Like I do, I wanted to fill in. But I kept my face to the window.

"She was on meds," Julie continued. "Maybe she stopped taking them. Or something."

Or something. I clenched my hands together. "Why didn't I know this?"

"I thought you did. Everybody knows, Linz." She exhaled. "If you were, um, if *you* had a problem . . . I'd be here for you."

She's afraid I might go bonkers, too. Correction: that I'll go bonkers again.

"Thanks," I said, fighting back tears. Julie was so sweet, but there was no way she would believe me if I told her what was really going on. I had tried to before, and she made me promise to get help. She had no memory of that horrible night, the night I had almost died.

Almost been *murdered*.

"You really took charge tonight," Julie praised me. She touched her short hair as if gathering up a phantom braid, and then played with her earring instead—a plain gold stud.

"You're so good. I think that's why you get . . . you have so much *trouble*," Julie said warmly. "You worry about people. That's nice." She gave me another hug, and I made her an unspoken promise—that I would keep her safe.

"It must have been so hard for you," she mused, dropping her voice to a whisper, "watching your mom get sicker. Not being able to help." She smiled sadly at me, and I shrugged. It *was* hard. It was horrible.

She looked thoughtful. "Mandy and those guys are still into all that ghost story stuff, like last semester. They're talking about holding this big group séance. Maybe we could ask if we could—"

"No." I was nearly yelling and she jumped. "No," I said more quietly. "That stuff is . . . " I shook my head. "It's not good for you."

A tiny hint of petulance flared across her features, and I could almost hear her snapping back, *You're not the boss of me.*

"It's not good for anybody," I added, seeing Shayna melt down all over again.   A flash of movement in Academy Quad caught my attention; the hair rose on the back of my head as Mandy and Lara slid through the snow, holding onto each other's arms and laughing. They looked like spiders as they darted along the icy path. As I started to step away from the window, Lara looked up; she jostled Mandy, and both of them smiled straight at me, and waved. I didn't wave back. Mandy twirled in a little circle, and they melted into the darkness, heading down the hill for Jessel.

"Tell me about the prank," I said, remaining at the window. Standing guard. "Go through the whole thing."

"It was kind of random," Julie said vaguely, as if she didn't want to talk about it. "Charlotte had to find this old locket, like a scavenger hunt. All she knew was that it was in the statue garden. Mandy has this mannequin and they dressed it up like a goddess and put it with the others. They put the locket around its neck and when Charlotte walked up to it, they made it move. She almost had a heart attack."

"How hilarious," I muttered.

"Charlotte was a good sport about it. Then she had to jump in the pool. Well you were there. Mandy's so pissed about that locket. Maybe it's back in the statue garden."

"Maybe," I said, but I didn't care.

I remembered the image on my camera and the light in the window. The footfalls. Had that really been Shayna, sneaking up to spook me?

If it hadn't been, who was it? Did Shayna see? Is that what had pushed her over the edge? I could almost hear her voice in my brain, ricocheting like an echo.

Suddenly, the light in Mandy's turret room went on. The door was open and she walked in, holding something under her arm. A white head. Lara brought up the rear, and when they turned sideways, I realized they were carrying a mannequin between them. They set it up at the window, positioning it just so. It was the figure I had seen, now wrapped in some kind of plaster-looking Grecian robe.

They waved at me again. I felt coldness seeping through me.

Mandy blew me a kiss.

A little while later, the lights finally went out in Mandy's room. I don't know how long I stood staring out the window. I thought it was only for a minute but maybe it was more, because when I turned and faced Julie, she was curled up around Panda, fast asleep.

TAKE CARE of the worst ones first. The ones who will try to escape. And then . . .

I woke up with Julie standing over me, gently shaking my shoulder. It was still the middle of the night, pitch-black through the windows.

"It's okay," she whispered. "You're having another bad dream." She looked tired and freaked out. "Again."

"Sorry," I said. Everyone had nightmares, I wanted to remind her, but coming so fast after Shayna's meltdown—and with Julie's knowledge of my own emotional shattering—a Lindsay Anne Cavanaugh nightmare took on special significance. Especially if it recurred at least a dozen times in the same night.

I couldn't keep doing it, or Julie would walk *me* down to the infirmary. Maybe I should pretend to have "an episode" of my own, so I could see Shayna and make sure she was all right—a relative term, if there ever was one.

But there was no guarantee a scheme like that would work—and so many possibilities for it to backfire all over me.

"I'm sorry," I repeated.

"Maybe it would help if you talked about it," Julie ventured. She sat on the edge of my bed and smoothed a corkscrew of hair off my cheek. Staring down at it, she pushed at it with the palm of her hand, fascinated.

"Hey," I teased.

"Sorry. It's just so springy," she said. Her weary, worn-out smile was kind. "So, what do you keep dreaming about?"

I could never tell her.

"I'm in Paris, at a fashion show," I said. She listened carefully. "And my platinum American Express card is *denied. And Paris Hilton sees it happen.*"

I smiled, and Julie batted me. "You freak! I almost believed you."

"And yet, you got better grades than me last term. How can that possibly *be*?"

She yawned, and I patted her on the shoulder. "I promise not to have any more nightmares tonight," I said. "Okay?"

"Okay." She gave my hair another pat, but I could see the

worry in her eyes. She honestly cared about me. But she really did think I was a whack job. Julie had been very sheltered—until she came to Marlwood, anyway. I wondered if her parents, like mine, pictured Marlwood as a protective cocoon where their little silkworm would metamorphose into a butterfly. We would have been safer in the Middle East.

After she got back in bed, she whispered, "Good night," turned out the light and settled in. Soon her soft breathing told me she was asleep. I lay staring at the ceiling, praying for the dawn, wanting so badly for the night to end. I tried to keep my eyes open, force myself to stay awake.

But I was exhausted. Before I knew it, I could feel myself falling asleep . . .

Take care of the worst ones first. The ones who will try to escape. And then . . .

THIRTEEN

January 16

"H'lo," Troy said, yawning, and I clutched the landline tightly. I was in the kitchen, sneaking a call to him before anyone else got up. I had tried to get reception on my cell, but my technology failed me. It was six in the morning. I wanted to be sure not to miss him.

"I need you," I said, then cleared my throat, because that wasn't what I had planned to say. "I need *help*," I amended.

"Lindsay?" His fuzzy voice was suddenly less fuzzy.

I looked over my shoulder to make sure no one was eavesdropping. The light from the kitchen spilled into the dark, empty hall. Bad art on the wall stared accusingly at me. Troy Minear was still officially Mandy's boyfriend, and no one at Marlwood would condone stealing another girl's guy, no matter how they felt about the girls involved. That hadn't been my experience in San Diego; no one leaped to my defense when Jane stole Riley. It was assumed that she should have him if she wanted him because she was Jane and I was not. Jane was entitled to have a cool boyfriend. I had just been amazingly—and temporarily—lucky.

I ran my hand along the marble kitchen countertop. I didn't need a boyfriend. I needed an ally.

"Things have been . . . " I began, and then, to my horror, I started to cry.

"What's wrong? Did she find out?"

That we drove up together, he meant. I didn't know if Mandy knew.

"Did she . . . do something to you?" he pressed. His voice was tense, angry.

"Troy, don't say anything about it to her. Please, don't," I said. "I-I didn't call you because of Mandy." That wasn't true, but I didn't know how to explain it to him. I began to cry again, covering my mouth so I wouldn't wake anyone up. I pressed my forehead against the wooden cabinet where we kept our candles and flashlights in case of a power outage. Distractedly opened and closed a door. Saw all the shiny, sharp kitchen knives.

"No. This entire situation is my fault. I've let it go on too long. Let me at least do something. I'm coming over there," he informed me.

"No," I blurted, but of course, that was exactly what I wanted. I pressed my fingers against my forehead. "Yes," I said. "Please."

"We'll get together tonight," he said.

We made a plan, and I was so relieved I cried some more. I felt like someone in the middle of the ocean who knew exactly when the rescue ship would arrive, and had only to keep treading water until then. I didn't know how I managed to get through all my classes. I fuzzed out a dozen times; I couldn't keep track. More than once, a teacher would dismiss us and I'd realized I hadn't heard a word she or he had said during the entire period.

More than once, Mandy caught my eye, narrowing her gaze at me, pursing her lips as if I smelled bad. Did she know Troy was going to meet me? Had he told her, out of a misplaced need to be honest and true?

I worried what she might do to me. Really worried. I worried about Shayna. And I pushed through the long hours; then, when Mandy and the others attended their extracurriculars, I loped back toward the abandoned library, staring at the disintegrating building in the light of day, and finding it no less terrifying. I had half an hour until Troy was due; I had brought my digital camera and I shot dozens of shots of the library exterior, holding my breath, listening to my heartbeat roaring in my ears. I didn't know what I was looking for—ectoplasm? Ghostly residue? I was afraid to look through the viewfinder—or at the picture on my cell phone. Maybe I'd have the courage to look when I was with Troy.

A weak sun blinked through tattered gray clouds, and the pines bobbed their branches at me as I kept taking pictures, raising the lens toward the window where I had seen the light.

I gasped. It was boarded up, moss-covered planks of gray wood nailed criss-cross over the frame. I lowered the camera and looked with my eyes. The moss traced patterns from the boards to the frame in an unbroken path. There was no way I could have seen anything through it, unless someone had come in last night to nail it shut, and smear moss over it.

As the wind blew, I could almost hear a voice I knew from my endless night of bad dreams: *Take care of the worst ones first.*

Fear fell over me like a net made of icicles; chills skittered up and down my spine. Had they "taken care" of Shayna? Were they going to take care of me next? Because we knew?

What had she seen? What had made her go crazy? Something slammed inside the building; I nearly jumped out of my skin. Wood on wood, hard. Maybe not a foot slamming into a wall; maybe a shutter, slamming in the wind.

But the wind was not that strong.

I turned half away, not willing to show my back, too afraid to look again. I raced to the chain-link fence, quickly locating the hole I'd first seen last semester. I had to drop to my hands and knees to crawl through, and I froze for a few seconds. I couldn't help imagining something racing up behind me while my back was turned, and grabbing me . . ..

"No," I said aloud.

Then I scuttled through the hole like a weird little crab. Fog swirled around me, and as I straightened, I saw Troy's T-bird at the bottom of the hill. I began to slip-slide down the hill, through the mud and the snow, straining my eyes to see if he was sitting inside the car.

"Hey," Troy said behind me. "I went to look for you."

As I stopped and looked back up the hill, he picked his way down to me. He was wearing a dark brown bomber jacket, a brown sweater, and jeans. His blue eyes gazed straight into mine. The wind was ruffling his dark hair, and he opened his arms as he reached for me. He was warm, and when I slid myself inside his jacket and pressed my face against his chest, I felt safe for the first time since getting back to Marlwood.

"Lindsay," he said, wrapping himself around me, cradling me. I shut my eyes and smelled clean cotton and a bit of sweat. I inhaled him, and whimpered and clung to him, feeling his athlete's muscles and the hardness of his chest. He was strong; he could fight off demons.

His lips kissed the crown of my crazy hair. And I wanted like anything to tip back my head and kiss him. It was so tempting . . . but I made myself step backward, giving my head a little shake as he reached for me.

"Troy, listen," I said. *Shayna's gone, and I'm alone*, I thought. *And I have no one except Celia. And what she's telling me, what she's saying . . .*

Taking my hand, he led me to a fallen log, and eased me down, carefully, as if I might shatter. "What's going on?"

I had rehearsed a dozen different things to say, and I still didn't have it right. "Everything is wrong here."

"Wrong?" he repeated, smoothing back my hair, looking, really looking at me. Listening hard.

How much could I tell him? "Things are happening over here. Bad things that are tied to the past. Something from a long time ago." I shook my head. I knew I wasn't making any sense. To him, anyway.

"Troy, please, just . . . just believe me," I said. "I need to find out what exactly . . . "

"I heard about Shayna," he said. After a beat, he added,

"From Mandy." He gave my hand a squeeze. "I know Shayna was Kiyoko's best friend."

I nodded. Of course he was talking to Mandy. She was his girlfriend. I couldn't forget that, couldn't assume anything. Slowly, gently, I eased my hand away and crossed my arms over my chest.

"Please, don't be mad at me," he said, misreading my body language. "You know how I feel, Linz." When I didn't reply, he stood up and combed his hands through his hair. "Why should you know? *I* don't even know how I feel. No, wait, I do. I *do*." His eyebrows wrinkled over his sea-blue eyes, as he peered through his heavy lashes at me. His mouth was pulled tight in misery, revealing his dimples, making him, if anything, harder to resist. I want to be with you."

I still didn't answer. I knew we were in a triangle; I could almost hear Celia saying, "*You see? You, Mandy, and Troy . . . Belle, me, and . . .* " And who? Celia had not said a name. "*She'll kill you before she gives him up. Like Belle killed me.*"

"How can I help?" he asked, coming back to the log, sitting down. He touched my cheek, examining my scratch. I felt his fingertips on my cheek, and I was sorry I had made such a point of extricating my hand from his grip. "How did this happen?"

"Do you think I'll have a scar?" I asked, touching it with my free hand. He ran his knuckles along my finger, then cradled my cheek.

He frowned. "Mandy didn't . . . ?"

It surprised me that he'd sense she was capable of hurting me. How could he know this, and still date her? Yet it gave me hope, in a twisted way. He was realizing how truly screwed up she was. That *she* was the unhinged one. Not me.

"The help that I need," I said carefully, wiping my eyes and trying hard to take care of my nose without his noticing, "is for us to do some research on Marlwood. It was a home for wayward girls a century ago, and then it closed."

"Really?" He smiled faintly, and I saw those amazing dimples, which deepened as he cocked his head, studying me. He reached in a pocket and handed me a paper napkin. "That's cause for tears."

I didn't join in his amusement. "Seriously. They did terrible things to the girls. I-I think they performed lobotomies on them."

He blinked and almost let go of me. "*Here?*"

At fancy Marlwood, I translated. "It's not exactly in the brochure," I drawled, and I could feel my snarky self coming back to life.

"Unless you flip through all the pages backward. Then the secret is revealed on page 666," he explained, nodding wisely. "Every thirteenth word—"

He *was* my friend, and my snarkmate. I couldn't help myself; I glommed onto him and gave him a tight hug.

"Oof, you're going to make me fart," he joked, to acknowledge that he was my snarkmate. Because snarkmates knew a snarkmate when they saw one.

Then he wrapped his arms around me again and squeezed me just as hard.

"Go for it, Linz," he urged. "Let it all out, once and for all."

He made me smile. And I finally felt just how exhausted I was from my nightmare-filled nights. As if I understood things that hadn't been clear before. I knew he was still officially Mandy's boyfriend, and I knew what Celia had shown me about what jealous rages could do. But I also understood why Troy was having trouble letting go of Mandy—he *cared* that she was hurting, or at any rate pretending to be. Because he was kind. And good.

"Can you look at something?" I asked. He nodded, and I pulled out my cell phone.

"Wait." He waved his hand at me. "Backtrack for a sec. Why would they perform lobotomies?"

"To make the girls sweet and obedient. That was the fashion, a hundred years ago."

"Wow, too bad those days are gone, eh?" He smirked. "Seriously, though, how did you find this out?"

"Look at this," I insisted, holding up my cell phone. I flicked on the photo screen. "It's not a lobotomy," I added.

He held the phone. "You look cute. It's too close up and you're all washed out, but you're still cute. Who's behind you?" He cocked his head, studying the picture.

So you see it, too, I thought, sagging inside with relief. But I was still too afraid to look.

I felt that terrible cold on the back of my neck, then all over inside me, as if my blood was frozen. Celia was with me. Or controlling me, or guiding me. Before I knew what I was doing, I reached for the phone and stared hard at the image. Willing it to be something; but it was a white shape, and nothing more. No features, no hair.

"I don't know." My voice was steady. "Who does it look like to you?"

"But . . . didn't you see him? Didn't you know he was there?" *He?*

"How do you know . . . ?" I began, and then I realized: whoever it was, was much taller than me. I'm only five-two, but the . . . blur . . . was at least six feet tall. Despite the models in our student population, no girl at Marlwood was that tall. That meant that a guy had snuck up behind me while I was waiting for Shayna. Mandy liked to invite Lakewood boys over to observe her pranks, and sometimes help out with them. Maybe it was one of them?

"Where was this taken?" he asked.

"At an old building," I hedged, in case he wound up telling Mandy about our meeting after all, "and I thought I was checking the time, but I accidentally took this picture. I didn't know anyone else was around."

He was quiet for a moment. I could practically see the wheels turning in his brain, and I wanted to hug him again, and thank him for not dismissing me and telling me I was seeing things. Whatever—whoever—it was, he saw it, too. He took the phone from me again.

I licked my lips. "Remember when we were driving up here, in the fog, and you thought you saw—"

"Miles," he snapped, shutting my phone. "That's who that is." He brought the phone closer to his eyes. "Yeah. I can see that stupid fifties haircut of his. It's that freak."

He turned the phone around and showed it to me. All I saw was a blobby, vaguely human shape.

"And now he's stalking you," he said, clenching his teeth. A muscle jumped in his cheek and his free hand balled into a fist; his eyes went as cold as I felt. "Like he does with every other girl Mandy tries to be friends with." His voice was as flat and solid as concrete and I pictured him pushing Miles off a cliff, and Miles landing hard.

Note to self, I thought. *Never piss off Troy Minear.*

"He does that, isolates her."

"She has friends here," I argued.

"Which is my point." He got up and started pacing. Fast. The change in him was startling. Beyond hurting my feelings, it was scary.

"What he did to her . . . " Then he shook himself, as if he was saying too much. So maybe he did know about the Lincoln Bedroom rumor.

I looked down at the phone pic again. It still didn't look like Miles. A wave of desperation roared over me; he wasn't going to help me after all. He was too busy being outraged on Mandy's behalf. Closing the flip top, I stuffed it in my pocket, averting my head so that he wouldn't see fresh tears welling.

"Okay, well," I choked out, wrapping my jacket around myself. "Thanks . . . "

"Show me where you took this."

"Okay, I—"

He took my hand and headed toward the fence.

"*Now?*" The thought of going back there, ever—

"Yes. *He's* what's wrong over here." Then he pulled me around to face him. The faded yellow light bleached his face; his eyes looked gray, and ghostly. He bent to kiss me again.

"*Let him*," Celia whispered inside my head. "*Then he will be bound to you. Then he will protect you.*"

I closed my eyes, and sealed my fate.

FOURTEEN

IT WAS DARK, and it was late, and before I was ready, Troy and I were standing outside the derelict library. Poised on the threshold, I listened for banging noises above my head. And I froze. I couldn't go in there. I just couldn't.

"This is where I took the picture," I said. "Right here."

He gazed around, then took his cell phone out of his jacket and punched on the light function. Trash and spiderwebs shifted in the icy air. He stopped, listening, and turned to me.

"Stay here," he said.

"I'll go with you," I replied. I didn't want to be alone; so I slid my hand through his, and he drew me close.

"Okay, but be careful. If it's not Miles, there might be some homeless guy sleeping in here. The Marlwood Stalker."

"Don't make fun," I implored him.

"Oh, I'm not. Believe me." His voice took on that hard edge again. "I'm *so* not."

I didn't know how I did it, but I walked with him down the

hall. It was cold, and it smelled like mud and mold. Graveyard smells.

The first turn led us into the reading room. It was as I remembered it: Bookcases in various stages of disarray lined the cracked walls. More books were scattered on the floor, and here and there old display cases with broken glass fronts stood on spindly legs. There was a rotted carpet over the destroyed wooden floor; across the room, a trio of glassed-in bookcases hung open. Mushrooms and mold spilled down their faces. Piles of rotting books spilled out.

"What a lot of stuff," he said. He bent down and picked up what appeared to be a ledger book, and shone his light on it. "David Abernathy, M.D. Huh." He flipped it open. "There's some kind of class list." He shrugged and put it in his pocket. "And look at this—"

I had a sudden feeling that we weren't alone. It was so strong that I whirled around, startling him. He straightened.

"What is it?"

"There's someone here," I said.

He froze, listening. I saw his frown, so intense it etched lines in his face and made him look old.

"Where?" he said. He headed back for the hall.

All I could think of were Shayna's dead eyes. I didn't want him to look for anything. I wanted us both to get out of there.

"Troy, please," I whispered, "it's dark and—"

"If that asshole is here . . . I'll just take a quick look—"

"Please, no," I said. "Please, I-I'm just so freaked out."

I reached up on tiptoe to kiss him, to distract him. The cell phone light was still on and I saw uncertainty waver over his face like clouds. The uneven glow made him look like someone else, someone I didn't know. For a tiny flicker, I was afraid.

"Lindsay, if Miles is here . . . " he whispered back.

"I want to leave. *Please.*"

I kissed him again, hesitantly and slightly embarrassed to be manipulating him like this. Then he sighed, frustrated, and I knew I had won this round.

He held his cell phone up, surveying the hall, looking up at the ceiling.

"You're sure."

With another sigh, he led the way down the hall. I kept turning around, half-expecting to see . . . what? A transparent figure floating after us? Miles, laughing his head off? Mandy, Lara, and Alis, with murder in their black eyes?

Unaware, Troy skirted a broken beer bottle, shining the light down to help me avoid the pieces of glass.

"We should come back here again with better light," he said.

"Sure," I said, although nothing in me wanted to do that. But I knew we should.

We went back outside; beads of sweat on my forehead practically crystallized in the frigid air. Troy spent a while patrolling while I shivered, hardly able to look at the building. I listened to an owl hooting through the rushing of the pine trees, braced to hear a twig snap, a giggle. I felt split in two—one half of me waiting anxiously for Troy, the other screaming like a banshee through the woods. My fear was reaching a level where one of my two halves was going to win, and I was afraid it would be the banshee.

"I don't see anything," Troy announced, coming back to me. He put his arms around me. "You're trembling." He kissed me again. "I'm glad you called me."

"Me too." I just hoped it had been the right thing to do.

We returned to the chain-link fence, and Troy squeezed back through the hole. For someone so tall, he was very agile. Hard to picture someone like him falling. Easier to imagine his being pushed.

Miles's target?

"So . . . " he said. "We'll come back. And we'll bust Miles."

"Thanks," I managed. "But if it isn't him . . . "

"Oh, it's him," he said. "*God*, I'd love to put him out of his misery."

His words hung there, and I swallowed hard. Then he laughed bitterly.

"Or at least, get him sent back to rehab."

"Or . . . find out what's been going on here," I reminded him.

He patted the ledger book in his jacket. "I'll keep this, okay? See if I can figure anything out."

"Thank you." I sounded humble, and maybe a little pathetic. "I know it sounds weird. But there's more to this place than we realize. And I just want to be sure everyone's safe."

His face grew soft and again, I felt ashamed that I was taking advantage of his protector instinct. But I was desperate.

"You're so sweet," he whispered, touching my fingertips with his through the metal diamonds. I knew we had to go; our everyday lives, with school and futures, demanded their share of us. I didn't know how Troy had managed to get away, and I hoped he wouldn't get in trouble.

"If anything happens, *anything*," he said, "call me."

"Same with you."

He kissed me again. "I'll call you anyway. And . . . Fartgirl? Please don't think I'm a total jerk. I've known Mandy all my life. Our parents are in business together. I know it seems like it's been going forever but trust me, I'll get free."

Even though I was thrilled to hear his reassurances, I remembered my Jane-lessons, and tossed my hair. "Whatever."

FIFTEEN

January 17

I didn't sleep. I just waited for the sun to rise, and around five, I ran down to the lake. Celia was there, waiting, staring up at me with tears bubbling on the surface.

"*You're stalling,*" she accused. "*Get it done. Then I'll rest.*"

Then she would leave me, I interpreted.

"Working on it," I said. "I have an ally now," I added.

"*Her boyfriend?*" she scoffed.

"*My* friend," I corrected.

She vanished, and I was looking at myself. And I looked . . . half-dead. Dull eyes with circles under them, pinched face. Like I was halfway to wherever Shayna had wound up.

When I returned to Grose, I found Ms. Krige standing fully dressed on our porch, in a red-checked flannel shirt, a black turtleneck, and black wool trousers. She waved at me and I waved back; as I came onto the porch, she said, "I was worried about you."

Because, after Shayna, I was the resident loony? I made a show of running in place and said, "I went jogging."

She looked past me, surveying snowdrifts and icy walkways. "You need to be careful," she said. "Next time, please write me a note on our board."

"I'm sorry. I will," I replied.

"Dr. Ehrlenbach would like to talk to you," she continued. "She's . . . off campus. She'll be back tomorrow. Go during free period."

"Oh." On red alert, I followed her into Grose. "Do you, um, know why?"

"She's visiting with the Maisels."

Making sure Shayna didn't reveal anything? Not dissing the school? Destroying her credibility?

"I mean, why she wants to talk to me."

"Oh, I'm sure she's just checking in with you, too." *Checking in on you.*

I decided to do some checking on my own. After dinner, I headed for our current library, the one we actually used, like, for studying. On the way, I hurried past the commons and then I crossed into the statue garden. The marble statues of the ancient gods and goddesses blended with the snow; their blank faces reminding me of zombies rising from their graves. Apparently, Edwin Marlwood had been very proud of these statues, which was a little off because the goddesses were chesty and the gods were well-endowed. Unlike the naked figures in the frieze over the entrance to the gym itself, the male statues wore fig leaf thongs, but that left little to the imagination.

I tried to remember which goddess statue Mandy used in

her prank, bracing myself in case the robotic version was still there. Athena. She stared straight at me with her pupil-less eyes. I flashed a little grin at her to prove I wasn't afraid; then I bent over in the snow, feeling around with my gloved hands for the locket Charlotte had lost. If it was that important to Mandy, she'd probably sifted through every snowflake in the garden— or had other people do it for her—so I figured I was wasting my time. I began to shiver and gave up. It was just too cold.

As I straightened, something brushed my cheek; there was a flash of white out of the corner of my eye—had she moved? I took a step back, and another, feeling the wrongness of the place. I forced myself to look away, my gaze caught by the frozen figures, so lifelike they seemed to be breathing, then looked back again. *Had* she moved?

Freaked, I pushed off, weaving my way among the statues, catching glimpses of their faces, afraid I would actually see one turn my way. Puffing, I skidded on black ice, and had to grab onto the very last statue—Aphrodite, goddess of love and beauty. And I swore she moved; *I felt her move*—and I almost lost it.

Then I remembered the details of Mandy's prank: she had wired up a mannequin. Still, I didn't linger. I flew to the steps of the library, an old brick building covered with ivy, and flew inside.

I rushed past the librarian's desk—Mr. Claremont was on duty, and he looked quizzically at me as I remembered, too late, that in snow country, you were supposed to stop and kick the outside world off your shoes—and I headed for the reference section. I'd done some Googling on Marlwood's history, but hadn't come up with anything, not even the fire. I crossed my fingers that Marlwood's own library would contain actual archives about its past.

The book stack reached from the floor to about half a foot above my head. To my right stood a bank of flat screen monitors. Two girls from Gordon House were sitting at two computers, clacking on the keys and giggling. They were watching YouTube videos.

One of them saw me and gave me a little wave. I waved back, and then I turned a corner . . . and came face-to-face with Lara.

She was holding a large book bound in black leather. Her emerald eyes widened in surprise; then she narrowed them and smiled thinly, like some evil villainess in a bad high school play.

"Oh," she said. "I just lost a bet. I figured you'd have left by now. Too bad. For you."

The hair on the back of my neck rose, but I stood my ground. She rapped the book with her knuckles.

"People are talking about you. Everyone you make friends with dies or goes crazy," she said. "Do you have a virus?"

I took a step toward her. "Just stop it, Lara, I *know*."

She wrinkled her forehead, then tilted her head. She gave it a shake, shrugged her shoulders, and said, "I don't know what you're talking about, breakdown girl." She shifted the book in her arm and pressed her palm against my forehead. "Wow, do you have a fever? Maybe you have brain damage."

I balled my fists. "Don't. Don't even try it. Y-you tried to kill . . ." Suddenly, I felt very dizzy. And confused. I remembered

Lara holding onto me, dragging me to a large pile of trash inside the abandoned operating theater. I remembered Rose and Sangeeta preparing to set the trash on fire. I remembered getting free, and running to the lake. There was a boat ... Troy's boat ... I got in, and it began to sink. But I got out, and I swam to the other side of the lake ... that enormous, frigid lake ...

Did I dream it? It was as if everything I had been sure of had popped like a soap bubble above my head. *Did it happen?*

"What did I try to kill?" Lara said.

"At the lake house. You three came after me." I was sure of that. I remembered that. Yes, I did remember that.

Or had I had a dream?

"What are you *on*?" Lara asked, peering at me. Her confusion sounded genuine.

I felt the iciness inside me and focused on that—on the reality of our lives at Marlwood. *We were possessed.*

I looked at her. Really looked. I couldn't tell if she was faking or if she really didn't know what I was talking about.

"It's Mandy," I said. "Sh-she's made a deal, a bargain with the dead. And she's sucked you in ... "

"*Excuse me?*"

"And it's out of control. Lara, Kiyoko *died*."

She caught her breath. Her head whipped backward and I heard her whispering to herself. Then she raised her head and looked at me.

Her eyes were completely black.

"You'll be dead, too, soon enough." Her voice was not hers— heavy New York accent, higher pitched—and her smile was huge, and evil, and I took a step backward.

I couldn't even whisper. I couldn't make a sound at all.

She tapped the book. "There's nowhere you can go. Nowhere you can hide. We know who you are. And we're going to get you."

I covered my mouth so that I wouldn't scream. Then Lara jerked hard and rapidly blinked. When she looked at me, her eyes were normal.

"Lara, did you . . . hear yourself?" I asked her. "Did you hear what you were saying?"

"What?" She brushed past me. "When you come back to planet Earth, let me know. So I can go somewhere else. Freak," she added under her breath.

Lara carried the book over to an empty study table and carefully set it down. Then she pulled out a chair and sat. Flipping it open, she began to page through it slowly, carefully. I watched for a few seconds; then I stumbled into the stacks in the direction she had come, looking for the gap such a large book would have left. I found it on a shelf with the Library of Congress call numbers that began with BF. Other titles: *Possession: Hysteria and Its Manifestations, A History of Spiritualism, Revivalism and Possession in American Religious Thought.*

Possession.

I began to tremble. So she *must* know what was happening to her and the others. I kept walking past the shelves of books to a brass drinking fountain. I bent over, preparing to drink—

—Saw two black holes staring at me—

—Celia's reflection—

—And staggered backward.

A girl seated in a green upholstered reading chair glanced

up at me, then back at her book. I bit down on my lower lip and made a sharp left, run-walking back to the entry. Pushing my way out, I stood on the porch and watched the snow falling heavily from the black sky. Fresh drifts had already begun to pile up around the base of the porch, and the lights of the other campus buildings glowed a dull, weak yellow. I couldn't see a single star, or the moon. Marlwood was closing in on me.

"Let me go," I said aloud.

The wind howled. The door behind me opened, and I knew without looking that Lara was standing behind me.

"We never will," she replied. "Ever."

I pushed away from the porch, racing into the snow, as her laughter trailed behind me.

SIXTEEN

January 18

After the library, I stayed on high alert, but nothing happened to me. I didn't sleep, only paced, and avoided the head in our room, staring at the darkened windows of Jessel. I knew that if I didn't rest, I would break down. But I couldn't turn down my inner banshee. I couldn't stop screaming in silence.

Then at breakfast the next morning, Mandy joined me in the food queue. She was dressed in an ivory cashmere sweater topped with a soft gray three-quarter-length jacket and a black wool miniskirt. Her hair was up in a bouffant, held in place with a beaded gray clip. She was beautiful . . . and her warm smile would have melted a glacier.

"Linz, sweetie, good morning."

I said nothing.

"We're having a party a week from Friday," she continued, not daunted at all by my coldness. "You know, for my usual sweet BFFs and suckups." Her eyes were hard. "You should show."

No way, I thought; but I said, "Why? Is it my turn?"

"Oh, baby." She grabbed a spoon out of the silverware bay and held it out to me. "You already passed the test."

I turned my back, aware that the din in the commons was noticeably lower, and people were watching. I was shaking. My coffee was sloshing on my fingers, scalding, but I was so cold I could practically see steam rising from my skin.

I REMEMBERED when my mom was sick, and I had told my dad I wanted to stop going to school and live with her in the hospital. And when he'd asked me why, I said, "Because she's going to die. And if you loved her, you would quit your job and be with her all the time. She's lonely, and she's scared."

He said some things about how life went on and we had to go on living; and I hadn't spoken to him for three days. For three days, in fact, I'd hated him. But now, as I walked into the admin office for my meeting with Dr. Ehrlenbach, I got it. I felt as if I had just stepped onto the escalator back at Fashion Valley Mall, struggling to get over my present and move into my future. But life just glided along with you.

A ghost had told me to murder another human being—someone I pretty much hated—but life just went on. Maybe Jane had been right: having a breakdown was a way to bail. You just sat down on the escalator and covered your head. At the moment, I was totally tempted to do just that.

"Go on in," Ms. Shelley said, and I nodded at her as I passed. "By the way," she added, you look nice."

That caught me off guard. Besides, I had formed the

impression that Ms. Shelley never actually saw me; she just kept track of Dr. Ehrlenbach's appointments. If it was ten o'clock, it must be Lindsay Cavanaugh.

But I had dressed to please, so I was grateful for the compliment. Julie and Marica had pulled my "look" together for me. Everyone (except for me, last semester) understood that an appointment with Ehrlenbach demanded good clothes. The first time I'd sat in her office, I'd worn raggedy jeans and had died a thousand deaths under her withering disgust. Now I had on a simple black wool skirt of Marica's, Ida's highly polished black riding boots, and Julie's black wool boyfriend jacket with the sleeves pushed up in an attempt to disguise the fact that it was too big for me. Claire's black-and-white silk paisley scarf was wound around my neck and loosely knotted. The resultant "look" was total conformity but it was *Vogue*-style conformity— and I actually savored the feeling of wearing a perfect outfit of clothes I couldn't hope to afford.

The ferocious statue of our founder, Edwin Marlwood, stared down at me as I rapped on Dr. Ehrlenbach's door. There was no answer, but I knew that I was supposed to go into her office anyway. I opened the door into the freezing cold and shut it behind me. It was like stepping into a refrigerator, and I shivered as I sat down in a hunter-green upholstered chair on the visitor side of her desk. As usual, the rich wood surface was immaculate, nothing on it except a desktop monitor facing away from me and her brass nameplate. A watercolor rendition of the Winters Sports Complex was framed on the wall beside her Ph.D. from Harvard.

I heard a soft ding. Incoming mail, probably. I slumped in the chair and tapped my fingers on the armrests; then pushed my butt to the back of the seat and sat up straight. Then before I was aware I was doing it, I got up and leaned over the desk, craning my neck to look at the screen. There was a nested list of folders. The header on the topmost one, SHAYNA MAISEL, caught my eye.

It is unfortunate that Shayna's Generalized Anxiety Disorder has grown so acute as to necessitate withdrawal from Marlwood. She has presented marked deterioration despite increased dosages of prescribed medications including benzodiazepines and her biweekly therapy sessions with Dr. Melton . . .

Dr. Melton was our school shrink. Generalized Anxiety Disorder? Shayna? I would never have guessed.

Then I heard Rose's voice outside the door.

"I was in the statue garden, and it was laying on the path. All mangled."

"It was *lying* on the path," Dr. Ehrlenbach replied.

"Actually, it was all over the path," Rose said.

I couldn't hear Dr. Ehrlenbach's reply. I crept from behind her desk and crossed to the door, pressing my ear against it. Dr. Ehrlenbach was still speaking: *Something something something, Dr. Melton.*

"*I* don't need to see a shrink," Rose insisted. "Whoever messed up that bird does."

"Rose," Dr. Ehrlenbach said, and then her voice trailed away.

Suddenly, the knob on Dr. Ehrlenbach's door turned, and the door pushed slightly open. I was in the way, and I took a step back. A short bald man with black eyebrows smiled curiously at me. Dr. Melton. I had met him before, when Kiyoko died.

"Hello, Lindsay," he said.

"What's going on?" I asked, gesturing to the hall.

His smile stayed put. I was willing to bet that his psych training, not Botox, kept it there. "The girls found a dead bird. Looks like a cat found it first."

I tried to remember if I'd ever seen a cat at Marlwood. No. Lots of birds, though.

"So," he said, coming into the room. "I'm sure Dr. Ehrlenbach will be here in a minute." He took the seat next to mine and gave it a half turn, so that when he sat down, he would be facing both Dr. Ehrlenbach and me. "How are things going?"

"Fine," I said, too quickly. I saw him file that away. Maybe along with my appearance—black circles, sunken cheeks. "Well, except for Shayna."

"Shayna's home, and she's doing much better. She just needs a little break."

"Oh. What's her diagnosis?" I asked, because after you've had a nervous breakdown, you learn to talk like that.

He raised a brow. "You know I can't share that. Directly, at any rate. What do you know about schizophrenia?"

I felt the walls of the room closing in, and my body temperature plummeted as if we were sitting outside in the snow. Schizophrenia *and* anxiety?

"One symptom of schizophrenia is the manifestation of hallucinations," he said.

My face prickled. I fiddled with my Tibetan prayer beads, caught myself, stopped.

"When people are under extreme stress, sometimes they see things that aren't really there."

Not like at Marlwood. Like at my mother's funeral, when I was sure she was still breathing. When I went to my father and begged him to tell the funeral director that they had to get the formaldehyde out of her body immediately, or she would truly die. I got a Xanax for my trouble; later, Dr. Yaeger asked me about it, and I wanted to kill my father for telling him. Not literally kill him, of course. But it had been my own private moment of losing my mom to the ground, and Dr. Yaeger wanted to dissect it like a biology specimen. And maybe he wrote it up in the report—the same report that I was even surer he had sent on to Marlwood. Maybe that was the real reason Dr. Ehrlenbach hadn't wanted me to come to Marlwood in the first place.

"Schizophrenics hallucinate even when they're not stressed," he went on.

I didn't say anything. I didn't like where he was going.

At that precise moment, Dr. Ehrlenbach entered the room. She was carrying a wafer-thin hunter-green folder, which she handed to him. Her face betrayed no emotion; my school was being run by Vulcans.

Dr. Melton opened the folder while Dr. Ehrlenbach seated herself behind her desk. He scanned some papers, then flipped it shut. They exchanged glances; I couldn't read their non-expressions. But at nearly the same instant, they both looked at me.

"I asked Dr. Melton to stop by to see if there is anything we can do for you, Lindsay," Dr. Ehrlenbach informed me. "You were the one who found Kiyoko Yamato, and I know that had to be very difficult for you. Now another classmate you were fond of has left suddenly."

"Yes," I said, trying to understand if she was actually linking dying with "suddenly leaving." Abandonment issues. "But I just started to get to know Shayna," I added defensively. "We didn't move past fond." I was talking too much. I had to shut up.

"You've had nightmares. Frequent ones," Dr. Ehrlenbach continued.

Julie, how could you? I thought, gripping the arms of my chair. They would probably notice that. But then again, they already knew I had suffered from post-traumatic stress disorder last September. That I had come to Marlwood partly because word had spread all over Grossmont High that I was a quivering mass of cuckoo.

"I've had some nightmares," I allowed.

"Yet despite this, you're doing very well in your classes. This is most impressive," Dr. Ehrlenbach said. "If you continue to do this well, I believe Marlwood may be in a position to extend your scholarship for next year."

"No way," I said, stunned. The last I had heard, I had too many Bs. Dr. Ehrlenbach stared at me, and I shifted and cleared my throat. "I mean, thank you."

"It appears that the Board of Trustees has found some funds to cover an extracurricular for you as well," she went on. Her desk was so highly polished that I could see a vague reflection of her face in the wood. I dared not look down. If I saw Celia, there would be no more talk of how well I was doing.

"I think, given your position, you should think strategically about what extracurricular to take. Something that will elevate your transcript." She tapped on her keyboard. "Have you given any thought to where you'll go?"

"Go?"

"You need to think differently," she continued. "Marlwood is going to open doors for you. You need to get ready. For *college*."

I fidgeted, even more bewildered. I felt completely out of my element.

She tapped some keys. "Your current foreign language is Spanish. We might want to talk about that. There are other languages that are more desirable. It's a little too late to put you into the international relations club. Let's schedule some sessions with Dr. Rahmani." She glanced past her screen at me. "She'll organize your admissions portfolio and help you investigate financial aid."

"Portfolio," I said, and she looked at me as if I were speaking a less desirable language.

"You should have begun this process last year. We need to catch up. I'll have Dr. Rahmani available for you as soon as she has an opening."

"You and I will set up an appointment, too," Dr. Melton informed me. "Some colleges are administering Meyers-Briggs or other psychological tests. I'll have your housemother notify you."

"Ms. Krige," Dr. Ehrlenbach told him.

He took out a flat silver smart phone and typed into it, then put it back in his blazer pocket.

"Lindsay, I hope you'll take full advantage of these opportunities," Dr. Ehrlenbach said. "Marlwood intends to prepare students for a life quite unlike the one you would have led, if you had not come here."

"Okay. I mean, thank you," I said.

She kept looking at me. Then she blinked. Dr. Melton pushed back his chair, so I did, too. Dr. Ehrlenbach made no move to stop me so I figured we were done.

I followed Dr. Melton out of the room. He turned to the left, toward the statue of Edwin Marlwood, and I hovered, unsure what to do. He smiled and pointed in the opposite direction, where the reception was, and I nodded, reviewing what had just happened as I headed out.

Are they bribing me? To do what? Or not to do what? Not to say anything?

In the foyer, the light through the leaded windows was glum and gray, and shone down on four heads seated on the couch: Rose, Julie, Susi, and Gretchen. Julie's face was puffy and blotched. Ms. Shelley was behind her desk on the phone, speaking softly. Susi and Gretchen were pressing their shoulders together, and Rose and Julie looked up as I came in.

"Oh, Lindsay," Julie said, leaping off the couch, rushing toward me, and throwing her arms around me. "It was so icky!"

I looked from her to Rose, who seemed to be the chick in charge. Susi and Gretchen got up like old ladies. Dark circles like mine ringed Susi's eyes; beneath a mask of makeup, Gretchen's skin was dry and flaky. Signs of stress. They were slouchy and long-faced; yet, except for Rose, they were dressed like baronesses or at the very least, contestants on *Project Runway*. Rose was still stridently Rose; she was wearing purple high-tops, a long, ruffled skirt, and an oversized dark gray peacoat with a long lavender-and-olive scarf wound several times around her neck, like my black-and-white paisley. Her silver tube earrings were big enough to qualify as wind chimes.

"Here's your late slip, Lindsay," Ms. Shelley told me. "Girls, you need to go to your next class."

I took the note and we all turned to go. Rose pushed out the front door, holding it open as Susi and Gretchen filed out, followed by Julie. I was last.

"What was icky?" I asked, as I shut the door.

"We found these animals," Julie said. "A little black bird. And then Gretchen and Susi found some more, too. In the snow."

"Chilly con carnage," Rose chimed in.

Susi made a sort of groaning, growling sound and looked down at her feet. Gretchen gave her arm a pat.

"But the worst was a cat," Julie told me. She grimaced. "A black cat. It was *horrible*."

"Ms. Krige said there's a mountain lion in the woods," I ventured. Dr. Melton had downplayed all of this. He'd only mentioned one single bird. Did he think we didn't talk to each other about the things that went on? Was calming them down part of my new open-door job?

Rose traded looks with Susi, who looked positively green. Susi shrugged as if to say *go ahead*.

"Maybe a mountain lion got it," Rose allowed. "But we don't think so. Because, wouldn't a mountain lion eat the whole thing? This kitty was pretty much all there. Pretty much. We're not sure what exactly got taken, but puss-puss was disemboweled, which I know from dissecting in biology. Gutted, but most of the guts were still there."

"God, Rose," Gretchen snapped.

"So someone . . . hurt it?" I said. "Whose cat was it?"

Julie shook her head, weeping. Gretchen unconsciously twirled her hair. Her nail polish was chipped, a major offense among some. A sign of anxiety among others. Girls were stressing out. It hadn't been like this last semester. Before our break, most of the student population had been blissfully unaware that there were some things that huge amounts of money could not fix.

"So who did it?" I asked.

"It's the Marlwood Stalker," Gretchen said.

I jerked. That was the same phrase Troy had used.

"Did you make that up?" I asked.

Gretchen shook her head. "No. Mandy did."

I went cold. So they were talking. He had probably told her about the picture on my cell phone.

"No one's saying who the Stalker is," Rose replied. She gave me a look. I translated: Rose had her suspicions.

There was a long pause. I glanced over my shoulder at the admin building, as if they could hear every word, and lowered my voice.

"Tell me who *you* think it is."

Another silence. We began to walk toward classes. It was cold. I could see our collective breaths, rising like fog over our heads.

"Miles Winters," Rose announced. Susi and Gretchen nodded; he was their number one suspect as well.

"Did you tell Dr. Ehrlenbach?" I asked Rose.

"Winters Sports Complex," Rose drawled.

Julie pulled away. "I don't think it's Miles. He left. Mandy said he's in Hawaii."

Rose didn't bother to reply. Of course there was no guarantee that Mandy was telling us the truth. And why was Julie defending him?

"Ehrlenfreak said she'd 'look into it.'" Rose made air quotes, then pulled her cheeks back so tightly her eyes went almond-shaped. "Did she give you some lecture about stress, Cinderella? That's what she told us, that we should try to relax a little more. It seems like part of going to a top-tier boarding school is tons of stress. It's a known occupational hazard."

"I'm under stress," Susi said. "I was looking out my window last night and I swear I saw something in the trees . . . "

"Some*one*," Gretchen corrected her. "I saw it too. It was a face."

"The Stalker," Rose declared.

I stopped walking. "Did you tell Dr. Ehrlenbach about the face? Either of you?"

"No," Gretchen replied. Her eyelid twitched. "I didn't really think it was there . . . until we found the birds."

"And the cat," Susi added. Gretchen nodded, pressing her hand flat against her stomach, as if she were going to be sick.

I understood why they hadn't told Ehrlenbach right away. Before I came to Marlwood, I would have dismissed a face in a window as my imagination, or my own reflection, and I wouldn't have thought it was worth mentioning. That was then; this was now.

Julie wiped her face as if she were sweating; then she dropped her hands to her sides and said, "I'm going to soccer. I have a responsibility. I'm the goalie." I nodded, and she trotted away from us. Poor Julie had had enough. Susi and Gretchen hustled it up, too, leaving Rose and me in their snowy dust.

"Hey," Rose said, in a voice meant only for me, "this is bullshit. Why are you avoiding me?"

I had learned when I hung out with Jane that you didn't have to explain yourself if you didn't want to. So I changed the subject.

"They want to help me get into college."

"Listen," Rose said, making a sort of balletic quarter-turn, taking both my hands in hers, and swinging them. "Here's my theory. Miles is living on campus. Or near campus. At the lake house or somewhere. And maybe Mandy knows and maybe she doesn't. He's hanging around because he's obsessed with her. But he's nuts, and he's killing animals."

She swung my hands some more, as if this was the best news ever. "You and I were the school detectives last semester. We found out a bunch of weird shit and then kazinga! Kiyoko is dead and we all go home. It's time for us to pick up where we left off."

It wasn't like that, Rose, I thought. And I had watched her suck up to Mandy the night of Charlotte's prank. Still, I looked at it another way: if she was going to do some investigating, I might discover some things I needed to know if I was there alongside her. As long as I didn't let down my guard and start to trust her, I would probably be okay. If, for example, she invited me to a satanic ritual in the middle of the forest and her eyes were a solid black, I should probably pass. And there was no way that I would let her know I was also working with Troy. If I still was. He must have told Mandy about the Marlwood Stalker; what exactly *had* he revealed?

"Is that why you were in the statue garden?" I asked. "Detecting?"

"*Sí.*"

"Did you find Mandy's locket?"

"Tell me you're in and I'll tell you."

I suppressed a sigh. "Yes."

She closed one eye and made a show of peering at me out of the other one. "Dude, you can't be sort of involved in this. You are or you aren't. It's like being a virgin."

Which I am, I thought. I could feel myself blushing, and Rose guffawed.

"No way. How old are you?" She took a step forward and kissed my forehead. "I won't tell anyone. Around here, they'd probably sacrifice you to their dark gods."

Actually, I thought, *they will*.

SEVENTEEN

January 20

For two days, more complaints cropped up of someone sneaking around and staring in windows, and Dr. Ehrlenbach hired more security staff. We were told to walk with a buddy, like little Brownie Girl Scouts. Everyone was talking about the Marlwood Stalker.

I never slept. I was afraid the Stalker would come for me. The Stalker might be Belle Johnson, dead for over a century. Or Belle and the other dead girls possessing Mandy and her friends

Or it might be Miles Winters, in the flesh. But I was pretty sure I was on his list of things to mangle. I remembered the morning in the woods, nearly two weeks ago now . . . what he'd said about protecting Mandy.

Then on Tuesday morning, Troy called on the landline, identifying himself as my stepbrother Sam. That codename kept him safe from the wrath of Mandy, or so he hoped. He asked me to meet him tomorrow night in the old library. With all the security, there were few safe places left to meet anyway.

"I think I've figured something out," he said quietly. Then suddenly, "Got to go."

So I had to go back there. I was afraid, even if Troy would be there. As usual, I didn't sleep . . . but that didn't really hold my nightmares at bay.

I got dressed to go running. I accidentally woke Julie up; she took her duty as my "buddy" very seriously, and insisted on going with me.

Naturally athletic, Julie ended up running quite a few paces in front of me. With a little pant and a moan she stopped to get rid of a hitch in her side, and I took advantage of the moment to "catch my breath" in front of Jessel's privet hedge. I wanted to check in with Troy more privately, on my cell phone. I needed to know what he had figured out before I got to the library. On occasion, we could get cell phone reception if we were in the vicinity of Jessel. Some people said Mandy paid extra for cell phone coverage; others, that since Jessel was rumored to be haunted, the ghostly emanations gave our phones a power boost. Now that I knew what I knew, I thought that both might be accurate.

The once-lush wall of greenery was a fence of frosted twigs as I flipped open my phone and prepared to text. But Troy beat me to it, confirming our . . . date?

2nite library 8 p.m.

I caught my breath and typed back, *K.*

"Hey," Julie called from about ten yards up the path, waving to show she was okay; and I jogged to catch up with her. No new snow tumbled down, but the fog boiled up from the surface of the lake and poured into the bowl-shaped valley where the campus was located. I had such a secret; I was excited and nervous . . . and I couldn't tell anyone, not even Julie.

I slogged through all my classes. Icy rain poured down, so for P.E., we were sent to the gym to do cardio kickboxing. Freezing, I hurried through the door that led through the swimming pool area, and Charlotte followed close behind. Steam rose from the surface of the swimming pool, and I looked over at Charlotte, wondering what had gone through her mind when Shayna had gone crazy during her prank.

"Hey," Charlotte said, catching my eye. "You will never guess what I did last night." She waited a beat. "I went to a séance at Jessel." She puffed up, immensely proud.

No, Charlotte, no, I begged. *Don't let them do this to you.*

"We were talking to some spirit who died in a fire," Charlotte went on.

I worked hard not to react. Then Charlotte took off her black steampunk coat. Gone were her showy drama clothes, and in their place, a creamy cashmere sweater under a dark gray shrug and black pants. It was all too tight.

Her face reddened and she gave her streaked hair a toss. "Mandy gave me these clothes. Aren't they gorgeous?"

I'm going to free you, I silently promised her.

———

CHARLOTTE didn't join Mandy at dinner that night; she sat with the other girls from Stewart, her dorm. Rose chattered away with her; then, as we filed out of the commons, Rose galloped with Charlotte in tow over to me.

"Charlotte went to a *séance*," she announced, slinging her arm over Charlotte's shoulder. Out of Charlotte's eyeshot, Rose crossed her eyes at me.

"I know," I replied, feeling a little busted because I hadn't yet shared the information with Rose. "Isn't it cool?"

"Yeah." Rose brightened. "It is so cool that I want to go to the next one. Do you think Mandy would let me?" she asked Charlotte.

I stiffened. "Rose, no," I said.

"Rose, *sí*," Rose replied, clicking invisible castanets.

Séances were for calling the dead, becoming the dead. I thought of Shayna, how cold and lifeless she'd become. I couldn't stand it if something like that happened to Rose.

Or to me.

A terrible sense of doom zinged me like an electric current. People really did die. Memmy had died; Kiyoko had died. Maybe that was the source of Belle Johnson's murderous fury—not that she had died tragically, but that she had died at all. I could understand anger like that. Rather than feel it all, I had broken down instead—that's what Dr. Yaeger had told me. People who didn't want to feel their feelings drank or took drugs, or cut themselves, or ate too much or had sex too much, or just had breakdowns.

After dinner, in the dark, I felt even more alone as I stood on the porch of Grose and studied the wall of fog. I didn't want to walk through the thick white blankets of mist, but I did want to see Troy. My flashlight beam bounced off the whiteness, and I had no idea how I would stay on course for the abandoned old library.

Maybe we should wait, I thought. But Troy was probably already driving from Lakewood to our rendezvous. And I didn't want to wait. I wanted to see him.

Still, I debated a little longer. And then coldness pressed against my neck, urging me off the porch into the fog bank. I gritted my teeth, and went; I supposed Celia could see where she was going even if I couldn't, but that didn't make me feel much better about letting her take the lead. But I reminded myself why I was going—to find a way to stop Belle without hurting Mandy—

—Who was I kidding? Without *killing* Mandy—

—And so I shuffled anxiously forward, holding my arms out in front of myself like a zombie. There could be anything in the fog—*anyone*, I thought—and I wouldn't know until it was too late.

I walked a few steps more, colliding with a swag of what had to be the oversized white chain that hung from the horse-head mouths, and edged to the right. I heard a blare of rock music, then nothing. Laughter, then silence. I turned and walked forward . . . straight into a tree.

"This is stupid. I'm turning around," I announced. Celia made no reply; I felt no icy hand on the back of my neck. So I stopped and made a half circle, and began to head back toward Grose . . .

. . . Or so I thought. Because I walked straight back into the barrier of Jessel's prickly twigs again. Snow sprinkled off the desiccated branches and splatted on my face.

"Troy, you will be hung by the neck until you are dead if Ms.

Meyerson finds you here," Mandy's voice wafted toward me through the fog. Ms. Meyerson was Jessel's housemother.

"She won't," Troy said. "She never has before."

"That was before someone started skulking around," Mandy countered.

I had to be the biggest idiot on the planet. Troy had gone to see Mandy first. Of course he had.

I doubled my fists even as a weird sense of shame washed over me—for being so gullible, I supposed. For dreaming that Troy could—would—be honest and true. I tried to swallow down a lump, and it wouldn't go. Thank God I hadn't dragged myself across campus to the library.

My first impulse was to get out of there, but I was afraid I might give myself away. And in spite of how crushed I was, it was definitely to my advantage to spy on them for as long as I possibly could.

"Maybe you're the Stalker," she said. "Peeking in all the girl's bedrooms. Don't you get enough from me?"

There was silence. Then, "Mandy, don't."

Don't what?

"What's wrong? You've been so weird since break. Why didn't you come skiing?"

"You know why."

"Well, *Miles* likes *you*."

"Good for him."

"We had to go together. It was the only way my parents would let him leave the country. And why do you keep checking your phone?" she demanded. "Are you expecting a call?"

"You know, you could be nicer to me," Troy replied. "I came all the way over here to see you. Spider's covering for me. I'm supposed to be at practice. And as for skiing, Mandy, I was in the hospital."

Taking a deep breath, I shielded my phone inside my army jacket and flipped it open. I had a text message from Troy: *don't come.* My heart cracked along the same fissures it had broken before. Jerk, jerk, jerk, jerk, jerk.

"Did you hear something?" Mandy said.

"It's just the wind."

"No, it's something else. Oh God, what if it's *him?* Troy, I-I'm scared. C'mon, hold me tighter."

I swallowed hard, trying not to form the image of Mandy in Troy's arms. Even though, of course, I'd seen it dozens of times in real life.

"You love to be scared," Troy said. "I heard about your séance."

She laughed weakly. It sounded forced. "It was terrifying. We got in contact with these ghosts. Dead girls—"

"Stop. You know I don't believe in that stuff." He sounded irritated, a little bored. But also a little . . . uneasy? Was he thinking about the burning girl he had seen in the fog on our drive to school?

"You would believe, if you came to one of my séances."

"If you're scared, then why—"

"Sssh," Mandy said.

There was silence, and I wondered if they were kissing. I shut my eyes.

"So, we should have a party," she said, changing the subject. "Shake off the freakout. Live life as it was intended."

"I don't think I can," he said gently. "We've got all these games—"

"Come afterward. Nothing should get in the way of fun."

"Not even Jack the Ripper? Jack the cat-killer?"

"You think you're so hilarious—"

"Not even Miles?" Troy's tone was low. Angry.

"Miles is gone," Mandy snapped. "You want proof? Here. Use my phone. Call him. In Hawaii."

There was silence.

"*Call him*," she said. "I swear, Troy, what is wrong with you? You didn't used to be so jealous. You're acting like such a jerk."

No argument there, I thought.

Another silence. "Mandy, I think we need to—"

More silence. Then I heard her moan softly. He was *kissing* her. My throat clamped shut as I tried to swallow down my protest. I clenched my fists at my sides and turned my head, shutting my eyes. Somehow I'd thought that trying to break up with her included not making out with her anymore. I wondered if they did . . . more.

"That's better. I swear, all this . . . 'danger' is getting on my nerves. *Some* people around here are trying to stir things up to get attention. Because they don't have any other way to get it. No looks, no brains . . . it's sad, really."

"What do you mean? That all this Stalker stuff is made up? Who would do that?"

"Oh, some poor Cinderella, painting arrows on her forehead," she sniped. "Or a bull's-eye on her chest. Someone who really likes being a victim."

Rose liked to call me Cinderella.

"I don't know anyone like that."

"Sure you do, superhero." She chuckled, and it was low and cruel. "You take in strays all the time. Blink-blink-blink, they flutter their lashes at your dimples. Then they figure out you're one of *the* Minears and go all damsel in distress on you—"

"That's *your* game."

My lips parted. He was figuring it out.

"Oh, baby, I don't need a game." She laughed. "I've *got* game. I've got everything I need. Everything *you* want."

"Don't be so—"

"Face it, Troy. You and I? We can go anywhere. We live in a world most of these girls can't even imagine. And last I checked? No pets were allowed, not even service animals. They might have fleas. Or rabies."

Something inside me snapped. Anger just bubbled out of me, exploded, and I was so furious I had to bite the inside of my cheek to keep from shouting at her. Who the hell did she think she was? She was evil, but it went more deeply than that—she was so rich, and so sure that made her better than . . . me. And maybe she was right. Maybe she was better.

Maybe that was why I hated her so much. It wasn't just the little things—the clothes, the money, her unshakable security. Nothing Mandy ever did would have real consequences, because her wealth would protect her. But she got perfect grades anyway.

She played with girls' feelings anyway. Not out of any deep-seated need, but because she was a bitch.

I hate her.

If *her* mother ever got sick, Mrs. Winters would get the best doctors, and round-the-clock care. She wouldn't die. And the thing that had torn my life to shreds wouldn't even register on Mandy's emotional scale, if she even had one.

God, I hate her.

Mandy Winters would never suffer, or struggle, or have a breakdown. I had known that the moment I saw her; I knew it now, deep to the marrow of my soul, as she made fun of me—me, the girl she had tried to kill—in front of the boy who had promised to save me.

Life was unfair. It was unjust. My mother had been good, and funny, and kind. And she died anyway. It was unfair, and if Mandy knew it, she didn't care, because the balance was tipped entirely in her favor.

I hate her so much. Panting, I balled my fists, feeling as if I were flying out of my body and into the foggy black night, soaring with nothing to hold me back. No barriers, no restraint, no fear, no remorse. If I could tumble from the sky just then, let go and fall on top of her, crushing her . . . God, I wanted to hurt her. I wanted to . . . *yes.*

I was grimacing like a demon, my lips pulled back from my teeth, my eyes so wide they might pop out of my sockets.

I *wanted* to. Longed to. Couldn't wait.

"*Yes,*" Celia said inside my head. "*Yes, you hate her enough. You really do.*"

I was heaving. My chest rose and fell, expelling fog, pushing out my hatred and fury, and sucking them back in.

"Whatever, Mandy," Troy snapped. "I have to go."

"No, wait, damn it."

"*I am going!*" Troy yelled at her.

There was rustling, and I remembered almost too late that there was a wooden gate in the hedge. I heard the creak of hinges. Footfalls passed close by; they stopped, as if someone—Troy—sensed that I was near. I took a step forward.

If it's Mandy, I'll—I'll crack open her skull, I thought. I pictured hurting her, doing unspeakable things to her . . . and I loved it. Loved it.

"Troy," Mandy called.

From just a few feet away, I heard more footsteps. Shortly after that, my phone vibrated.

"Fine." She threw the words at him. "Just go."

More footfalls sounded on the concrete path leading to Jessel's front door; then the door opened, and slammed shut. Mandy had made her exit. For a second I thought about letting Troy know I was there. I didn't know if he was headed for the library after all; if that was the text message he had sent me. I hid my phone inside my jacket again, and looked at the new message in my inbox.

sorry couldn't make it. found something very weird.

I opened my mouth to call out to him; then I heard another voice. It was a man, singing, and his song chilled my blood:

My love is like a red, red rose . . .

Inside me, Celia screamed. I heard her shrieks over the man's voice, which was also inside my head . . . at least, I was fairly certain that it was.

My love . . .

Screaming *"No no no! Oh God, oh God, help me! No no no no no—"*

With a sharp gasp, I sank to my knees and put my hands over my head, shrinking into a tiny ball on the wet, snowy earth.

"Oh God, oh God," I whispered. "God, help me."

Then I went limp as my rage flew back up into the fog; my body fell face-first into the snow, and everything turned black.

———

HOWLING AND SHRIEKING, like dying cats . . . in the fire, in the water; the reformatory walls hiss into steam; the girls are screaming. My friend Lydia is running down the corridor, racing for her life. Rage is boiling over; and terror—

My skin is peeling right off my bones—

Who locked the door?

EIGHTEEN

SOMEONE WAS CRYING, but my eyelids were too heavy to open to see who it was. Fingertips brushed my hair off my forehead and cupped my cheek. It was Memmy. As soon as she knew I was awake, she'd bring me chicken noodle soup and a turkey sandwich with the crusts cut off. She'd read aloud to me: "*The woods are lovely, dark, and deep . . .* " We'd listen to Beethoven's "Ode to Joy" and cry with happiness that we were alive to hear it.

Her kiss on my cheek was feather-light. I heard her whisper, "I love you."

You didn't die, I thought.

"Of course not," she whispered. "You love me."

Then I opened my eyes.

"Hi," Julie said. She was leaning over me, and I was in a metal hospital bed. Colorful posters about AIDS and STDs served as wallpaper behind her; and there was an ebony clock with Roman numerals for the hours between two dark wood doors. It said one o'clock; judging by the subdued lighting, I guessed it was one in the morning, not in the afternoon.

The smell of rubbing alcohol stung my nose and my stomach clenched, hard. That smell, that horrible smell . . .

Dr. Ehrlenbach came up beside Julie, with Ms. Simonet, our school nurse. I sneezed. I felt warm and toasty; an electric blanket was spread across me. My forehead hurt.

"Hi, sweetie," the nurse said. "You scared us."

No one knew how long I had lain unconscious in the snow, but Ms. Krige had noticed I was missing during her eleven o'clock bed check. It had been seven forty the last time I'd looked at my phone—

"My phone," I murmured.

"You fainted. They think because of your insomnia, you just fell asleep in the snow! They were worried about frostbite," Julie said, digging into the pocket of my army jacket, which was hanging on a hook beside my bed. She handed me my phone. I held it in my palm and quickly flicked it open. There were two new text messages. Frustrated, I shut the phone. I would have to wait until I was alone to read them.

"Who found me?" I asked.

"Ms. Krige," Dr. Ehrlenbach said. "There are reasons for these new rules."

"I'm sorry," I told her. I meant it. I wondered if I was still getting all the freebies—extracurricular, psych testing.

"As long as you're safe, that's all that matters." Dr. Ehrlenbach turned to Julie. "Time to go."

Julie hesitated. Then she held out Panda to me. Avoiding Dr. Ehrlenbach's gaze, she tucked him beside me in the bed.

"I'll be sleeping in the next room," Ms. Simonet promised.

As soon as they were gone, I flipped open my phone again—and discovered, to my surprise, that I had five bars. Since it was the middle of the night, I couldn't call anyone. But I did read my third and fourth texts from Troy:

library=weird. had 2 go back 2 lakewood asap. i'll check in soon.

And the fourth one:

miss u xo.

Xo. Yeah, right. I texted him: *OK, thx.* And left it at that.

A deep chill ran down the center of my body and fanned out. I pulled the electric blanket up to my chin and noted the crookneck lamp on a nightstand beside my bed. I reached out to turn it off, but I knew I didn't want to lie there in the dark. I gave Panda a squeeze.

My phone vibrated. I had another text from Troy.

u up?

yes.

can call?

Before I could type back a reply, it vibrated again. I accepted the call and put the phone to my ear.

"Hey," he whispered. "I went back to the library earlier tonight. Scary place."

"You went inside?" I whispered into the phone.

"Yeah. God, Lindsay, I figured out what the ledger book was.

I think it was a list of girls who got lobotomies. There were a few notes. 'Difficult case. Skull damaged pick.'"

"*God*," I whispered.

And suddenly I remembered how angry I had been—so infuriated that I could have grabbed the nearest heavy object and bashed in Mandy's skull. I had never, ever felt so angry in my life. It scared the wits out of me now.

"I wanted to tell you in person. But I-I had to go back to Lakewood sooner than I planned."

Did anyone tell you what happened to me?

"Did you tell Mandy about them?" Before he could answer, I said, "Please don't."

There was a pause. "Lindsay," he said, "what's going on?"

"Please, just don't. You want to be loyal to her, I get that. But this is . . . for me, okay?"

"It's not that I want to be loyal," he argued, but then he huffed. Because, of course, he did want to be loyal to her. He did and he didn't.

"It's late." I didn't want to have this conversation again. It bordered on whining, or implying that he had to make a choice. I didn't work that way—even though I wished, bitterly, that he would make a choice.

And that he would choose me. My life might actually depend on it. I began to seethe. Clearing my throat, I pushed my anger away.

"It's late," I said again, more gently, "and I have POS." *Parents over shoulder*, the shorthand for no privacy.

"Julie's up? Okay. You want to text?"

So he didn't know I was in the infirmary. In the same place they had taken Shayna, before she had left the campus forever. Was she really home?

Was she even alive?

"I have to get some sleep," I said, even though I doubted I would sleep at all.

"I'm sorry I had to bail tonight. Something came up."

Don't lie. Please don't lie. "No problem," I assured him, and cut the call.

IN THE MORNING, when Ms. Krige escorted me back to the dorm, Julie, Claire, Ida, Marica, and the other girls from my dorm gathered around me, hugging me, and told me that I was lucky to be alive. I had picked a bad night to pass out alone in the fog: last night, while I was freezing to death, deep slash marks had been found in the trunks of several pine trees on campus. A search by security had yielded even more, on the outskirts of the forest. The administration talked about mountain lions, or maybe even bears. But *we* talked about the Marlwood Stalker.

The other girls left, but Julie stayed behind, glancing over her shoulder before she bent over the bed.

"Oh my God, Lindsay," she whispered. "The security guys nearly found Spider and me."

I was alarmed. "Found you? When? Where?"

"Sevenish, I think. Spider had permission to go off campus

and we were, um, kind of making out." She giggled and covered her cheeks.

"Jules, that would have gotten you expelled," I reminded her, even though I, of course, had been planning to do much the same thing with Troy. I wasn't sure Dr. Ehrlenbach would have actually expelled Julie. All that tuition down the drain? "You have to be careful," I continued. "It's dangerous out in the woods. As you can see."

"I had Spider to protect me. As you can see." Her voice was dreamy and gushy, and I tried not to make a face. My days of believing that guys were knights in shining armor were over, pretty much.

Then her face changed. "But, um . . . "

I looked at her; she lowered her eyes and moved her shoulders. I waited, wondering if this was how moms felt while they were waiting for the rest of the story.

She sighed a little, very ill at ease. "Well, Spider thinks that you and Troy are seeing each other . . . behind Mandy's back." Before I could respond, she looked up at me. "I think you two would be great together, Linz. Really. I'd like it. But . . . Troy should break up with Mandy first, you know?"

"I know," I agreed.

She nodded. "I don't like Mandy anymore. She's a real snot-head." I smiled faintly at Julie's choice of insults. "But she's still his girlfriend. It would make *you* look skanky."

It *so* would. "Plus," I said, "if Troy prefers Mandy, he's insane, and who wants a crazy boyfriend?"

"You got *that* right," she said, smiling. Her smile faded. "I hope you're not angry."

"Naw. I know you're just looking out for me." And watching me. Good to know. But I couldn't hold it against her. "Thanks."

"Welcs," she said, relaxing. "Oh my God, Spider is such a good kisser."

Back to the matter at hand.

"Be careful in the woods," I said. "Please."

NINETEEN

January 25

Another dead cat was found. There were more slash marks on our trees. Girls screamed in the middle of the night, shrieking that someone was looking through their windows.

On the Sunday morning following my collapse, I gazed down into Searle Lake, listening to Celia.

"She's making her plans," Celia insisted. *"She's setting it up so no one will suspect her when she comes after you. You have to strike first. With all you've got."*

"I can't just . . . kill her," I said, weaving with weariness. I felt as if I were being worn down to a nub, forced into a black place where no one and nothing would be able to touch me . . .

"You can, and you must," Celia replied. *"Until then we can't be free."*

I picked up a stone and dropped it into the center of her reflected face. Her face became harmless ripples, and then it disappeared.

Shivering in the cold, watching my breath, I trudged back to

Grose just as Troy called on our landline, identifying himself as usual, as my stepbrother. Maybe we'd been sloppy using that as our code. Julie knew my stepbrothers were very young.

"Mandy told me—I heard that things are getting worse with the Stalker," he said. "I want to get over there, but I've got all these practices. I can't get away."

"It's okay," I murmured.

"No, it's not."

———

FOR A FEW MOMENTS, news of a Valentine's Day dance overshadowed the gossip about the Marlwood Stalker. A school calendar of events had been handed out at the beginning of the year, and there had been no Valentine's Day dance on it. I wondered if the dance was an attempt to distract us. It worked, as girls got on phones with designers and fitters halfway around the world—a dance required a new dress, the best dress—a *killer* dress. Amounts were flung around—five grand, ten grand, fifteen grand. For starters. Then there were shoes and bags and *tiaras* to buy.

My appointment with Dr. Rahmani was scheduled; it would take place during extracurriculars. I still didn't have an extracurricular, so it was no great loss. I hiked toward the admin building, anxious and exhausted.

My horrible fury overhearing Mandy and Troy outside of Jessel the other day had frightened me. It wasn't like me to be that angry, to take pleasure in imagining doing horrible things to someone. Now, by light of day, it sickened me.

I knew Celia was thrilled by it. Nothing would please her more than for me to lose control and . . . I could barely *think* it now . . . kill Mandy. But I was barely functioning under the pressure I felt. I was so scared that Celia was right—that Mandy was going to make her move—that I couldn't think straight.

———

THERE WAS A PORTABLE HEATER in Dr. Rahmani's office and I pulled my chair close to it as she whipped through screens of data, showing me tables, graphs, and charts about different schools and analyzing my parents' financial data in relation to different aid "packages." I was shocked that she knew so much about us. She said the fact that my mother had died would be "useful and helpful," but she touched my shoulder when she said it.

"Please don't think me insensitive," she added. "When one is contemplating the Ivy League, one must be a barracuda."

She gave me a pile of handouts, including an enormous questionnaire all about me, and some not-so-subtle suggestions on how to properly fill it out. Then she consulted with Ms. Shelley for another appointment. Dr. Melton was going to see me in early February. Apparently, he had a very full counseling plate, trying to keep the high-achieving heiresses around me from going nuts.

———

THE NEXT DAY, Mandy formally invited Rose to her

next séance, set for that evening. Rose leaped at it. I begged her not to go.

"Jeez, what's happened to the Linz I picked locks with?" she jibed, grinning at me. "Hark, woman, the game's afoot!"

I realized Rose was going to the séance so that I could do recon behind Mandy's back. She thought she was helping me out. That and another thing I'd learned about Rose: she was drawn to trouble—whether uncovering it or taking part in it.

"Rose is going to a séance with the Man-demon," Ida told me later that day. She sounded indignant . . . and perhaps a little wistful that she had not been included. No matter how much they all claimed to hate her, they still wanted her seal of approval. An invitation from Mandy raised a girl's cool factor by thousands.

"Good, I guess," I replied, trying to sound unconcerned.

"I think it's ridiculous," Ida insisted, with an unconvincing scowl.

As the day darkened and girls made use of the lull between extracurriculars and dinner for homework and gossip, I made use of the current Marlwood library. I still wanted to find another way to stop Mandy, and Rose's invitation galvanized me into action. I searched for books about *dybbuks*. There had been four, but all of them had been checked out by Shayna Maisel. They had not been returned. I checked Wikipedia. It was as Shayna had said: *dybbuks* were souls who needed to find a way to make amends.

To pay, I thought, as another surge of anger washed through me and my hands pushed down hard on the keyboard, leaving a row of 1s on the screen. *Mandy should pay.*

I took my hands off the keys and twisted them together under the library desk. That wasn't what I wanted. It couldn't be. I was too nice. I wanted Mandy stopped, and I wanted to be safe.

So I kept reading online. Apparently, you had to ask the *dybbuk* why it was troubled. Make it confess, and own up to its sins. Once it faced the horror of what it had done, it was free to go on.

I deflated, disappointed and confused. *Mandy would never do that. And I don't think Belle Johnson would, either. She doesn't believe she did anything wrong. She blames me.*

At dinner, Rose flounced up to me and fluttered her lashes.

"*Hola, bonita*. Séance time in three, two, one. And we're going to the lake house to do it. Bwahaha."

No. No, don't go. Please, Rose, please.

"Cozy," I said.

"So you can snoop around in peace," she said, in case I'd missed the point.

After we got back to Grose, Julie changed into sweats and a hoodie for a late goalie session with Coach Dorcas, which was handy because it got her out of my way. While I packed my cell phone and a flashlight, I watched Jessel for signs that Mandy and the others were leaving again. Julie returned, worn out and chattering about the upcoming spring competitive season against other private schools. Soccer might give her the edge she needed to get into her top-tier universities.

Soon she was sleeping soundly, and I got up, dressed, and waited. Around eleven, Jessel's lights went out. Then, from the side of the hedge, a flashlight flicked on, off. I saw Rose's face highlighted by the beam as she gave me a little wave.

I waited a while longer, until nearly eleven thirty, pulling a black knitted cap over my hair, and putting on my Doc Martens. Then I crawled out of the bathroom and snuck down to Jessel, with its dark windows and castle turrets. Blending as best I could with the darkness, I crept onto the porch and gave the knob a try. It was locked, which is what I would have expected.

Refusing to be thwarted, I walked around to the left, to the kitchen door. It was locked, too. I tried to peer in through the panes of glass, but it was dark. But as I stood there, I could hear the TV of their housemother, Ms. Meyerson. Yikes. If she was still awake, it was just as well I hadn't tried to pry open a window, which had been on my to-do list.

I skulked around the outside of the house, shivering, feeling waves of anxiety just being near it. I hated that place. It was filled with ghosts and horrible memories. A chill went down my spine as I reached the back door. Facing Searle Lake on the cliff below, it was also the exit to a secret tunnel that led to the attic. The attic was the epicenter of all that was wrong with Jessel—a cursed room. So I was just as glad that that door was locked, too.

With no way to get inside Jessel, I decided to go back to the statue garden and look around for Mandy's locket. She was still on Charlotte's case about losing it. I could feel myself tensing as I walked through the quad, past the commons, and stared hard at the white statues. With their bases covered in snow, they looked like they were hovering above the ground, phantoms of another age haunting our present. Like Belle . . . and Celia.

I gathered my army jacket and sweatshirt more tightly around myself. I should have put on the parka CJ had given me. As my boots crunched through the snow, I watched my breath flow out with each *chuff chuff.* I looked for the moon, but the snow made me blink, and I turned on my flashlight. The beams hit the face of a male statue holding a spear. I didn't know which god he was. His name was covered up. But as my flashlight passed over his features, I could have sworn he smiled.

I jerked and moved away from him. Maybe this hadn't been a good idea. What did I care about Mandy's stupid locket? I only wanted to get Charlotte off the hook and—

I felt Celia's icy grip against the back of my neck, urging me to move to the left. And then forward. I pursed my half-frozen lips at this reminder that I *had* to care about things that mattered to Mandy. I had to find a way to free her, and myself ... or the next statues I saw might be angels weeping over graves.

Our graves.

"Okay, I get it," I said aloud, as Celia guided me forward. The statues were white blurs as I trudged past them, nervously avoiding their posed, outstretched hands. What would I do if one of them moved? Would I start screaming and babbling? Would they haul me away? The thought was more than tempting.

Then I stumbled over something beneath the snow, and fell onto my knees. I cushioned my fall with my gloved hands as I sank deeply into the powdery white.

There was something underneath my right hand. Something sharp.

I jerked up my hand, then grabbed my flashlight and shone it into the indentation I had made. Kneeling, I peered into the circle of yellow light.

There was something shiny. The locket!

I bent to retrieve it. It was stuck on a twig, and I felt the fragile rusted chain break as I picked it up. I lifted it to my face and shined the flashlight on it.

Sure enough, it was a gold locket, etched in silver. There was a little clasp on the side; I pushed it, and the lid popped open.

A small tea-tinted photograph of a man stared back at me. Dark, deep-set eyes, short hair parted in the middle and slicked down with oil. And afterward, some refreshing rosewater. I could smell it. He had a thick, lustrous moustache and when he kissed—

I gasped. I knew him. I knew he had kissed me. And his name was—

I jerked, hard, and dropped the locket on the ground. Quickly, I picked it up; the photograph was really a thick disk, and it fell out in my hand.

For dear Celia,
David Abernathy,
June, 1886

It was the same name as had been in the ledger book Troy had found. I examined the face again. Was he the lobotomy doctor? But why would Celia love him then?

I wanted for more response from her. But there was nothing.

I started to put the picture back in the locket; then I heard a noise. Someone was coming into the garden, the footfalls distinct, and rapid.

Had someone followed me into the statue garden?

I got to my feet and darted forward among the statues, looking over my shoulders, seeing only snow and darkness. I kept going, all the way through, the back of my neck prickling. What was I doing out here alone? How did I know that Rose was really on my side? Maybe she had told Mandy I was going to snoop around tonight. Maybe they were following me right now . . . and I would be the next one to die. I hadn't seen the birds or the cat . . . but I had seen Kiyoko. Her hair, so frozen.

I broke into a run, following the path, which canted down sharply. I flew past the library and the commons, realizing I was headed back toward Jessel. Was I being herded there? Maybe they would be waiting for me; maybe this was a mistake. But I kept going, faster, so fast I almost fell over my feet.

A twig cracked. As I passed beneath a pine branch, it dipped, showering me with snow. Startled, I cried out, and ran into something hard. The impact sent me reeling, and I shouted aloud.

It was just the tree trunk. Eyes welling, I pushed away and kept running. I could see Jessel's hulking, hunchbacked shape growing larger. I was outside Jessel, in their backyard. But as I whirled around in a circle, I saw no one else. I was alone.

And still alive. With the locket firmly clenched in my hand.

TWENTY

I HEAVED IN, out, lungs bursting. Tears dripped off my chin and I staggered forward. Then my cell phone vibrated, and I fumbled, trying to grab it out of my pocket.

Rose had texted me.

help call.

"Oh no, Rose," I whispered, as I scanned my surroundings. I saw no one, only the inky blackness of Searle Lake slightly below me. As I headed for it, I texted back, afraid to speak aloud.

u ok?

drunkkkk. ok, Rose texted back.

Not in immediate danger, then, I translated. Maybe she really did need me, and wasn't just setting me up to come to Mandy. Or maybe Mandy was bating me, double-thinking as much as I was, seeing if I was going to nibble.

Maybe whoever had followed me into the statue garden had let Mandy know that I had gotten away.

By then, I was at the lake, in the spot where I had found Kiyoko. The flowers that had been left for her had dried up;

there was a fresh circlet of roses lying on top of some melting snow. I hurried past, placing the locket and the loose picture in my pocket and calling Rose.

"Linz? Oh my God," she said, laughing. "I'm so trashed. I can' neven walk."

"Where's Mandy?" I asked.

"Left. I wenna pee an' they said c'mon an' I said I'll catch up inna few but there's *one* more vodka shot. . . . " She cracked up. "I'm gonna get expelled. Scholarship . . . "

Behind me, lights blazed on in Jessel's living room. The drapes were open; Mandy and Lara appeared. How convenient. Next, the light in Sangeeta and Alis's room on the second floor went on.

"Troy," Rose said.

I waited. For about two seconds. "Troy what?"

"Was here. Julie. Spider."

I blinked. "At Mandy's séance?"

"She lied. It was jussa party." Rose guffawed. "A *great* party." She swore. "I can' get up."

Damn it. I huffed. "Rose, just get up and—"

She snickered. "I'm total rubber."

I checked the time on my cell phone. It was a little past midnight.

"You have to promise me this isn't some stupid prank," I said, warily. "You give me the key to Jessel; then you call me to come help you. And what am I going to do, carry you?"

"Mean, mean, meanie," she slurred. "Linny, you're my bes' frien'."

"Okay. Okay, I'm coming. Stay on the phone."

"I'll sing. Lalalala," she bellowed. "Lalala . . . "

A few more steps, and my cell phone cut out. I had left the sacred circle of cell phone coverage. I put it in my pocket and pulled out the picture, walking to the lake, bending over, holding it face down. I held out the locket.

"Did you love him? Did he love you?" I asked loudly. *Is he the man you and Belle fought over?* I remembered what I'd dreamed in the shower a few days back.

I pushed on, picking up my pace as I walked to the lake house, all my senses on high alert. I heard an owl hoot. Birds swooped above the water, then shot back into the air, as if what they saw gave them such a fright that they didn't want to land.

I heard no voices, no laughter, no cracking branches to give away movement. In dim moonlight, the lake house loomed ahead, just a jumble of boards and disconnected gables hanging over the water as if, at any minute, it might break apart and tumble in. I shined my flashlight over the weathered walls; something skittered away—a raccoon, maybe, or a mouse.

Or a cat.

As I went inside, the hairs on the back of my neck stood straight up. I hated this place; it was haunted and dangerous, and I was alone and vulnerable. The old-time photographs still hung on the walls, faces covered with mold, the glass cracked, picture frames worm-eaten. An old sofa sat beneath a rotted sheet. A real party zone.

"Lalala," I heard. Rose was in the basement. One way in, one way out—more stairs. I had no idea how I would get her back to Stewart.

I had no idea if she was alone.

I tiptoed across the filthy room and aimed the flashlight down the steep basement stairs, A bluish glow framed the door, which was cracked open. Taking a deep breath, I scooted down as quietly as my big clunky shoes would take me and pushed open the door.

Yikes. There were a couple of mattresses heaped with blankets and low tables cluttered with bottles of wine and a flashlight aimed at the ceiling. The light bounced off spiderwebs and sections of molded tin ceiling cover. I winced at the mattresses, thinking of Julie and Spider, and trying not to think of Mandy and Troy. Then one of the heaps groaned and moved, and I realized it was Rose.

"Oh God," I whispered, and raced over to her. Rose's arm was flopped over her eyes. There was a Ouija board and an oval mirror the size of a dinner platter beside her mattress. On the mirror sat six white candles, out, three of them knocked over on their sides. "Are you okay?"

She chuckled low and moved a little. It was so cold in the basement; left there alone all night, she might have frozen to death. I gently took her arm and laid it at her side. Her head was turned and I cupped her chin and turned it toward me. Her mouth was parted.

And her eyes were black.

She was possessed. By one of the girls who had died in that fire a hundred years ago . . . one of the girls who had sworn with her dying breath to exact revenge on Celia Reaves.

I flung myself away from her, grabbing onto one of the tables to push myself up so I could run. It cracked under my weight, and I fell back onto my butt.

"*Celia*," she intoned. Her slack mouth didn't move. The voice was coming out of her, but she wasn't speaking. "*You killed us.*"

"Rose, no," I said. "Fight it. Fight *her.*"

"*You're going to pay.*" Rose weakly raised her arm. It fell. I realized she was trying to get up, too, and she couldn't. She was too drunk. I pushed myself up harder, getting to my feet . . . and saw both our reflections in the mirror, Rose from the back of her head, and me, from the front.

A gauzy white image floated over her body and her face, a white, shapeless gown glowed over her clothes. Her face was bone white, gouged with dark circles for eyes, and a black hole for her mouth. She had two tear-shaped holes for a nose, and no skin.

"*Kill her,*" Celia urged me. "*Stop her.*"

On the mattress, Rose groaned.

I backed away, tripping over an empty Grey Goose vodka bottle, throwing out my arms to maintain my balance. I lost sight of my reflection—of Celia—in the mirror, but I heard her voice in my head.

"*It will be easy, sweet bee. She's weakened by drink. Just put your hands over her mouth and press. It won't take long.*"

"No," I said aloud, as Rose flopped over on her side. Her black eyes glared at me, but she didn't speak. A white glow shifted and moved around her, and I covered my mouth with both hands, my eyes widening.

"*Then light a candle, and set her blanket on fire.*"

I shook my head, over and over and over; but my gaze shifted to the pillow beside Rose's elbow. All I had to do . . .

Rose got up on her elbows, staring at me, the rotted face of a long-dead girl superimposed on her features, eyeless sockets focused on me. No black eyes; no eyes at all. Her hands were nothing but bones and as she began to crawl toward me, in a disjointed, inhuman way, they clacked like wind chimes. I heard her sliding over the floor. Her hair swinging, her jaw rattling with two or three loose, decayed teeth. She stared at me with no eyes. She smiled with no lips.

I whimpered.

She kept coming.

"*She's still down,*" Celia said. "*But she's going to stand up. And when she does—*"

Rose—the spirit inside Rose—laughed again, low and unearthly, an echo of an echo of an echo. My skin prickled and I whimpered again. Backed away again.

"*Don't be a coward. Remember that girl in the lake. Kiyoko. They made her do it, because she was fighting them. They killed her. Stop them.*"

Hand flopping down on a plastic cup, Rose crushed it, and kept coming, crawling a little faster, still laughing, a low, nearly sub-audible rumble in what sounded like an empty chest. The expression on her face was pure hatred. I knew Celia was right. I had to do something, or Rose was going to kill me.

Rose's head lowered to the floor and she pushed back on her elbows, hunching her back as she worked herself onto her knees. Why didn't I do something? Why didn't I stop her?

I felt myself take a step forward. And I understood—if I didn't do something on my own, Celia would *make* me.

"I won't kill her," I insisted.

"Lalala," Rose sang, her face obscured by her hair, laughing low and deep and crazy in her chest.

"Stop it, Rose, stop," I bellowed at her. She began to raise her head—

"Rose, it's me," I said. "Lindsay."

"*Celia*," she said, stumbling to the left. "*Kill you.*"

"You have no reason to kill her." I started to cry. "She didn't do anything to you."

"*Fire. The fire.*" She threw back her head and I saw her black eyes. "*Set us on fire.*"

I didn't know if that was true. But I knew that *I* hadn't done it.

"Rose. You're Rose Hyde-Smith, and you like me," I insisted. "Rose, listen to me. I know you're in there."

She went silent. And then I heard a strange, wheezing, rushing sound—as if a heavy wind gushed out of her and rushed around the room. She heaved hard, and threw up, turning her head and groaning.

"Oh man," she said, in her own voice. "I'm so sick."

I crossed the room and shined my flashlight on her face. Her eyes were normal.

"Rose?" My voice shook.

She threw up again. "Jesus," she said, gasping, "I'm freezing."

I grabbed a blanket as she wiped her mouth with a paper napkin and dropped it on the littered floor. Afraid to touch her, I did it anyway, wrapping the blanket around her shoulders and easing her up the stairs.

"Bad dream," she muttered. "Vodka's evil."

"Yes, very evil," I agreed.

We had to walk through the scary upstairs room again. I made a vow to myself that I would never, ever come back here again. Rose stirred, muttering something about her purse.

"Oh, God, did you leave it downstairs?" I asked her shrilly.

"No, when I wenna pee," she said. "By the shed."

I didn't know about any shed. "Show me," I said.

We staggered onto the porch, off the stairs, and then she turned left and wove to the back of the lake house, where I had never been. A plain wooden shed stood beside a rotted rowboat. The door was open, and I examined it with my flashlight. There was another mattress, fresher looking than those downstairs, and a Lakewood Academy blanket. And a brown hobo bag.

"Yeah," Rose said. "My purse."

"You go in there," I said. "I'm not."

"I didn't pee in there," she huffed, doing as I asked. She tottered inside.

And at that exact moment, I heard a horrible scream. It was Julie.

"Julie!" I shouted.

"Lindsay, oh Lindsay!"

"Rose, stay here," I said, pushing her onto her butt. "Stay."

I ran to my right, into the dark trees, flinging frost-covered branches of needles out of my way. The earth cracked and crunched beneath my heavy shoes. I heard running and crashing, and crying.

"Julie! Where are you?"

Trees shook to my left; then Julie staggered out. She was half-naked, one sleeve of a dark sweater torn away at the shoulder and draped halfway down her arm, wearing leggings and flats but nothing else. Her hair was a rat's nest and her face was scratched. She stumbled toward me and fell into my arms, sobbing.

"What's wrong?" I demanded. "What happened?"

She sobbed against me, smelling of pine. I stared in the direction of the lake house and drew her away. "Is someone after you?"

"There, he was there," she cried, pointing into the trees as she backed us both away in the opposite direction.

Taking her hand and pulling her toward the beach, I shined my flashlight over the laced branches and thick trunks. Wind made the boughs lift and fall as if they were breathing. The moonlight played tricks—was that a hand? A face?

"Where? Who?"

She half-ran, half-staggered toward the water, crying, trying to hold her clothes on. I charged after her, taking off my army jacket and slinging it over her shoulders. She didn't even notice. I stopped her from grabbing at her top and made her hold onto the jacket. The scratches on her cheeks and chin were superficial, but in the moonlight they looked like black stitches on white, dead skin.

"Oh, Lindsay," she wailed. "Oh God. I was supposed to meet Spider—"

"*He* did this?" I was shocked.

"No. Well . . . " She kept weaving, kept crying. "It was so dark. The moon was gone and I got lost. And someone came up behind me, a-and put his hand on me, so I thought it was . . . Spider."

She nearly fell over. I caught her arm and steadied her, grabbing my jacket. She was hiccupping with sobs.

"But his voice was lower."

"He talked to you?"

"He whispered. He said, 'Come to me.'"

I sucked in my breath. "He said that?"

"And I felt his breath on my neck, and his grip was too tight; it *hurt*. And I said, 'Stop,' but he was clutching my shirt and I tried to pull away. And he ripped it."

She pulled her shoulders in tight inside my jacket, weeping, terrified. Her eyes were practically spinning. "I begged him to let me go. I thought . . . I thought he was going to *rape* me. And then I screamed and you came."

"So he's still out here," I finished. She nodded mutely, and my heart pumped even faster. We were in danger.

Maybe he's watching us right now. The Marlwood Stalker.

"Was it Miles?" I asked.

Her teeth were clenched and tears created rivulets of black down her cheeks. She looked as if someone had tattooed spiderwebs underneath her eyes, which were hazel. Normal.

"Maybe. No. He's in Ha-Hawaii," she stammered. "I talked to him on Mandy's phone."

"When?"

She shook her head, weeping. "I don't know," she wailed. "I don't remember."

"Okay, okay. You have to stay here," I said. "Wait for me. Watch the trees and yell if someone's coming. Rose is back there. She's in the shed."

"No." She started to run down the shore, toward Marlwood. "Lindsay, just come, *please*." She broke away from me and stumbled on ahead, weaving along the shore, losing my jacket and grabbing at her torn sweater. Then she tripped and fell onto her hands and knees, sobbing.

"Wait here," I begged her.

I went back alone, knowing someone was out here with me. A rapist, someone like Rose, who was possessed? It didn't really matter. All that mattered was that he could hurt me.

"Come on, Rose," I said loudly, opening the shed. Bracing myself in case she wasn't Rose again. In case there was someone behind me.

Julie was still staggering down the beach, crying, when I returned with Rose, who was still very drunk. Seeing Julie, Rose fell down beside her on the ground.

"Wha' happened?" Rose looked at me. "Wha's going on?"

"Come on," I said. "We'll talk later."

"Julie?" Rose took Julie's hand. "Julie? You all right?"

"No," Julie said. "No, I'm not. I'm not."

"C'mere, c'mere," Rose said, gathering her up. I helped them both to a standing position and guided them along the ice-cold water. Julie cried all the way back to the dorm and Rose kept saying, "What's wrong? What's wrong?"

Over and over and over.

TWENTY-ONE

I GOT JULIE IN BED, walked Rose back to her dorm, and miraculously managed to sneak her into her room, despite all the noise she made. Without my army jacket, I was nearly frozen solid by the time I walked back to Grose.

Julie was wide-awake, fetal in her bed, holding Panda.

"We have to tell someone," I said.

"No." She sniffled. "I'll get everyone in huge trouble."

"*Julie.* That doesn't matter. This is big. This is attempted rape. Everyone deserves to know—"

"No," she pleaded. "Everyone already knows, Lindsay. We're supposed to walk in pairs and we're not supposed to go drinking in abandoned buildings or meet up with our boyfriends in the woods. *Okay?*"

"No, not okay," I insisted.

"Maybe it was Spider. Maybe he had too much to drink. And he lowered his voice to scare me. In a fun way."

"That was *fun?*" I echoed.

"I definitely drank too much," she concluded.

Then she pulled the sheets up to her neck, and settled in with Panda. "Please, leave me alone, Linz. Please." She rolled over and turned her back to the wall.

I'd had no sleep; and I was probably going to get a horrible cold from going out in the elements; and I'd been scared to death. I blamed Mandy Winters for all of it. I was so angry. Julie, my sweet little Julie, nearly *raped*. And what about Rose? If I hadn't come after Rose, she would have frozen to death.

And then Rose tried to kill me because of the games she'd played with Mandy at her "party." Belle was gathering her forces, getting ready to take me out—just the way Celia insisted. This was more than a one-on-one duel between us. This was war. I was beginning to understand that.

Julie finally dozed; it was about four thirty in the morning, and as I paced, I saw Mandy's light go on, then off. She was leaving her room. Then the front door of Jessel opened and she flew onto the porch, dressed all in black—black cap, black maxicoat, black gloves.

Bitch, I thought. *Where are you going? Are you off to celebrate with your coven of dead girls?*

White-hot with fury, I put on my jacket and climbed through the bathroom window. The air blasted me and sleety snow dripped onto my hair. I slipped on the boulder and nearly fell headfirst into mud and dirty snow littered with pine needles and crushed pinecones.

By the time I slid off the boulder and dropped down to the ground, Mandy had crossed Academy Quad and was headed up the path to the admin building. I followed, rehearsing my ultimatum in my mind. This had to end, now. All of it. And if she didn't swear it was over, I would . . .

. . . I would . . .

I'll make her swear, I told myself. *Or I'll make Dr. Ehrlenbach listen to me. I'll tell the media that this place is dangerous. This is over. Now.*

Mandy reached the parking lot. I wasn't far behind. I was gaining on her, in fact. Beneath the thickening snowfall, a wicked, low-slung Jaguar was parked in the snowy lot. The passenger door opened.

And Mandy climbed in.

The momentum of my rage pushed me on, and I stomped toward the car. Mandy was in the front seat, her back against the window, facing the driver. Her black-gloved hands stroked his face.

It was Miles.

Miles, who was supposedly in Hawaii. Miles, who had attacked my best friend.

Their faces moved close together. Were they kissing? I felt the ground shift beneath me. Everyone said they were lovers. Mandy and her own brother. Even Troy had practically implied it. Did his lips rub across hers, then nibble her earlobe? Or was he whispering into her ear?

I was too stunned to do anything. Suddenly, I was aware of the imbalance between us—two against one, the rich against the poor, the insane against the at least marginally more sane. It wasn't a good idea, confronting them together.

Then Mandy turned, and saw me. We locked gazes, and I was rooted to the spot.

The car door opened.

Mandy got out and started walking toward me. I heard her boots thudding in the snow like small falling bodies. Bird bodies. Her breath flared around her head like the ghostly face I'd seen superimposed over Rose's.

Behind her, the Jag roared to life.

"Did you get a good look?" Mandy yelled at me. "Did you take a picture?"

I pivoted on my heel, and bolted.

Snowy trees waved in the stiff morning breeze on the eastern perimeter of the parking lot. I ran for them. Gazing over my shoulder, I gasped to see that Mandy was charging after me, yanking off her cap. Her blonde hair came loose from a chignon and flapped haglike around her beautiful face.

"Come back, you bitch!" she shrieked.

Like an animal run to ground, I ran deeper into the trees, as afraid now as I had been righteously angry a moment before. Branches slapped my forehead and cheeks. I gasped as the cut on my face ripped open again.

I couldn't see her or the Jag, but I could hear them both—her rapid footfalls, branches snapping, animals scurrying out of her way. The Jag quietly rolling.

"Oh, peeping Tom, where'd you go? You like the show? Want some more? Since you're not getting any yourself?"

Her voice dripped acid. I heard a sharp *crack*—the breaking of a thick branch—and I crept slowly backward, panting, trying to escape. I slid over rocks glazed with ice.

The Jag engine purred, predatory. I thought of Julie, how I'd found her. I wondered if anyone would find me.

I moved faster—or tried to. The underbrush caught at my shoes like grasping hands, and fear made me awkward. The trees grew together so densely they formed a wall; as I tested them for weak spots, I found no way out. My lungs burned as I kept trying, pushing, now kicking.

"So," Mandy said behind me.

I whirled around, slamming my back against a tree. It knocked the wind out of me, and for a moment, I reeled, too dizzy to see.

She was standing less than five feet away with a jagged stick in her hand. She was panting as hard as I was, and her face was red.

"Spy," she hissed. "Just what do you—"

"You disgust me," I flung at her, scared past common sense. "You think you're so sophisticated and powerful? You're just pathetic! You're a crazy, stupid loser!"

"Shut up," she spat. "Just shut up!"

"Wait until *Troy* hears about—"

That set her off. Her mouth dropped open and she flew at me, flinging her stick at me, grabbing my hair. She gathered it up and pulled. The pain was like fire; she was yanking it out by the roots.

"*Whore! Slut!*" I screamed at her. It wasn't my voice. It wasn't my hand that reached down for her stick, and found a rock instead, and brought it up over my head. Not my legs that propelled me toward her, as she backed away, screaming for help. And—

I knew they would take the worst ones first; I knew they were coming, that they would take me and grind a hole through my forehead and let out all that was I, Celia Reaves, before I could tell them what Belle was, what she was doing. Murderess, liar. If they carved a hole in her head, no soul would pour out. Belle had no soul.

Even then she leered at me, laughing and dancing, as she often did on the upper floor of the library, where she would steal away—

—steal him—

She didn't know he was going to save me.

But now . . . we are here, now, finally, and we can stop her:

"You cannot live!" I shriek, and I close the space between us. She is no match for me. The rock is big and heavy and I grab her around the waist, whirling her in a circle till she falls to her knees. I rake my fingers through her hair and yank back hard; I'll hit her in the face with it, break that pretty nose, drive in those eyes.

"Lindsay, free us now!"

I felt Mandy squirming, heard her sobbing.

"No," I gasped. "I'm Lindsay Anne Cavanaugh. I'm Lindsay."

"—No, Lindsay, do it now, hit her! Beat in her face! Quick, in the name of all that is holy, do this thing and drive this evil from the world—"

Celia's desperation overwhelmed me. I couldn't hear myself thinking; couldn't feel myself moving. I had no choice.

"Oh, dear God, I beg you, do this, do it—"

"No," I rasped. Then I, Lindsay, leaped away from her.

Her face yanked back, her skull-face clicking and slashing at my hand, Belle screamed.

"*You took my love from me!*" Belle shrieked. "*And then you killed me! Damn you to hell, Celia Reaves! You killed me!*"

As Celia stared into Belle's black eyes blazing at her from Mandy's face, she dropped the rock.

We dropped the rock. I dropped the rock.

Celia was squirming and shifting inside me, agonized and confused. I felt her. I was her.

"*What are you saying? I didn't,*" Celia said, in her voice, although it came from my mouth. "You *killed* me. *And you want to kill me still.*"

"*Why would I bother?*" Mandy retorted, and I didn't know who was answering me, Mandy or Belle.

"*Because you loved him. And he loved me. He chose me.*"

Then Celia fished in my jacket and pulled out the locket. And as she did it, a wave of dizziness rushed through me; I saw the locket in a blur, as if someone had wiped Vaseline over my eyes. Mandy's face stretched and glowed, becoming the skull again, as she threw back her head and laughed in a bizarre, mewling way, like a cat falling down a well. And somehow, I fell down that well with it. Celia was here; and I was . . . gone.

"*I have the sister of that locket, harlot,*" Belle said. "*I sent that poor child into the statuary to retrieve it. To proclaim David's love for me among these ridiculous, posturing tarts!*"

Celia was thunderstruck. "*But he said that he loved me.*"

Belle stared at her, placing her hands on her hips, shaking her head. "*Why would he? You're insane, and loose, while I—*"

"*Who was mad, you or I? You tortured me at every turn, to*

force me to give him up. It was your madness that killed you. You set that terrible fire—"

"*I didn't,*" Belle insisted. "*It was you. I was there. You did it.*"

"*The years have burned away what little was left of your brain,*" Celia decreed. She held out the locket. "*It was for him that you burned us all alive. If you couldn't have him, you wanted no one to. Especially not me. Your rival. The victor.*"

But as she spoke, Celia's hand shook. Suddenly, she was not as clear on the events of the past as she once had been. The memory of the flames—the pain, the agony—feeling such sharp regret, and remorse for the evil she had done. Reaching as the flames licked her flimsy hospital shift dress for her locket; her skin cracking and peeling away from her bones as she felt around her neck, screaming, "Where is it? Where is it?" Wanting to die with it in her hand.

Feeling again her tears turning to steam as she became the moth that soared full tilt into the flame.

"*Lockets are cheap, Celia. Think, girl,*" Belle said, shaking her. "*If he gave you one, and me another . . . and then we perished in a fire . . . think . . .*"

"*No,*" Celia whispered, shaking her head from side to side. "*David loved me. He said . . .*" Her mind slid inside the brain of the girl she had possessed. The girl who was so like her—passionate, raging against the injustices of her life; and yet afraid of the power of the world and its capacity to harm her. Wrenched from her mother, as Celia had been. Sent to a strange place, as Celia had been. Tortured by a girl of means, a wanton, spoiled, privileged girl who had been granted favors by another . . . a lackey she had charmed—coffee, blankets, while Celia and the others froze and starved.

But David . . . he had seen how horribly she suffered, and pitied her; pity turned to softness; and softness to love.

David Abernathy had loved Celia.

And Celia only.

"*Me only*," she said aloud. "*Me!*"

"*Then* he *was the liar!*" Belle shrieked. "*His promises sealed our deaths! You fawning, weak fool, don't you see? He tricked us!*"

She hit Celia hard, on the shoulder; and again, on the arm. Then Celia grabbed her fist and forced her to stop. Belle lurched forward, then backward, and started sobbing.

"*He lied to us,*" Belle ground out. "*He did, Celia.*"

"*No, not David. He would never—*"

"*He did, and if he loved us both, or didn't . . . it wasn't fair. We weren't ready to die.*" Belle wrenched her hand away from Celia. "*Do you hear me? It wasn't fair!*"

And those words penetrated; like pleas for mercy bouncing against the icy bricks of a well, they surrounded Celia. They wound around her like ropes, piled like stones in her pockets. I felt my body get heavy, like I was sinking.

It wasn't fair. What had happened to her . . .

An ocean of sorrow, rage, and terror closed over her head. Over *my* head. Not fair, not fair . . .

Waves of dizziness overcame Celia as she sank into the snow, settling back into the girl, Lindsay, for whom life had been so terribly unfair; she was overcome. Collapsing in the snow, her eyes fluttered half-closed as she gazed over at Belle Johnson, in the person of Amanda Winters, who was sobbing as if her rotted heart were breaking.

Celia wept, too. The wind blew across her lashes and cheeks; she could hear herself but she couldn't feel herself. Belle looked as if she were dying. Her lips were turning blue and her eyes were closed.

TWENTY-TWO

February 14, 1889

"*Celia Reaves, Celia Reaves . . . you wear your heart on your sleeve, Celia Reaves.*"

David Abernathy kissed her. Newly out of surgical college, with his sandy hair parted down the middle and his rough chin stubble, a pensive look in his eyes, just three months at Marlwood and so beautiful in his frock coat and white surgical apron. She was about to learn, as she knelt beside his library desk and wrote in his journal, that he had discovered her name on Edwin Marlwood's list of girls scheduled for the calming operation. But first he pulled the ribbons from her hair and kissed her on the center of her forehead. Then his hand moved toward the cameo at her neck, so fine and fair an object, the only memento she had of her life before this wretched place. Her father had come at her, and she had stopped him; and for daring to raise a hand against such an important man, they had exiled her to this hell.

She touched the cameo, suddenly shy and unsure. Smiling at her modesty, he reached into a drawer and pulled out a small velvet box. Opening the lid, he gazed at her with lovesick eyes.

"A token," he whispered huskily, "of my feeling for you. Of my love."

It was a golden locket, shaped like a heart. He took it out of the box, laid it across his palm, and pressed it open. There was a daguerreotype of him in one oval and lock of his hair in the other.

"Once we are free, you may wear it," he murmured. "Until then . . . " He closed the box and placed it back in the drawer.

And the strapping young physician reached for her. This time, she did not stay his hand.

"I love you and only you, Celia, my darling. Now listen, my girl, we must make a plan."

———

"*BELLE JOHNSON*, Bella mia, Bella fortuna."

Fine young David Abernathy stole his hand down the opened bodice of Belle's blouse. Beneath, the whalebone of her corset shaped her heaving bosom, and his fingers knew where every tingling nerve lay in the land of her soft skin. He braised her flesh with the fire of passion. He was her love, and her lover; and he had promised to take her away from this nightmarish asylum, this bedlam, this chamber of horrors.

"I will come for you and steal you away like a thief in the night. I will not let them have you. You are mine. We'll be together soon. . . ."

"Promise me," Belle moaned, clenching the locket he had given her, and was keeping safe for her, in his desk.

"I promise you. Now, come to me."

———

"SING TO ME," Celia whispered, in the darkness beside the lake, where they rendezvoused.

"My love is like a red, red rose ... Let me, my love. Love me." He swung the locket, as if to mesmerize her. But she was hypnotized already, by serious blue eyes.

She put her arms around him. "Promise me."

"I pledge you my word. Now ... come to me."

But his only promise was death.

And the flames rose, licking at my skin, her skin, the white-hot fire searing us. The pain, the awful pain ... who locked the door?

———

I CAME BACK to myself.

It was like my dreams—or memories—had mingled with Mandy's—or Belle's. I didn't know how else to explain it—except that I had been somewhere else, living in Belle and Celia's time and place—experiencing things that Belle had seen and done, and hoped, and dreamed ... Two girls, locked in so much yearning, and wanting ... Did it make Belle go crazy? Had it dogged her relentlessly from beyond the grave?

Footfalls crunched in the snow, and I—Lindsay Cavanaugh—forced my eyes open. Miles Winters was staring down at me and Mandy both. My heart stopped. He could hurt me. No one would see. No one would know.

The wind ruffled his light blond hair as it whistled across the valley where Marlwood School squatted like a hunchback. But Miles was tall, towering over me, and there was something, some kind of energy, that I felt as he locked gazes with me. His eyes seemed to darken, like the stormy sky and he smiled, thinly, oddly.

Snow fluttered onto the crown of his bare head. His blond hair was disheveled. There was a scar on the right side of his jaw. I'd never noticed it before.

I heard my heartbeat thudding in my temples. I was afraid, but I was also . . . fascinated. I couldn't explain it. I didn't want to feel it. But I couldn't break his hold on me. I couldn't stop staring at Miles Winters, or feeling as if I had just received the most powerful shock of my life.

"Well, Lindsay," he said, in a husky, low voice. He looked at me for one more long, measured beat, and I stiffened, sure that he was coming to some sort of decision about my fate. I still couldn't move. It was as if he had hypnotized me.

Then he bent down, scooped his arms beneath Mandy's neck and knees as if she weighed nothing, and straightened.

He cocked his head at me, and for a second he looked very, very sad. His full mouth drooped, and snow dotted his lashes as he blinked.

Then he turned and carried Mandy away.

The spell broken, I gasped as I picked myself up from the snow.

"He played them," I said aloud, looking around me at the deserted woods. Played them and betrayed them. Promised them both his love if they would give him what he wanted. So did he kill them? Lock the door to be rid of both girls at once?

My heart was beating so hard I was afraid I was going to pass out again. It all made sense. Unfinished business. Terrible business. That was why a *dybbuk* had found a home in Mandy. If Belle had not killed for love, had she died for it—a love that was not returned? A false love?

I knew that kind of betrayal. I knew that kind of anger. The same thing had happened to me with Jane. But rather than deal with it, I had had a nervous breakdown. Whereas, in an attempt to deal with it face-on, Belle Johnson had wormed her way into Mandy Winter's soul . . .

I shuddered, hard, so sad, so angry . . .

Come to me.

Come to me.

Come to me.

Come to me.

Come to me.

The ice pick. We were tied down. Deep into the center of our foreheads. She dunked me in the bath. She hated me.

He set us on fire.

Come to me.

Come to me.

Come to me.

Come to me.

I was shaking.

"God," I whispered. "Celia, did he do it? Did he start that fire and lock them in?"

TWENTY-THREE

possessions: him

My love is like a red red rose
That's newly sprung in June;
My love is like the melodie
That's sweetly play'd in tune.

As fair art thou, my bonnie lass,
So deep in love am I;
And I will love thee still, my dear,
Till a' the seas gang dry.
Till a' the seas gang dry, my dear,
And the rocks melt wi' the sun:
And I will love thee still, my dear,
While the sands o' life shall run.

And fare thee weel, my only love,
And fare thee weel a while!

And I will come again, my love,
Thou' it were ten thousand mile.

—Robert Burns, "A Red, Red Rose"

———

I WAS RATTLED, and frightened, and I cried for a long time, but it wasn't enough. Maybe grief was Celia's unfinished business—that a guy she had loved so much had left her to die in that fire. Belle's response was rage, and an unquenched need for revenge. Except Belle was venting her fury on the wrong person—a fellow victim. If I was right. If David Abernathy really was the one to blame.

I staggered back to Grose, and retrieved my cell phone out of my pocket. Both a text message and a voicemail had come through.

"Hey, it's Troy. I found out some more stuff. Meet me tonight? Old library?"

Before I met up with Troy, I had to get through a day filled with question marks. Mandy was nowhere to be seen. And Miles—where had he gone, and had he been in the woods all along?

Julie was claiming to be under the weather, but I knew she didn't want to face the world so soon after what had happened. Rose had a hangover, but she didn't remember her possession. No one ever did, except me, and maybe Mandy.

Then I was summoned to a visit with Dr. Melton. I could barely drag myself to the admin building. Ms. Shelley was photocopying a flyer for the Valentine's Day dance, featuring a pen-and-ink drawing of a laughing cupid being pelted with stars and hearts by three girls in Grecian robes. I pictured Mandy slow-dancing with Troy, and turned away. I wondered if anyone knew that Valentine's Day was also my birthday. No more sweet sixteen. My mom used to say my face was heart-shaped because I'd gotten a kiss from Cupid, and that I was the best Valentine's Day present she had ever received.

I wondered if there was a statue of Cupid in the god-and-goddess garden.

"Lindsay?" It was Dr. Melton.

He escorted me into his office. It was warm and inviting; there were Ansel Adams photographs of the redwoods on the walls, along with several framed diplomas. He had gone to Princeton. On his desk a miniature waterfall trickled water over polished gray stones. He had a fish tank, too. Dr. Yaeger had also had a fish tank. Maybe it was a thing with psychiatrists.

"Everything good?" he asked, as I settled into an oversized padded chair. My feet didn't quite touch the carpeted floor. There was a vase of red roses on a bookshelf, probably silk, and I remembered the song David Abernathy had sung to the two girls who had died in a fire.

I nodded. "Super. Great." I sounded too eager, and he looked penetratingly at me. "Except for right now," I added, and he grinned.

"I will take my therapist hat off." He pantomimed doing so, tossing his invisible hat across the room. But I knew therapists. They never stopped checking you out. Mental health—wise.

"I'm thinking we should look at universities that are attracted to free spirits," he began, and I started. "Reed, Oberlin, places like that."

I didn't know those names. I hadn't done any research on higher education; all I knew was that my mom went to UC San Diego and my dad graduated from the University of Maryland.

I was planning to ask him what he meant by "places like that." Instead, I said in a rush, "Why did you talk to me about schizophrenia?"

He didn't blink. "Did that bother you?"

"Yeah," I retorted, as in *duh*. "You know I had a breakdown—"

"*Oh*." He smiled and waved his hand. "No, no, no. I'm so sorry, Lindsay. I didn't mean to give you the impression that I was referring to *you*."

I met his "*oh*" and raised him one. In the ensuing silence, I replayed our original conversation. "You meant Shayna."

He gave his head a discreet little shake.

My lips parted. I got it.

"*Kiyoko*?"

"I must honor patient confidentiality," he said slowly, as if giving me time to catch up, in the event that I needed it. Basically, he was saying yes. Kiyoko had been schizophrenic. And he was telling me that why? To explain away anything she might have told me before she died? Did he *know* that the sordid past had possession of Dr. Ehrlenbach's fancy rich-girl school?

And if so, would he fully enlighten me as to what precisely had occurred here?

"Let's move on." His tone was firm but pleasant. "Oberlin."

———

OBERLIN is fifty thousand dollars a year, I thought, as I made my way to the old library after dinner. *Two hundred thousand for four years.*

Now *that* was scary.

But I could no longer distract myself with thoughts of colleges. I was standing outside the library again. By the bluish light of the battery-operated lantern Troy had left for me in the hall, I knew he was already in the reading room.

I shook my head, unable to go inside. How was I supposed to take charge of my survival when I couldn't even walk down the hall?

"Lindsay?" he called, unaware that he might summon the dead if he spoke aloud in a haunted house.

"Yeah," I said. "Coming."

I shut my eyes tightly and took a breath. Then I flicked on my flashlight and surveyed the doorway. I turned quickly around, staring at the waving trees, listening to the wind as it pinched my earlobes.

I tottered down the hall as if I were drunk, and turned into the reading room. Troy was kneeling on a blanket the he'd spread over a section of the carpet, and there were piles of rotting books all around him. They stank. Another lantern sat on a small stack of books that were in much better condition.

Troy smiled up at me and patted the blanket, gesturing for me to sit with him.

"Here's the ledger book," he said. "I have to warn you. It's gruesome."

I sat down on the blanket, and coldness seeped into my bones. I felt as if my spine and ribcage were made of ice cubes, strung together on brittle silver wires. Troy handed me the book. The cover was black and charred; he pulled a flashlight from his jacket, angling it downward as I carefully opened the burned cover with both hands and turned to the first page. It was dark, with a small light-colored square pasted in the middle. A lit candle was burning on top of a skull.

Semper Curatio
Ex Libris
David Abernathy, M.D.

"It means something like, "Always attentive. This book belongs to David Abernathy, M.D."

"With a candle burning on top of a skull," I said. Then I turned the page of the ledger book, or journal, or whatever it was.

"Oh my God," I whispered. In a faded black-and-white photograph in an oval black cut-out frame, the eyes of Belle Johnson stared malevolently out at me. The fury in her expression took my breath away and I didn't move, didn't speak.

Then I turned to the next page. In tiny, elaborate handwriting, on a page with brittle, curled edges, was a list of girls' names; it started at the top of the page and extended all the way to the bottom. My mouth dropped open.

"A hundred and twelve. I counted them." Troy pointed

to the topmost name. There was a date beside it: January 4, 1889. Different day, different year, same calendar month. Coincidence?

I dropped my gaze to the last seven names. There they— there *we* were:

Belle Johnson
Lydia Jenkins
Anna Gomez
Martha St. Pierre
Pearl Magnusen
Henrietta Fortescu
Celia Reaves

None of them had dates after their names.

I waited for a reaction from Celia, for something inside me to snap. None came. Trying to contain my dread, I began to turn the page. Troy put a hand over mine, and my skin tingled.

"I have to warn you, there are drawings and some old photographs. And I-I think that some of the girls in the pictures are dead. And others have been . . . butchered. Lindsay, you were right. Dr. David Abernathy performed lobotomies on the girls here at Marlwood. It's creepy—you can't find any evidence online or in the Marlwood or Lakewood archives. It's Marlwood's dark secret."

Troy's voice shook a little. I looked up at him. His expression was grim. "The operation didn't always work. Especially at first. He had to practice. A lot." He gestured to the book. "He treated them like lab specimens. Like experimental *things* whose brains he dissected."

I studied their names. I traced *Celia Reaves* with my fingertip.

Why was there no date? No date on any of the seven? Had they been spared?

I smelled smoke. I felt heat. I looked down at the book and saw the charred edges smoldering, glowing red embers releasing sparks that flared toward Troy's chin. He was unaware of them . . . or else, I was imagining them.

Or Celia is making me see it? I thought, as the coldness lay across the back of my neck. The pages curled in the flames as I leaped up, dropping the book on the ground. Then I moved away, crossing my arms, and turned my back. I began to shake so hard I was afraid I was going to throw up.

"Are you okay?" Troy asked me.

I shrugged, unsure how to answer. "It's just . . . horrible."

"It is," he agreed. "First he drilled holes in their foreheads and dug around with knives . . ."

I shut my eyes as the ground whirled around me.

"Later, he changed his method. He'd take an ice pick and a hammer . . ."

Everything began to melt—the library in front of me, the sky, the trees . . . and Troy's face. They bubbled into globules like wax, like soured milk, like a bad dream, a hallucination, like I was losing my mind.

"I did some research," he went on, unaware of my panic. "There's no information in any medical literature about lobotomies until around 1935. So he was just making it all up as he went along."

"*Save me, David,*" Celia whispered inside me. "*For the love of God . . .*"

Troy fell silent. There was a beat. Then he said, "Lindsay? Did you just say something?"

Don't. Stop it. Please, I silently begged her. *Troy will help. Don't scare him away.*

My head throbbed.

"Linz, I'm sorry. I know it's gross. I shouldn't have shown it to you."

Troy bent over me, draping himself around me as he tried to lift me to my feet. I was a mess, boneless, limp, in shock. Then, as he lifted me in his arms, I fought hard not to cling to him, and scream and scream and scream . . .

Instead, I kissed him. He kissed me back. He kept kissing me, too much, too long. We both wanted to move on to other things and I knew it; we were panting and clinging and pressing and touching; his hair was soft and his skin was warm and everywhere he touched me I felt alive again; and we began to go too far. I gasped, and he jerked away.

"I'm sorry," he said, the perfect gentleman. The dimples on either side of his mouth deepened. "I didn't mean to do that. I know you . . . " He blushed and took my hand. "Things should be nicer than this, for you."

He knows I'm a virgin, I thought. I didn't know how I felt about that. Embarrassed, I supposed. Very shy.

"Hey." He lifted my chin. "In my world, we grow up fast."

Mine too, I thought. *I had to grow up when my mom got sick.*

"I'd like . . . I'd *really* like . . . to slow down." The lamplight danced in his hair. His eyes gleamed with genuine kindness as he bent forward and kissed my forehead. "Let's take our time.

Okay?" He took my hand, turned it over, and his forehead wrinkled. "You're shaking. I'm so sorry."

I swallowed. I didn't know how to explain, where to begin. It wasn't him.

Mostly.

"Listen, I know things are . . . strange. I'm going to make things right." He took my hand and waggled it. "Okay?"

"Okay."

"After this, I can't come over for the rest of the week," he said, then guffawed at how that must sound—making things right. "I'm on our baseball team and we've got stuff to do." He took a breath. "But, uh, there's a dance coming up. Here, at Marlwood. Valentine's Day."

My stomach did a flip. I forced myself not to betray any emotion as I waited for him to go on.

He put his arms around me and hugged me. "There's this spa resort, Pine Meadow. Near here. They've got a nice restaurant. I thought maybe we could go there before the dance for dinner."

Before I could stop myself, I smiled. A date! He was asking me on a date, and on my birthday, even though he didn't know it. *What about the dance?* I almost said, but I played it cool.

"Sure," I said. "Great."

He smiled back. "Let's get real dressed up," he said. "I'll get a sweet car."

"You have a sweet car," I replied. "Just ask my dad."

"Even sweeter." He looked really happy. Until we heard a light thump overhead. I held still, listened. Troy gave me a questioning look, and I pointed upward.

"I heard something," I murmured.

"The stairs are this way," Troy said quietly, pointing to the right. "I'll go look."

No, I thought. *Don't go up there. Ever.* I shook my head. "Let's just go."

"But if someone's *here* . . . " His face clouded. "If it's Miles . . . "

"It's dark, and it's late," I said, as icy fingers tiptoed up my spine. "And maybe . . . maybe I didn't hear anything."

He looked unconvinced. "Mandy told me about those birds, and those slash marks . . . "

And the cats. And we were supposed to go everywhere with a buddy . . .

He trotted off, and I let him. I told myself I could handle being in the room alone for a few minutes. I was sure I could.

I looked over at the little stack of books beneath the lantern. Lifting up the light, I held the top book in its glow. *The Dybbuk: A Classic of Yiddish Theater*, said the cover. My heart skipped a beat as I examined the spine. BM call letters, then numbers, and a sticker with the Marlwood crest. It had been checked out from our *new* library. By Shayna.

I looked from it to the rest of the stack. There were two more books from our library: *Exorcism Rituals from Around the World* and *Jewish Folktales and Legends*.

I settled back down cross-legged and put them in my lap. I opened each one in turn, looking at the titles, the section headers, some of them in Hebrew. Did *dybbuks* only possess Jewish people? Maybe Shayna had been all wrong.

Someone was watching me. I lifted up my head, expecting

Troy; and I exhaled very slowly. Celia's face was reflected back at me from the surface of the glass front of the center bookshelf across the room. Black eyes, slack face . . . but her mouth was moving.

Dizzy, I got up and walked toward her.

"*Don't trust him*," she said. "*Don't trust Troy.*"

"Why not?" I whispered. "He's not like David Abernathy, if that's what you're worried about." But I paused. Could he *become* David Abernathy?

"Did you find something else?" Troy asked me, coming back into the room.

I stared at Celia. She stared back. He didn't see her. Then she faded away, leaving me with no clue what to do or say next.

"Linz?" he said. "Are you okay?"

"I'm fine." I came to the blanket and sat back down. He joined me. My chest was tight as he took my hand again, smiling quizzically. I felt his warm skin on mine. Solid, human, normal, wonderful. He smelled like soap and cotton. Good smells.

"No one there. All clear. Find anything else down here?" he asked, indicating the books in my lap.

"Yeah, maybe," I hedged. "What else do you have?"

He picked up another book. "*First Lessons in Female Comportment*," he read. "There's a zillion ones like that. They even had lessons on how to hold your fan. After a while, they all look the same. The books, I mean."

He turned my hand over and traced my palm. It tickled. "Let me see vat I see," he said in a singsong fake German accent. "Oh, Fraulein, youz is cuckoo."

"*Ja, ja*," I replied, trying to match his light tone.

I glanced over my shoulder at the glass cabinets. The merest whisper of Celia's white face stared back at me, and I shuddered, suddenly very cold.

"What time is it?" I asked.

"I know." He tapped my palm with his finger. "We have to go back."

I didn't argue. We both got up, he lifting up the lantern. I was still holding Shayna's books and he didn't seem to care or notice as he led the way back into the hall. Light bounced off spiderwebs and skittering insects in bulging, off-kilter circles.

Celia's warning irked me.

"I really do have to go," I said.

He looked at the ceiling. Then he sighed as he gave in. "I'll walk you back to the main part of the campus. As close as we can get without Dr. E's *guards* catching us anyway."

Taking my hand, he began walking me out the front door. Once we were outside, he studied the windows, his jaw clenched, his eyes narrowed. His face changed. Hardened.

"Someone should just shoot that guy," he said.

"Miles?"

Troy didn't reply. But his hand around mine became too tight, and my finger bones rubbed painfully together.

"Ow," I protested.

"Oh, I'm sorry." He wrapped his arms around me and kissed me. "Sorry, Lindsay." He kissed me again. "I'll miss you."

"Same here."

"But we'll have a great time." In my head I heard Celia's words again: *Don't trust Troy.*

In the shadows, he left me, brushing another kiss across my

mouth. I walked back to Grose alone, turning my head automatically toward Jessel.

Mandy's mannequin was dressed in a camouflage jacket and a pair of jeans. It was hanging out of her window, its bare feet nearly brushing the top of a thorny bush in the yard.

And there was an expertly tied hangman's noose around its neck.

TWENTY-FOUR

February 8

I didn't know if I was glad that Dr. Melton had to cancel our next appointment. As I started reading Shayna's library books, I began to obsess over alternate ways to get rid of Belle and Celia. Some of the rituals seemed so silly—pouring salt across your threshold—but others held what felt like a germ of truth— smashing all the mirrors in your house. Some said that restless spirits took control of the "sinful minded"—that would be Mandy—or those whose will had been weakened in some way. I thought of my bid for popularity and how I had bowed my will to Jane. I watched Mandy as she continued to pull pranks on my fellow Marlwood girls, forcing them to humiliate themselves to prove their desire to be one of her followers. Breakdowns in the making. Like mine.

And Shayna's.

Knowing now that someone—Shayna—had watched me from afar and figured me out, I shut down a little more each day. Celia was wild inside me; I could feel her impatience—and sense Mandy's eagerness for . . . what? For something to happen to me?

I felt like I was going crazy, or crazi*er* . . . sweaty and panicky, unsure of what was really happening . . .

. . . except for the occasional landline calls I got from my "little brother Sam," and the friendship of my sweet Julie, who, I could see, was getting more and more worried about me.

And my nightmares . . . they were real.

THEY TIE US DOWN to the table. They press cloths soaked in chloroform over the faces of the lucky ones; but those who have been especially bad, those girls get no help at all.

He picks out the victims, Edwin Marlwood does, and he gives us numbers, like cows to the slaughterhouse. He gives the list to David Abernathy, who does the dirty work for him. Belle is Number One, and I am Seven; and between us are the girls who love Belle and hate me. The girls who have nearly drowned me, for her sake, to force me to deny my love for David.

What do I care of them? Marlwood and his henchmen have moved us into the cells inside the operating theater, Numbers One through Seven. The others have come back slack-faced and empty of all care and all passion. They're like dead things. That's how he wants us, Edwin Marlwood. That's how David leaves them, on his orders.

Belle has been flirting with Mr. Truscott, the young orderly. She's after a way to escape; and if that is the case, I say, God send His angels to her aid, and release us all from this pit of vipers.

But I fear that I will not benefit from her acts of cunning; I will be left behind, to suffer the wrath of Marlwood. Unless, of course, David can manage to free me. My hated father sends money to ensure my continued imprisonment. If Dr. Marlwood were forced to tell him that I have escaped, surely my father would exact his revenge. I believe that it is only fear of scandal that keeps me alive, as it is.

I hear the clank of the keys, the thud of men's footfalls; and distantly, I hear Lydia's screams. Oh God, they're coming for us! That's why we've been moved. They're going to strap us down and wheel us into the operating theater.

The stench of smoke slides down my throat like sorghum molasses. The fire is the whirlwind of hell. Now Pearl is shrieking. And Martha. Anna, and Henrietta. But I hear laughter, and singing. My love is like a red, red rose. Am I fleeing, or am I dancing, in his arms?

Am I . . . am I really dying? Or is the hot wind carrying me up to the stars, the cold, unfeeling heavens, where I am saved? I feel so cold. I am so icy, in the hellstorm.

She is pushing me under. Belle is pushing me under . . . in the tub? Or below the depths of the lake, where phantoms swim, and grab at me? And kill me?

And kill me?

But I cannot burn . . . I cannot die.

I burn already . . .

. . . For David . . .

"David, help us," I whispered, as I woke up.

I was swaying inside the operating theater, in my pajamas and my Doc Martens. Half-frozen, teeth chattering, body quivering with cold, I had no memory of getting out of bed and walking there. None.

I had nearly died there, two months before. Once a round, two-story structure of wood, slate, and metal, it had collapsed in on itself decades before. The balconies where eager young doctors and ghoulish spectators had watched Marlwood's brilliant surgeon at work on the helpless inmates were rusted ribbons of iron and straight-backed seats. A basement sprawled, containing the cells where they had imprisoned their victims—Celia and the others—and the burned-away corridor with its missing door, still covered with ashes—the ashes of the dead, unmourned girls.

My Doc Martens were coated with ash.

I turned and gagged, and fell to my knees in complete, blind panic, on more ashes. I heard myself wheezing as if someone had drilled holes in my lungs, and I threw up. From the hole in the ceiling above me, the moon glowed down on everything that remained of the fire that Mandy and the other five had set last semester, trying to burn me alive.

"Why did you bring me here?" I croaked, crawling as fast as I could over scraps of metal, bottles, and memories. "I know we're in danger, I know, I know . . ."

And the word became "*No, no, no*" echoing and ricocheting off all the walls, girls screaming for their lives; hitting me like solid fists, knocking me over on my side. I smelled the smoke and as I sprawled, dazed, transparent flames shot up from the floor like geysers, flickering at first, then hotter. One licked at my hand and it *burned*. I smelled singeing hair—mine.

"Don't lock it!" I yelled, "Please, don't!" and then I was racing up the stairs to the second level, as the floor of the theater crack-led and girls screeched in agony. I barreled through the pas-sageways, bashing into walls, slamming into rotted posts and tripping over piles of rubble. Heat engulfed me . . .

. . . And then I flew outside, throwing myself into the snow. For a moment I could only pant; then I flipped over on my back to look at the building. It stood beneath the moon, no smoke, no fire, which is what I had expected.

"Oh *God*," I whispered, pounding my fists into the snow. "Just stop it."

Then I got up and ran as fast as I could—which wasn't very fast, because I was half-frozen—back to Grose. I tore off my pajamas and wadded them in the trash. I cleaned up in the kitchen, and made myself some tea. No way was I going to go to bed.

I picked up *Exorcism Rituals from Around the World*.

And a card fell out. I picked it up. It was a calling card, like some girls used, with SHAYNA MAISEL, her email address, and her phone number.

Her phone number.

It was only eleven; I raced back into the kitchen and dialed it, wincing at the sound of each ring, hoping that she, and not her dad or her mom, would answer the phone.

"Yeah," she murmured.

"Shayna, oh my God, Shayna," I blurted. "It's me, Lindsay."

There was a pause. For a minute I thought she had hung up.

Then I heard weeping. "Lindsay," she said. "Lindsay, they think I'm crazy."

"You're not. *You're not*," I promised her, listening to her sad, low keening. I wanted to ask her what had happened to her. I wanted to know if Mandy and Lara had done anything to make it worse.

Instead, she said, "Tell me what's going on."

So I did, filling her in on everything, including tonight's visit to the operating theater. She listened intently; when I was done, she exhaled.

"Oh God, I'm sorry I'm not there to help you," she said. "If only you had told me, Lindsay."

Please come back, Shayna. I need you to come back.

"I-I saw a man in the library. A ghost," Shayna said. "He was sitting down, like at a desk, only no desk was there. And he was crying. It scared me so badly I just lost it. That's what happened to me, Lindsay. That's why I left."

"Oh," I said, "Oh, Shayna—"

"He was young. And he was holding a piece of jewelry."

Maybe it was one of those lockets, the ones David Abernathy gave to both of them.

Shayna was quiet, thinking. "Maybe the ghost wants to say he's sorry. Maybe he needs to be forgiven, so he can move on."

"Do you think . . . do you think that he's possessing Troy?" I asked.

"Possible. Look at him, torn between you and Mandy. Celia and Belle. It's the same triangle."

"I-I really like him."

"Then you should finish it. Stay in it, and force it to be over."

"But what if—"

"You have to," she cut in. "Do it for Kiyoko. And for yourself, and everybody you care about." She took a deep breath. "And do it for me. Because I can't sleep. I never sleep anymore."

She hung up. I figured one of her parents had walked into the room. I stayed up pacing, counting down the minutes, waiting until it was a decent time to call her back. Shayna was back, and she was going to help me.

But when I dialed her number again, it had been disconnected.

VALENTINE'S DAY

Courage is tiny pieces of fear all glued together.
                                        —Irisa Hail

There is only one difference between a madman and me. I am not mad.

                                        —Salvador Dali

TWENTY-FIVE

February 14, my birthday
possessions: me

> the pieces of the puzzle; i can almost feel them fitting
> together. but do i have them all?

> am i possessed, or am i obsessed?

> *haunted by*: too many questions
> *listening to*: who should i listen to?
> *mood:* fragmented

possessions: them

> my answers? all the answers?

> *haunted by*: dead girls who don't care if they live or die
> *listening to*: Mandy. *mistake.*
> *mood*: bitchy

possessions: mandy

> she thinks she owns Troy.
> she knows she owns Miles.
> but she doesn't own herself. Belle does.

> *haunted by*: unfinished business
> *listening to*: lies
> *mood*: mean, edgy, ready

possessions: troy

> well, that remains to be seen, doesn't it?

A CANDY-RED LOTUS hummed in front of the admin building, and as I hesitated, the driver's side opened and Troy stepped out. He was wearing a tux, and it showed off his broad shoulders and nonexistent hips. His dark hair was slicked back, accentuating his eyes and the angles of his face. He looked older and, if humanly possible, hotter than ever.

I had never been on a date with a guy in a tux before, having not gone to the winter formal with Riley, of course. And I had never even seen a Lotus outside of a movie. I suddenly felt very shy, and weird. All this was way beyond me.

I hadn't expected him to get out of the car. I thought I'd sneak in and he'd peel out, as if we had committed a crime. To him, going out with me was sort of a crime, since he still hadn't officially broken up with Mandy. To me, it was . . . wonderful at one level, highly terrifying at another. I knew now that at least on *some* level, I really was repeating the past. But this was different because Troy was good. Wasn't he?

"Lindsay," he said, gawking at me.

"Troy," I retorted, highly self-conscious in the clothes my dormies had lent me—a red halter top of raw silk that loosely crossed just above my bra line, a little black leather motorcycle jacket, eensy gray jeans which made my legs look really long, and a pair of towering ebony slingbacks that, frankly, were a half size too small. Marica's. Everything had been "created" by designers with single names. I had on rubies and diamonds, including a few that Marica had glued on my cheeks and left shoulder. Real? Probably. My wild dark mane was pinned partly back to show off the angles of my face, and I wore a faint berry stain on my lips. I had never looked this stunning in my life. Happy Birthday, me.

In my pocket, I held Celia's broken locket, as well as the silk crochet necklace with the crescent moon pendant that Troy gave me for Christmas. Knowing nothing of possession, but plenty about the true meaning of Valentine's Day (the claiming of hearts), my friends had decided that in the case of Mandy, the honor system didn't apply after all.

Ever since our confrontation in the snow, Mandy had transformed into a crabby diva and hardly anyone could stand her. Where before she ruled the roost with some style, now she acted like an overtired, indulged two-year-old, sending her minions to fetch more bottled water or to go back to her room to grab her history book, or even to take notes in classes they shared with her because she didn't feel like it.

Mandy wasn't sleeping well either.

I thought somehow she would remember what had happened—that Belle would let her remember. But Mandy obviously didn't recall our mutual revelation about David Abernathy, or maybe she didn't think that had anything to do with her, and me, and Troy. Or maybe she did, and was plotting something way beyond my scope.

Whatever the case, I was the one my dormies cared about, not Mandy; and I wasn't acting like a bitch. So all gloves were off in the Troy sweepstakes; they styled me into the hottie I never was and served me up on stilettos.

"You look amazing," he said. "Not that you don't in real life."

The "real life" comment reminded me that he was my snarkmate; while he was flushed and happy to be all dressed up and driving a Lotus, he acknowledged that there was an unreal aspect to it. Maybe even for him.

"Don't get used to it," I ordered him. "This is just for . . . because." That made no sense, but he grinned and swept a bow. I almost curtseyed before I thought just how wonky that would look. I *felt* wonky, and unsure. I had only gone out with one other guy in a boy-girl way—Riley, and that hadn't turned out very well in the end.

Riley could *have turned out well after all. He was checking you out in the theater,* I reminded myself. *Before you started channeling Celia.*

Well, I was channeling her now, so there was no telling what would happen tonight. The thought made me itch, badly. Or else I was allergic to the glue Marica had used to apply the jewels.

I had finished all of Shayna's books. There were a lot of

exorcism rituals in the world, and a lot of them required special equipment—rattles, bones, talismans, holy water, and crucifixes. I had even learned how to say the Ninety-First Psalm and the Ten Commandments in phonetic Hebrew, although I had no idea which word was which. Just in case.

Troy walked me to my side of the car and opened the door. The seats were real leather.

"Sweet," I said.

He smiled. "Borrowed from the same guy who told me about the restaurant."

"Your other car was really nice."

"T-bird, Lotus. No comparison."

I was flattered—and awestruck—by his rich-guy logic. He was actually trying to impress me. Me, the girl who had been stupid enough to believe that Riley the quarterback really liked her best. And the small-minded section of my heart—located in the same quadrant as all the scar tissue—wished that Jane and Riley could see me now.

Or Mem, I thought, and choked back a wistful sigh.

"Thank you, same guy," I said. My big ruby earrings tickled my neck. I was tingling from head to toe, feeling gorgeous, edgy, guarded, giddy, and close to overwhelmed with how simply happy I was to be with him. Fragmented. Amazed I could feel so many different ways, all at once.

The Lotus didn't so much roll as glide; the motor purred. I thought of Miles's Jag and pushed that comparison firmly aside.

Diamond stars, pearl moon. Troy was breathtaking behind the wheel, moving one hand behind my neck and playing with tendrils of my hair. His smile was positively radiant. I had never seen a guy so uninhibited about expressing his delight, unless it had been on the football field. *I* was making him smile like that. Me. Fartgirl.

We went down the bypass famed for the appearance of the burning ghost. One of the seven who had died in the fire? I almost wanted to see her.

Almost.

A few minutes later, we pulled up a circular drive starring floodlights on pine trees, a towering rock waterfall, and an enormous bronze statue of an eagle scooping up a fish.

"Jeez," I said. "Cheery. It's just like Marlwood."

Troy chuckled and drove up to an alpine-style hut. A guard inside was dressed in a navy blue suit. Troy gave him his name and a white barrier lifted.

That waterfall was only a prelude to a far more amazing waterfall at least two stories tall, in front of what looked like an infinity pool. Beyond that, a beautiful multi-storied stone lodge snuggled against the incline of the hill, like a couple sleeping like spoons.

A guy—a valet—took the keys from Troy and another guy helped me out of the car while Troy came around. I stared down at the gravel walkway and then at Marica's beautiful shoes. I could never hope to replace them if I scuffed them up—and they were probably one of a kind. Make that two.

Troy looked from me to the gravel, to my shoes, and grinned. Then he bent down and scooped me up in his arms, one arm under my knees and one around my back. Troy was muscly and he smelled like cotton and soap, with maybe a dash of tuxedo. Clean and sexy. He smiled at me happily, and I took that moment and held it closely—no matter what else was going on, right then, right there, a handsome, rich guy in a tux was carrying me like a hero in a fairytale.

"Wow, you are dinky," he said. "I knew you were short but you don't weigh much either."

I laughed and we sailed into the restaurant. The foyer was a circular room, water cascading down a wall of black marble behind a black marble podium. A woman with chestnut hair tied in a knot, wearing a simple but elegant black gown, smiled at us and said, "Mr. Minear?"

"Yes," he said, setting me down. I tottered briefly on Marica's heels and he steadied me. His grin was impish.

Then she walked us around the black marble wall to a dining room with a black-and-white marble floor, dominated by a sweeping spiral staircase. Black sconces on the walls held white candles, and the tables were covered with black tablecloths and white candles set in crystal. Prisms of light danced against the walls. Other diners, most in suits and nice dresses, but at least one other man in a tux, smiled at us as we passed. Everyone sort of gleamed, fit, trim, healthy, ageless.

She led us to the staircase; then we went up to the second level, to a small round table for two. Other couples smiled at us, and we smiled back. A man in a white jacket arrived, explaining that he was Missou, our waiter.

Our table bounced with candlelight. In front of a black vase with a single red rose, a white tent card read "Lindsay Cavanaugh and Troy Minear, Valentine's Day."

Troy pulled out my chair. His body heat warmed the nape of my neck.

"We have the menu in hand," Missou informed Troy. "Would you care to change anything?"

Troy turned to me. "Are you a vegetarian?" I shook my head. "Beef okay?"

"Yes," I said.

"I think we're all set, then," Troy told Missou, who kind of wafted away.

Then another man came, wearing a chain around his neck. He introduced himself as the wine steward and asked Troy if he should bring the Bollinger. I knew that was a kind of champagne because Jane and I had taken a trivia quiz about James Bond; 007 used to drink Bollinger, but he switched to something else.

There was no way I, at least, looked old enough to be twenty-one. I decided that liquor licenses just didn't apply at a place like this—just like Marlwood, where the rules didn't matter.

"Yes, thanks," Troy said, as I sat there, floundering.

Missou popped our bottle of champagne, poured, and put the bottle in an ice bucket. Wine came, and steaks and all kinds of side dishes—little potatoes and asparagus, which I loved.

"You've got the strangest look on your face," Troy said, finishing a bite of steak. The candlelight glimmered in his dark blue eyes. "What are you thinking about?"

Actually, I had been thinking about Julie, and wondering how she was doing. She and Spider were going to the dance as a couple, but she wasn't as excited about it as I'd thought. She'd insisted on keeping what had happened in the woods a secret; not even Spider knew, apparently. I hated the shadow that had fallen over her life. Hated whoever had done that to her.

"This is really nice," I replied instead. "Thank you."

He leaned across the table, took my hand, and gave me a look that was more than a look—a Valentine's Day look, an *I am serious* look.

"I'm going to break up with Mandy at the dance tonight," he announced. He was perfectly calm. As if he had planned this entire dinner to tell me this. Which maybe he had.

My heart soared. I was so happy I almost started crying. *Don't trust Troy*? Celia was *so* wrong.

"So watch out for fireworks," he added. "Because there will be some later."

Why *did* mean girls get good guys? I opened my mouth to blurt that out, then firmly shut it. I was the nice girl and I was getting the good guy after all. The impulse to babble was enormous, because I felt so . . . *extreme*. I tried to think of something to say. I had never told him about seeing Mandy and Miles probably-kissing in the Jag. I hadn't even known how to go there—*your girlfriend was cheating on you with her brother*—or maybe she was like Angelina Jolie and her brother, in a tease relationship that exploded my middle-class boundaries. I thought about saying it now, to make sure the deal was sealed. But it would make me look small and mean, and besides, I wasn't sure exactly what I'd seen.

"You're so quiet," Troy whispered with a grin as he tugged apart his dinner roll. He was leaning toward me, and I saw his dimples, and the candlelight reflected in his eyes.

I knew that quiet was good. I picked up my glass of champagne and took a deep swallow.

"You don't believe me, do you?" He hunched a little, sighed. "I don't blame you. I've been such a wuss . . . "

I swallowed more champagne. A lot more. I knew I had to let him dangle. He had to be sure.

"I need to use the ladies," I said after a few seconds of silence.

Troy pointed to the left. "I think it's down that corridor."

I wondered how he knew, but I didn't really care.

"I won," I murmured aloud, as I tottered down the hallway and came to a black door with a white *W* on it. "I won," I said to myself again, giggling. I had had way too much to drink, I suddenly realized. And tonight was the night. "I won, I won, I won."

I opened the door and stepped onto black marble, very slippery. I reached for the dish-shaped black marble sink and held on with both hands; then I stared into the huge oval mirror that reached to the black marble ceiling mirror.

And I saw her. Her mouth was moving and for the first time ever, since I had seen her, I saw her eyes, taking on definition and color—they were chocolate brown.

My color.

It was as if they were rising to the surface of her skull from somewhere very far away; and it was one of the most terrifying things I had ever seen. My stomach tightened and I gripped the sink edge so tightly my fingers ached.

She stared straight at me. Then a single tear trickled down her bone-white face, dripping from the mirror onto the sink. It was a real tear. I stared at it, disbelieving, and backed away.

"*Listen to me. Don't trust him,*" she said. I heard her voice echoing on the hard surfaces—the marble, the ceramic, the mirror. "*He's part of it.*"

"What the hell?" I said. "He's not, Celia."

"*You don't know. You can't know what it's like,*" she said, "*but you have to trust me. The web's being woven around you, and you can't see it. But they're going to ki—*"

"No, you're wrong. They're *not*," I insisted. Then I corrected myself. "*He's* not." I looked away from the mirror, but I could feel her staring at me. I sensed her moving around me, like a ghost about to materialize. I turned in a circle on Marica's stilettos, a little tipsy. My wits were not about me.

"He's been *helping* me. And not all men are like David Abernathy," I said.

"*How dare you!*" she shrieked. The hammered-bronze doors to the stalls rattled. The huge oval mirror over the sink made a cracking sound. Backing away, I stared fearfully up at it, afraid it would detach from the wall and crash on top of me.

"*How dare you! How dare you! I've done everything to keep you alive—*"

"No," I cried. "You've done everything to exact your revenge." I kept staggering backward, hugging myself. "I know it looks like your triangle with Belle and the doctor. I understand that. But he's not like that."

"*I thought David was true.*"

"He was performing lobotomies on helpless girls!" I cried. "And you knew that! Did you conveniently forget that when he kissed you?"

"*He thought he was helping them. He* did. *And then he saw the horrors he was inflicting, and he wanted to stop. He was going to stop.*"

She'd been gullible. Unbelievably naive. But *I* wasn't. And Troy wasn't hurting people for a living.

"Go away. *Please*," I begged her.

Just then, the door opened, and a woman in a teal wraparound dress came into the bathroom. I jerked, almost slipping off my heels again.

"I'm sorry; are you waiting?" she asked me, glancing at the stalls.

Mutely, I shook my head and bolted.

Back in the corridor, I leaned against the wall. I didn't know why I'd let Celia get to me; I was still certain she was wrong. Trying not to lose it, I went back to the table. Troy's back was to me. He had broad shoulders, and his hair was thick and shiny, and tousled; he was so sexy and so hot and he was going to be mine.

I tiptoed toward him, thinking to surprise him with a little kiss on his cheek, when I heard him humming.

"*My love is like a red, red rose . . .*"

And I stopped.

Dead.

"Lindsay," he said, turning and looking over his shoulder. And his deep blue eyes . . . were they still blue? . . . locked on me.

The candle on our table flickered and blew out. Troy jerked; his head lowered slightly toward his chin, and he wiped his forehead.

"Whoa," he said, taking a drink of water.

"What?" I asked, not sitting down yet. He reached over to me and took my hand. His fingers were cold.

"Nothing. I'm just a little . . . dizzy . . . " He trailed off, blinking a few times, and drinking a little more water. "You dazzled me."

Our waiter arrived.

"Would either of you care for an after-dinner liqueur?"

"Just coffee for me," Troy said. "Lindsay, go ahead; you're not driving."

Maybe that was the problem; he'd had too much to drink and he knew it. He had to drive in the fog in someone else's Lotus, on the winding, hilly roads.

"No thanks," I said, although at any other time, I would have loved to try an after-dinner liqueur. I didn't even know what they were. But it was time to keep my wits about me. Because maybe Troy was more than drunk.

Troy sucked in his breath again, and half-turned his head, murmuring to himself. His coffee arrived and I drank more water, watching him. He sipped slowly; then he set down his cup.

"We should go," he said. "I have to go back to Lakewood to get Spider. He can't wait to see Julie."

"Yeah," I said vaguely.

He grinned at me. "And I've got another big surprise planned for you. You're the only person on the planet who would love it."

"Oh?" I asked anxiously. "What is it?"

He cupped my chin. His eyes *were* dark. But not black. It was just the lighting, I told myself. Repeatedly.

"It's a *surprise*," he emphasized.

"Not big on 'em," I said.

"It'll be worth the wait. Trust me."

I want to. I want to. I want to.

Troy stood and pulled out my chair, and all our servants thanked us for coming. There was no mention of a bill. Then, after we went outside, he scooped me up in his arms once more.

Cold seeped through me, aching, into my bones. He gazed down at me but the moon was hidden, and I couldn't see his eyes.

"Lindsay, serious, what's up?" he asked. "I thought you'd be happy . . . "

I tried to smile one of those semi-reserved smiles I learned from Jane. If I could keep him guessing, maybe he *wouldn't* guess that I was suddenly afraid of him. Worried that Celia was right, and I was wrong.

"You probably don't believe me." He sighed against my cheek. "I said I'd break up with her almost two months ago, and I haven't."

I still said nothing. By then he had finished walking across the gravel and he set me down, tipping back my head with both hands, and kissed me deeply. I wanted to enjoy it, I really did, but I was too afraid.

Way too afraid.

TWENTY-SIX

THE LOTUS GLIDED to a stop in the same spot where Troy had picked me up for our dinner. It was seven thirty, and very dark. The dance would start at nine. Troy opened his door; I tried to get out before he came around to my side, but between Marica's heels and how low the car was to the ground, I couldn't manage it. He wrapped his hand around my forearm and pulled me up until I settled into my shoes, kind of like a marionette, and he kissed me. So maybe my inner—and as yet unrecognized—suspicion was unfounded: that he had borrowed the Lotus not so much to impress me, but so that no one would see me getting out of his car. I was so cold, and his lips were warm and soft, like melted chocolate.

I wanted to give in to that kiss. I had a terrible feeling that it would be our last. Celia had warned me, and Troy had hummed the wrong tune at dinner; and I broke away from him, staggering in Marica's shoes. I took them off and began to rush away.

"Lindsay," he called after me, "your feet. I probably have something in my gym bag—"

"No problem," I said, giving him a wave. "I'm good."

He laughed. "You're crazy!"

"It's not far," I said, although of course he knew that it was far. My feet were already on fire from the frozen ground that was littered with twigs and rocks. Sticks and stones. Words will never . . .

Possessed.

He kept laughing, the sound distorting in the wind. "Don't forget the surprise."

"Yeah, okay," I said, taking giant strides now to make my trip shorter. I could see the blacktop path to Grose peeking through the snow, its lines of horse head sentries mutely observing my flight. Did one of them move? Did a chain clank?

The wind blew, and fog drifted across my path. When I turned and looked back the way I had come, the Lotus was gone. I thought I heard laughter echoing off the buildings, but when I looked left and right at the veils of mist, I saw no one. In our school of hundreds, I felt as if I were the only person on the fog-choked grounds. Everyone else was getting ready for the dance.

I was feeling spooked—but when had I stopped being spooked? Fear was a current that jittered through me constantly. It was like when Memmy was sick—I would go through five minutes, ten, maybe an hour, forgetting that she had a terminal illness; and then when I remembered, I would be astonished that I could forget. And with that horrifying reboot, it would feel worse, like finding it out for the very first time . . . again and again and again.

I had been terribly afraid each time I relearned that she was going to die.

Now I was terribly afraid that I was going to die.

I didn't have a death wish. I wouldn't go to the dance. I'd stay in my room with the door firmly shut, all lights on, and let someone else deal with the unfinished business of Marlwood—including Celia's. I was done. Especially if Troy was being dragged into it.

I couldn't stand the idea that he'd been part of it since the beginning. All the more reason to bail.

Not bail, stop.

"It's over," I said aloud, not so much to make sure Celia heard me, as to make sure that I heard myself.

Decision made, I rounded the corner . . . and leaped into the shadows, shaking so hard my teeth chattered.

Miles Winters was standing in front of our door, smoking a cigarette. He was wearing a long black overcoat and black gloves. An overhead spotlight shone on his white-blond hair as he stood in profile, slowly blowing smoke out of his nose as he turned his head in my direction. I caught my breath.

"You can come out," he said. "I know you're there."

I didn't move, only hugged my short jacket around myself, watching as he flicked his cigarette into the snow and walked briskly along the concrete path in my direction. I squeezed myself into the darkness, my heart beating painfully against my ribs. My feet ached but I stepped to the right, off the blacktop and into the snow . . . just as he darted forward, cornering me. He came right up to me, and smiled. He smelled spicy, like clove cigarettes.

"Hello, princess," he said. He plucked Marica's shoes out of my grasp and let them drop to the ground; they landed with two soft thuds, like apples falling into wet straw. "They can't hurt *that* much."

I swallowed hard. "They're not mine."

"And yet," he said. The tension in his face accentuated the sharp angles beneath his eyes, his jawline. "You use a lot of things that aren't yours, don't you?"

I shivered as if someone had just walked over my grave. "That's none of your business."

"It is." He looked from the shoes to my feet, then swept his gaze up my body, to rest on my face. "My family is investing in this school. So what happens at Marlwood . . . " He smiled thinly. ". . . Better not hurt any of us Winters."

"Don't threaten me," I snapped, hoping he didn't hear the catch in my voice. I was scared. We were alone.

"Or what?" He reached out a hand and touched my cut, the cut I'd gotten from a branch the day we'd run into each other in the woods. I jerked my head away. "Poor little poor girl, out in the cold. Troy's father has been in business with my father since before we were born. You can't fight that, baby."

"Maybe *you* can't, rehab boy," I shot back. "But your family's tribal affiliation has nothing to do with me."

He laughed. "Oh, sweetie." He snapped his fingers. "One word and you're out on your ass."

For a moment I believed him. And then I realized that if that were true, Mandy would have gotten rid of me two months ago. I stared at him, working overtime not to let my fear show. I hadn't seen the birds or the cats, but I had seen the slash marks in the tree trunks, thick and deep.

"You know, in the old days, a cut like that was called a dueling scar," he said, gesturing to my wound. "A young man would wear it as a badge of honor. It showed his courage."

"What do you want?" I said harshly. "Because I'm cold and I want to go inside." And as far away from him as possible.

"You'll grab a warmer coat and some walking shoes, yes?" he asked. "All your friends are going to the dance. And your housemother's going over to Stewart to watch a movie. "In a little while, no one else will be home."

"You just pump it up, don't you?" My voice rose an octave. "If you can't scare someone one way, you just try another."

"Scare . . . " he said slowly, blowing out breath like smoke, like a ghost. He cocked his head, and the overhead light gleamed in his eye. He looked almost like an animal himself.

"The birds. The cats," I flung at him.

He blinked. Then he snickered. "Oh God, you mean the Marlwood Stalker. You think it's me?" He guffawed. "Really?"

"Most of us *know* it's you," I said. I was scanning the path behind him. It was deserted; no one else was out. If he tried anything, and I screamed . . . he could clap his hand over my mouth in a second.

"Oh, Linz. I haven't got the energy." He smiled ruefully. "And I'm too old for pranks."

Pranks. God, was I so stupid? Was Mandy doing it all? Pulling one big uber-prank on the entire school?

Or is Belle?

Maybe Belle had come back to wreak revenge on *the living.* Maybe she wanted her story told, the guilty brought to justice, if only through the judgment of history.

"*But she is the guilty one,*" Celia said.

"What?" Miles said, narrowing his eyes. "Are you talking about Mandy? What's wrong with your voice?"

I cleared my throat. "I'm cold," I declared flatly.

"Then go and get a jacket," he said. "And some better shoes. Not that those aren't beautiful. I'll wait."

My eyes widened. Was he serious? "I'm not going anywhere with you. In fact—" I tried to push past him "—all I have to do is tell my dorm that you're out here. And *you'll* be going straight to hell."

"Wrong. Been there. Got the T-shirt. Now I'm here." He brushed his black- gloved hand over my lips. I jerked back my head. "And if you decide to hide out in Grose, I'll still wait."

"For what?"

"You." He moved his shoulders as if to protest his innocence and gave me a lopsided smile, revealing his own white scar. It did look edgy, as he had said mine would look. "I think you're kinda nifty."

I shivered as if ice water had splashed down my spine. I wanted to come up with a sharp retort, but I was fresh out. Miles was diabolical. He was really, really good at scaring me.

"C'mon, admit it," he said. "You're a smart girl. Smart girls like smart guys. And I'm way smarter than Troy."

"I don't think Troy . . . " *makes out with his sister*, I was about to blurt. Probably not the right thing to say to a psycho.

"I'll go get that jacket," I said.

He bowed with a flourish, stepping out of my way. I held my breath as I brushed past him, trembling, then opened our door and sailed inside. I leaned against it and closed my eyes. My body flooded with adrenaline and I shuddered for nearly half a minute. Then I propelled myself down the hall to find Julie.

She wasn't in our room. Her top dresser drawer was open; a pink and silver scarf hung over the side. I asked; no one knew where she was, except that she'd left hours before and said she'd meet up with us at the dance.

Everyone else except Ms. Krige was there, trying on and rejecting outfits; spraying each other with perfume; borrowing makeup and jewelry. I returned Marica's shoes and jewels and everyone else's clothing; down to my panties and bra, I wrapped myself in Elvis's fluffy sky-blue blanket and went back to my room. I crawled under the covers, watching the clock; it was eight thirty by then. I walked to the window and saw Miles standing on the porch of Jessel. He waved at me.

Was he even allowed on school property? Or, as usual, did the rules not apply?

"Hey, what's up?" Claire said, hanging in my doorway. "You'd better hurry. We're almost ready to go."

I could keep my distance from Troy at the dance, but Miles appeared more than willing to invade my territory. Even if I locked all the doors and windows, I couldn't be sure that I could keep him out. I'd have to rely on safety in numbers, then.

"Give me a minute," I said, turning away from the window.

TWENTY-SEVEN

"HERE, WEAR THIS," Ida ordered, bustling in with a very sexy, low-cut emerald green bubble dress, a pair of silvery tights with jewels creating seams up the backs, and yet another pair of arch-stretching heels, this pair silver.

"Dude, she'll look like a Munchkin," Claire protested.

"If she wears green, we have to take off her body jewelry," Ida added. "Or she'll look like a Christmas tree."

"Let's put her back in her dinner outfit," Elvis said.

"She can't dance in that," Ida replied.

"Simple is best," Marica declared. "American girls get too complicated. We'll take all these colors away."

Claire brushed her fingers against my cheek. "We have to leave on her jewels. She'll look puffy if we take them off."

They bustled around, and Marica sat on my bed with me for a few moments of quiet. She played with my hair, and then she smiled.

"Listen, Linz," she began. "I think Troy is very nice, and I think he is trying very hard to let go of Mandy. I think you'll win."

"That's very nice of you," I said. My voice was a little shaky, and I cleared my throat. "But I'm not so sure."

"I hope you don't mind, but I've had a couple of little chats with him." She wiggled her fingers as if to emphasize just how little they'd been. "To speak on your behalf."

I burst out with a laugh, partly because I was so surprised and partly because of the way she put it, with her beautiful Mexican accent. She smiled gently, as if she knew I was a basket case, and tapped the cut on my cheek.

"We can conceal that," she suggested.

"It'll heal faster if we don't." I grimaced. "That sounds so deep and philosophical."

"Don't worry so much. You're very beautiful. If you made an effort . . ." She held up her hands. "Sorry, sorry, I won't push my luck." Then she kissed my cheek. "Tonight I think you'll enjoy yourself very much."

In the end, they left on my rubies and diamonds and put me in a slinky strapless black dress, no stockings, and strappy black heels. Marica added a silver cuff, which I clasped over my red thread, reluctantly leaving off my Tibetan prayer beads. I insisted on wearing my Doc Martens to the gym. And my too-cute parka from CJ. Suddenly I was determined not to dress to kill. I didn't care if all these rich kids thought I looked low-rent. I *was* low-rent.

Then the five of us left Grose. I glanced at Jessel's porch, to discover that Miles wasn't there, and I wasn't surprised. It wouldn't be as much fun if I knew where he was. Or maybe he'd gotten tired of the game and had moved on. In a way, I was almost disappointed. If this was a power play, I wanted him to know not to mess with me. I didn't want him to think I was scared. Though of course, I was.

As we slid through the snow, I looked at my excited, giggling friends and wondered if I should tell them what was going on. But I was afraid Miles would extract some kind of payback, and if that meant harming any of them—

"You will never guess who I saw lurking around after extracurriculars," Claire told me. "Miles. He was waiting for Mandy. Who was not around."

"Where'd she go?" Elvis asked.

"Out to buy some coke and pick up a sailor," Ida snarked.

"Who cares?" Marica said, sniffing.

I licked my lips. "Miles confronted me. For going out with Troy."

They all looked at me. Really looked.

"Oh my God," Ida breathed. "Why didn't you say anything about it?"

Claire gazed fearfully around. "Where?"

I was ashamed now, and mortified. Why *hadn't* I told them? I was too used to keeping everything to myself, dealing with it alone. But every time I tried to get some help, my helper paid. Look at Julie. And Shayna.

And Kiyoko.

"I'm sorry. It was right outside Grose." More staring, more disbelief. "He was all dressed up. I think he's going to the dance."

"With a hatchet," Claire said.

"And a chainsaw," Ida put in.

"I swear I'm bringing a rocket launcher next year," Claire muttered. "Or a bodyguard."

"I'm not coming back next year," Marica declared. She was looking around, peering at the shadows. "This place is too bizarre. But you should have told us, *chica*. We have a right to know if the Stalker is around."

I apologized again, and we slid along to the gym, which was brilliantly lit with spotlights outside, the entrance bordered by six-foot-tall ivy topiaries shaped like hearts, festooned with white twinkle lights. Above the door, a vintage large plaster cupid was shooting a red fifties-style neon arrow that flew tick-tick-tick into the center of a glowing white heart. The freeze-frame movements of the arrow pulsed in time to the frenetic, booming beat inside the gym.

"When did they do all that?" Ida wondered aloud, as the anticipation of the dance began to overshadow their collective fear of Miles. "They must have hired some locals to do the set up."

"There are no locals," Elvis retorted. "We're two hours from civilization."

"Actually, there's that resort near here." I caught myself zipping and unzipping my parka. "Very fancy." I didn't think they used words like fancy.

"Oh, right, where Troy took you," Claire said, and I nodded shyly.

We faced the gym. The music was practically blowing back my hair. I didn't know Dr. Ehrlenbach had it in her, to let her students have a party that was actually teen-friendly.

"So . . . what do we do if Miles is in there?" Claire asked. "Linz, did you bring the crosses and holy water?"

Marica smacked her arm. "That's not funny. He's a menace."

"It's a public place," Ida said. "What could happen?"

"I'm going in. I'm freezing out here," Elvis announced, opening the gym door.

I twisted my little red thread. I couldn't remember a single word of Hebrew. Or any of the words for any of the rituals for keeping the Devil at bay.

And then, as we swept into the gym, I could barely remember my own name. The vast, plain warehouse-like space had been transformed into a breathtaking fairy forest rich with the scent of honeysuckle. Both real and artificial trees rose to the vaulted ceiling of the gym; the artificial trees were purple, lavender, violet, and gray, with curling, mossy branches from which dangled thousands of heart-shaped leaves, shaking with the pounding bass of the music. Little cupids with wings and arrows darted on filament wires, appearing, reappearing, truly magical. The gym floor was covered with carpets painted with fallen purple and lavender leaves, from which rose fairy rings of giant glass mushrooms glowing with muted colored lights. The room was warm, and everywhere, people were taking off their coats, scarves, hats, and boots as they queued at a bastion of coat check tables.

There was a painted parchment scroll tacked to the nearest tree:

> WHOSE WOODS THESE ARE, I THINK I KNOW.
> HIS HOME'S ON MT. OLYMPUS, THOUGH . . .

"It's a little bit mixed-mode," Elvis said. "Fairy forest, Greek god of love . . . "

"Maybe it's Shakespearian," Claire ventured. "*Midsummer Night's Dream* . . . in the middle of winter. They definitely spent some major bucks."

"Speaking of Greek gods," Ida drawled, elbowing me. "Please, I'm begging you, lose the parka *now*."

Through the trees, the main center of the gym was unadorned, except for a vast portable dance floor ringed by tables whose glass tops glowed with inset optical filaments. And seated at one of those tables was Troy, alone. We could see him, but he was unaware of us, and as my innocent girlfriends pushed me forward, my heart thundered. Could I have been wrong at the restaurant? Had he been humming a different song, but I was so jacked up and anxious I only thought I heard it?

Maybe Mandy's been singing it and that's where Troy picked it up, I thought, clenching my hands together. I had heard it a hundred times in the last four months. She must have, too.

We passed several glass tables loaded with Marlwood girls and Lakewood guys. I avoided looking at the reflective surfaces, and focused on Troy, who didn't look like a guy who had broken up with his long-term girlfriend. Was Mandy even there yet? I didn't see her, or her brother, Mr. Insanity Plea, anywhere. Maybe they wouldn't show.

Maybe I was dreaming.

As we neared Troy, the girls bunched up behind me, as if they had to keep me from cutting and running. Preparing me for combat, Ida and Claire forced me out of my Doc Martens and into my heels. Then they stripped off my parka, leaving me half-naked in the tight black dress.

"Oh, sweet Jesus," Claire muttered, examining the parka, "this thing is polyester."

"Yeah, but Troy is 100 percent natural fibers," Ida said. "What a fantastic tux."

"Should we go with her to say hi, or leave our two lovebirds alone?" Elvis wondered aloud.

"Group," I croaked.

"Why are you so nervous?" Ida asked. "You just spent three hours alone with him."

"She wasn't braless," Marica declared. Then she slid a glance at me. "At least, not that we have heard about. I'll put these in a bin for you," she said, peeling off from the herd.

Then Dr. Ehrlenbach swept into my line of vision. Her dark hair was pulled back as tight as always, her face the same wrinkle-free mask. Red heart earrings of some kind of stone matched a red raw silk boat-neck blouse with three-quarter length sleeves and a draping black skirt that fell to the floor. Strands of sea pearls were wound around her neck like the colors on a barber pole, and I suppressed a giddy laugh at the thought. She was wearing silver cuffs with red enamel hearts on them, like handcuffs.

And she came fully accessorized with Miles.

He stood beside her, his coat and gloves off, in a black nubby sweater, a simple black belt, and black wool pants. Very Euro-sophisticated, and the boy version of what I would wear if I had the clothes—off the grid, not quite playing. He wore his white-blond hair in a ducktail, and his icy eyes bored into me with unmasked pleasure. I had to admit there was something breathtaking about him.

"Lindsay," Dr. Ehrlenbach said, "Miles was telling me about your discussion with him. I think it would be wonderful if you interned with one of their companies over the summer. If you went overseas, you could also do a language immersion."

Ida made a choking sound. Marica dug her elbow into her side.

"We'll just go dance," Elvis announced, and they abandoned me, just like that.

"Dr. Ehrlenbach's very excited about it," Miles said, smiling at me.

"It's very generous of your family." Dr. Ehrlenbach's face never changed, but she turned her head toward him; maybe that was her version of a smile. "An affiliation with the Winters name will open doors for our Lindsay."

I am not yours. I am not.

"Let's continue that discussion over a tango," Miles said, coming toward me. He put one arm around my waist and took my other in his hand, ballroom style. His skin was warm and smooth. I had expected it to be cold. He smelled of clove cigarettes and wine.

Dr. Ehrlenbach moved aside to give us space to dance. The music blaring through the speakers was in no way, shape, or form a tango. It was weird and bouncy, and the vocals sounded like French.

"Welcome to my parlor," Miles said. "You're not shaking. I'm impressed."

"I'm getting ready to stomp on your instep," I informed him, and his smile could have lit up the room.

"Oh, spirited wench," he drawled, "sarcasm poureth from thy lips as from others, sweet nothings."

I ignored his joy in mangling Shakespeare. There was no way he could know that *Romeo and Juliet* was my favorite play in the entire world.

"What do you want? And what's all this bogus crap you're feeding Dr. Ehrlenbach?"

"Bad words. The weapons of anxiety." He cocked his head. "No bogus crap. I think it's a great idea. We've got a beautiful building in London. Comes with its own dungeon."

"Where they keep *you* every full moon."

He just smiled and moved me smoothly in a circle. I had the sense that we were actually performing some kind of specific dance, but I came from the shake-your-butt school, and I wouldn't have known a tango from a waltz. Or maybe a rumba. I was aware that other people were watching. I turned my head slightly, looking for someone, anyone to save me. Dr. Ehrlenbach dipped her head in my direction, her seal of approval.

Then I saw Troy—or rather, the back of his head, and I started to pull away from Miles. Miles kept me close, and I glared at him. His eyelids drooped over his chilly eyes.

"Cocky, aren't you?" he drawled, looking over my head in Troy's direction. Then he smiled faintly.

I turned around and looked for Troy . . .

. . . Who had just begun to dance with Mandy. She was sleek in a thirties-style black satin halter dress with her hair wound into a smooth bun, and an oversized red rose tucked behind her right ear. And from the way she was smiling, it didn't look like he was breaking up with her.

With the same cold and triumphant expression on her face, she looked straight at me. My cheeks burned. Then she pressed her bright red lips together and blew a kiss at Miles.

I broke from him and began to walk away, across the dance floor. Tears threatened to spill and I knew I had to get out of there. I didn't want to go past Miles again, or Troy and Mandy, so I headed for the door that led into the pool room. I lifted my chin, holding my head high, my back to all of them. Let them bask in their dysfunction; let them go around and around in their stupid drama. I was out.

I was so out. When would I learn?

At least I got rejected by someone even cooler than Riley this time, I thought. But I didn't think I was being funny.

I thought my heart was breaking.

TWENTY-EIGHT

DESPERATE to get out of there, I half-blindly pushed open the door on the opposite side of the gym. It read POOL NO ENTRY but no one stopped me as I crossed the threshold, hit by a blast of chlorine smell that mingled with the welling tears in my eyes.

The door shut behind me, and I stood alone in the swimming pool room. The pool lights were on, sending waves of ghostly white illumination through the steaming turquoise water. I thought of Shayna, catatonic. Of Charlotte, chubby and naked like a pathetic cupid, humiliated by the girl now currently dancing in Troy's arms.

She's so evil, I thought, as the tears slid down my face. *She really is.*

It was cold, and I was afraid to get too close to the water. I didn't want to see Celia, for her to tell me she'd told me so. Okay, maybe I shouldn't have trusted him.

"I should get my head examined," I said aloud. Bad joke, bitter Fartgirl. I wanted to be done with triangles and Celia and

Belle, but I was fairly certain it wasn't really up to me. Maybe that was the real secret—*I* had unfinished business to resolve before I could really be Lindsay 2.0—a normal girl with a nice boyfriend.

Maybe he *was* breaking up with her. Maybe this dance was their last, and I had jumped to conclusions.

But how long did it take to say, "It's over"? Jane had given us a little seminar. Key points: You had to go straight for the jugular. You couldn't try to let them down easy; it was confusing and left too much open to interpretation. The longer Troy hemmed and hawed, the less likely it was that he would pull it off.

It didn't matter, or so I told myself. I would never die for love, even if it felt like dying.

I smoothed back my hair. I was stuck in the pool room, unless I bit the bullet and went back to the dance. Maybe it would be easier just to kill her.

"That's just a joke," I said, so Celia wouldn't get her hopes up. Then I cleared my throat. "And don't you think this whole joke's over? Can't you leave me? After Kiyoko died, the spirit who possessed her moved into Julie. There's been some shifting around, yes? I'm not the right one, Celia. Go find someone else."

"*You're the perfect one,*" she replied. "*I couldn't have chosen better.*"

"You *didn't* choose," I argued, blinking because somehow, I had walked to the edge of the pool, and I was staring down at Celia. Her eyes were brown. There was color in her cheeks. She was taking on a life of her own. "I brought you into myself by accident."

"*No. It was meant to be,*" Celia responded, and I moved away from the water. The person most in need of an exorcism was me. Maybe I should just leave now and find somewhere quiet, see if I could make it work.

Coldness poured through me and the icy-hand sensation on the back of my neck made me gasp. After all this time, it was always a shock. The image of Celia crawling inside me bloomed in my mind and I whirled around . . .

. . . And saw a shimmer of whiteness hanging in the air. I jumped away from it, and it hung, unmoving. As I backed away, it thickened and took on a shape—a person shape, my shape, only taller. Like in my cell phone picture; like in my nightmares.

My nightmares: I had forgotten one of them, only jerked awake each time I dreamed it:

I couldn't move, and it was coming, and it was here. I was panting, screaming, clawing. Sweat rolled off me. The back of my neck was cold but my forehead . . . my forehead, oh God. I couldn't move and it was crawling toward the bed; one hand was on the mattress oh—

Come to me, come to me, come to me, come to me, come to me. It was on my chest, it was pressing down—

I shouted. I was sprawled on the cement floor, clutching my hand to my out-of-rhythm heart, furiously knocking against my ribs.

Let me out.

Let her in.

Let me out.

Let her in.

Let me out.

Let her in.

I was swamped with cold as it gushed over my skin and rushed into my brain; and I whispered her name, protesting: "Celia, Celia, Celia."

Trembling, I opened my eyes and stared at the red thread on my wrist. It would be much easier to go crazy, then and there. A birthday breakdown—tempting, enticing—and then none of it would be up to me. But I took deep breaths of chlorine-scented air and forced myself to sit up on the hard concrete floor. No white shape. With a hard swallow, I stepped out of my heels, gathered up the hem of my long dress, and awkwardly stood. Because of the way the light wavered on the surface of the pool, the whole blue room looked like it was tilting.

Then the door from the main gym crashed open, slamming hard against the plaster wall. Troy burst into the room, stumbling backward.

I braced myself for the fireworks, expecting Mandy next, but instead, Spider charged over the threshold. He was wearing a tux, and his face was a mask of rage as he took a swing at Troy.

"You bastard!" Spider shouted, and Troy ducked away. Spider's words slurred; he had been drinking.

Dressed in a fuchsia gown with bronze criss-crosses across the bodice and a bronze half-jacket, Julie appeared behind Spider, crying, trying to grab his arm. It didn't seem to register to Spider as he swung again, staggering from the momentum, spreading his legs wide to keep from going down.

"Lindsay!" Julie cried. "Lindsay, help!" She ran toward me, her gold high heels clattering on the cement. "Stop them!"

She ran into my arms, hugging me, then took my hand

and dragged me toward Troy and Spider, just as Spider's right fist connected with Troy's chin. I heard a crack as Troy's head jerked backward; he clutched his jaw and wobbled out of Spider's reach.

"Oh my God, oh my God," Julie choked out.

"Stay back. Stay away from them," I told her, yanking on her arm. "Why is he doing this?"

"I told him," she said, "about th-the attack. And he thinks Troy is the one who . . . *the guy*," she said. She looked as if she were about to throw up.

"*What?*"

I could barely hear her over the yelling and the music as the door opened again. Mandy, Lara, Charlotte, and Rose rushed in, and everyone froze for an instant, like in an opera, staring at Troy and Spider. Lara was wearing a tux, and Rose had on a black satin top with white ruffles and a wide black skirt stretched over half a dozen fifties-style black petticoats with black lace hems showing. Black footless tights and ballerina flats finished off her prom beatnik look.

Charlotte's black dress was elegant and boring. All the colorful streaks had vanished from her hair. More boring.

Troy wasn't hitting back; he was trying to deflect Spider's attack without hurting him. But Spider was going crazy, pummeling the air, battering Troy, and Julie burst into more tears.

"I didn't touch her at the party!" Troy yelled.

"You're a liar!" Spider shouted, landing another punch, this one on Troy's chest. Troy grabbed Spider's arm and pushed him backward. Spider was drunk enough that he lost his balance and staggered, barely staying on his feet.

"Spider, I would never do that," Troy replied, stepping forward and shoving Spider hard. Julie's fingers dug into my shoulder and I winced but kept quiet; then Spider swayed for a couple of seconds and landed hard on his butt. The wind was knocked out of him and he groaned, loudly.

Troy was panting, his face tight, red, and angry. I looked from him to Mandy. She went white, and her eyes welled.

"What's going on?" Lara shouted.

"Troy tried to rape Julie at that party at the lake house," Spider announced. "And I have proof."

The girls gasped and looked at each other, then at Julie, and then at Troy, who stood with his hands balled at his sides, staring in disbelief.

"That's *insane*," Mandy said, coming up beside Troy. She took his hand as though she were trying to keep him calm. "He was with me the whole time." Her cheeks glowed bright pink. She was lying. I suddenly felt a cold wash of certainty. "He didn't leave me alone for one second, right, Lara?"

But I remembered seeing Mandy and Lara return to Jessel after the séance, the night I'd gone to find Rose, the night Julie was attacked. Mandy was lying. Troy had no alibi.

Fingering her black cummerbund, Lara nodded hard. She kept nodding, as if the more she did it, the truer the lie would be.

"Charlotte? You saw him. Couldn't keep his hands off me," Mandy pressed, her voice shrill. Lara stood beside Mandy and crossed her arms like a bar bouncer. On Mandy's other side, Troy clenched his jaw. He looked furious. He looked . . . like someone else.

Charlotte stared at them both, her forehead wrinkled with

confusion. She glanced over at the pool, as if remembering what Mandy had done to her.

"I don't remem . . . " Charlotte began, but she wasn't brave enough to go through with it. "Oh, yeah, right. He came back and hung out with us. Yeah," she said.

Mandy looked as if she wanted to hit her for her less than halfhearted attempt at backing her up. I wondered if Charlotte was doing it on purpose, so we would know she was being badgered into it.

But Rose put her hands on her hips and bombastically shook her head. Her skirt and petticoats swayed like the plunger of a washing machine.

"You guys ditched us," Rose said. "You weren't even there."

"You don't even remember half of what went on," Mandy said shrilly. "You were drunk!"

Mandy was losing control, not the smooth I-am-Queen-of-the-World diva I knew and loathed. It occurred to me to wonder if she was handling this badly because Troy had just dumped her back inside the gym. *Had he?*

"You were trashed," Mandy said to Rose, and the look she threw at Troy blazed with fear. I didn't know how to read it—was she afraid that he *had* hurt Julie? Or afraid that it was really, truly over between them?

"He was with me," Mandy said again, putting her arms around Troy, then easing his arms around her. Caged by her, Troy looked over her head.

At me.

Looked, but didn't let go of her.

Spider got to his feet. "Today I rowed over and Julie and I met at the lake house. To be alone."

To have sex, I filled in.

"And we found Julie's skirt," he continued. "Someone tore it off her that night."

Another gasp from the girls. Julie kept crying. Her fingers were gouging my shoulder.

Spider pointed at Troy. "It was all wadded up, on the shore. Troy's ID bracelet was snagged on it. Then I found out that he rowed back after he dropped me off. He never mentioned it. And nobody remembers seeing him. Except Mandy, who's lying. And Julie."

I looked at Julie. She blanched. "I remember a little. His eyes . . . " She looked down. "His eyes," she whispered. "I'm sorry, Lindsay."

"You're sorry, *Lindsay*?" Charlotte blurted. Then, "*Oh*."

The non-Grose girls looked at me with new eyes. Figuring it out. I had a thing for Mandy's boyfriend. I was a boyfriend thief.

"Troy?" I said.

His lips parted in shock. He saw that I doubted him. That in my mind it was possible that he had done—or tried to do—this terrible thing to my best friend.

Spider took a menacing step toward Troy but Mandy shifted, making a show of placing herself between them.

"*I* know he didn't do anything," Mandy declared, staring straight at me. "I know him better than anyone in this room. He would never, ever do something like that."

Then and there, she won. She had declared herself. I couldn't explain myself—that I thought he might be possessed by a hateful, murdering butcher who *could* do something like that. In agony, I kept silent, and Troy stared at me in disbelief.

"Then why do I have *this*?" Spider yelled, and he pulled a simple ID bracelet from his pocket. "TAM. That'd be you, huh?"

He threw it at Troy. It landed on the concrete with a clink.

Spider's footfalls echoed as he stomped over to Julie and me; ducking her head in abject humiliation, she let go of me and took his hand.

Was I wrong? I made a list as I trailed after them, knowing that if I walked out the door, I would lose Troy:

The dark eyes at dinner.

The song.

His inability to pick between Mandy and me.

And now . . . this horrible accusation.

They all pointed to one thing: He *was* possessed by David Abernathy. Celia was right. It was all coming to a head.

Troy grabbed Mandy's hand. "Come on," he said.

She narrowed her eyes at me. "I know what you tried to do," she said. "I know *everything*."

Then the two of them swept from the room, back through the door into the gym.

No one called for them to stop. I stared, open-mouthed, and then I turned and ran out the other door, the one that led directly outside, into the snow.

"Lindsay, wait!" Julie cried, but I kept going, letting the door bang behind me. It was snowing again, and the crystal flakes stung like whips.

I ducked down my head and walked between the topiaries, the cupid display casting red globules of light against the snowy walkways. This night. This night was beyond me. It was easier when you were positive that someone had cheated on you; when you opened your parents' bedroom door and there he was, tucking in his shirt. It was like my late start leaping into the pressure cooker of Ivy League college apps; I was a minnow among barracudas.

The hem of my dress was soaking wet; I gathered it up as a bone-hard sob erupted from my chest and—

—I was in the statue garden.

The blank marble faces of the gods and goddesses stared mutely at me. Just like Marlwood, and Troy, I had blundered in, not paying attention to where I was going, only focused on where I didn't want to go. And now I was there, among Edwin Marlwood's rock-hard, six-pack, semi-pornographic pantheon. It was so amazingly absurd that I began to laugh.

"Evil surrounds me," I intoned in a mocking, bitter voice, waving my arms as I made a little circle. I walked up to the nearest statue, of some broad-chested Greek god with curls like Troy's, reached up, and knocked on his forehead. "Hello? Jerkface? Cupid?"

Did the statue move?

Jumping away, I balled my fist and caught it in my other hand. Snow fell off the branches of a tall pine tree about ten yards to my left, as if someone else had shaken it, hard.

"Hello?" I called, but my voice was swallowed up in the music.

More snow fell—off the tree beside the first one, slightly

closer to me. I took a step back, then darted behind the statue, my face pressed against his back. Had I forgotten everything there was to be afraid of?

And then I remembered something: Troy had given his ID bracelet to *Mandy* when we'd come back from the break. She'd worn it a couple of times. I'd noticed, of course. Then she'd stopped wearing it.

"*Jewelry,*" Celia said. "*Like the lockets.*"

"No," I said, "not like that."

"*Like that. He's toying with you both.*" I thought of the crocheted necklace with the crescent moon.

"No," I whispered again. Then I remembered his "surprise." Maybe David Abernathy was the *dybbuk* with unfinished business—he had never gotten to finish what he'd started— silencing the two girls he had betrayed—by drilling holes in their brains—or killing them in a fire—

They haven't been silenced, I realized. *And he's still setting them against each other, when they should be joining forces to bring him down.*

"Not Troy," I whispered.

A shadow broke from the tree and glided toward me. I couldn't make it out; it was a black-hole blackout; darkness folding into the snow-laden night. The wind shifted, and the pine trees bobbed. The coldness on the back of my neck pressed down hard—*Celia*—and I waited to see if she knew what was going on. If she knew what I should do.

The shadow drifted closer. As my eyes adjusted, I could make out a shape gliding just in front of the trees. It was a person, moving carefully, trying to sneak up on me. Was it Miles? My stalker? *The* Stalker?

I licked my lips and pressed them together, knuckles white as I held onto the statue, staring at the figure; I dared him—her?—to show himself.

Then someone raced up behind me and tapped me on the shoulder, and I screamed.

TWENTY-NINE

"WHOA," Rose said, as she and Charlotte raised their hands and took a step back. She was holding my parka, my Doc Martens, and my gloves. "It's just us, Lindsay."

I checked their eyes. Normal. For the moment.

"Oh my God, did you really try to steal Troy from Mandy?" Charlotte asked. "You've got a pair, woman."

"I think there's someone over there," I said, gesturing with my head. "Someone hiding."

"Someone making out?" Rose asked.

"I don't think so," I said.

"Then . . . ?" Rose prompted. "Hello? We skedaddle?"

Rubbing my freezing hands between her cashmere mittens, she started walking with me as Charlotte trotted backward, staring at the spot I had indicated. My kneecaps ached. I had stood still so long my bones felt as if they'd begun to freeze together.

"Do you think it's the Stalker?" Charlotte asked me, looking anxiously over her shoulder. "Should we go tell Ehrlenbach?"

Before I could answer, Rose said, "Yeah-huh, we should. Come on, let's hustle it up. If there's some psycho out there, I don't want Ehrlenbach to miss him."

I went back inside the gym with them, my mind working overtime. Troy had promised me a surprise—something only I would like. Was it something to do with Mandy besides breaking up with her? Something happening to her?

I suddenly realized I *had* to find them. Mandy might be in terrible danger. Of all the ironies in the world . . .

"*So are you. Don't go,*" Celia pleaded.

And I didn't know where to go. I hadn't asked any questions about the surprise because it was meant to be . . . a surprise. And I'd been afraid. I didn't want to know . . . *to confirm* . . . that something was wrong with him.

That *he* was what was wrong.

I felt sick. I should have asked, should have pushed.

I had to ditch Rose and Charlotte, had to get out of there. I tapped Rose on the shoulder. "I'm going to the bathroom," I yelled, so she could hear me.

She nodded, swiveling her head right and left; then she pointed. "*Voilà,*" she said, and I followed her line of vision. Dr. Ehrlenbach had her back to us, speaking to Dr. Melton. I wondered if they'd found out about the fight in the pool room. About Spider's accusation.

I didn't see Miles. Or Julie, or anyone else who'd been in the pool room.

"Where are Julie and Spider?" I asked Rose, but she and Charlotte were already heading off toward our headmistress. I would have to check on Julie later.

For a flash of an instant, I wondered if I would ever see her again. If Troy hurt Mandy, or me . . . or worse . . .

Don't think like that, I told myself, feeling the flutters of panic. My chest got tight and I couldn't breathe. As I dashed back outside, I became light-headed. I gripped my hands together, glancing fearfully around, in case whoever had been lurking in the statue garden had followed me back to the gym. Maybe it was just someone making out.

Maybe pigs could touch down on Mars.

Shaking, I put on my parka, my Doc Martens, and my gloves, and checked my cell for just the tiniest possibility that a text message from Troy had come in. Nothing. I stashed it back in my pocket and took a ragged, but deep breath. I tried to clear my head but I couldn't quell the panic.

Where was Troy? *Who* was Troy?

Then I struck out for the old library. That was where we had been meeting of late, so it seemed likely that would be where he—or David Abernathy—would spring a "surprise" on me. Shayna had seen his ghost, crying over a piece of jewelry—one of the lockets he had promised to two desperate, terrified girls.

Cold pressed over the back of my neck. "*Liar. Deceiver,*" Celia said, through me.

I felt her anger boiling inside me. The snow tumbled and fell, creating bulky objects in the air, like giant foggy vampires swarming over the mountains. I tucked in my head and began to run, partly to keep myself warm, but also in hopes of outpacing anyone who was trying to follow me. As before, I had no idea how I would find my way. I assumed Celia was sufficiently motivated to do it for me. Last semester, Julie had served as bait to lure me to the operating theater. This semester, Mandy—

—I slowed. Would Troy want me to meet him at the library, or the operating theater? He and I had never met there. But that was where the fire had happened.

And the lobotomies.

The same panicky sensation caught hold of me as when I stared into our swimming pool and saw Celia again, after I thought I was free. I lurched forward, unsure of my path in more ways than one. At least if someone was trying to follow me, they'd have as hard a time as I did. Unless they saw with different eyes, like Celia. Then nothing could keep them from me—not the snow, or the dark, or the past.

THE LIBRARY WAS CLOSER.

As the snow flurried around me, I stood in front of it and stared at the upstairs window. The shutters were open, banging against the side of the house. I remembered seeing them open at night, then nailed shut by light of day. I even had pictures on my cell phone.

I took another deep breath and walked through the doorway. I was out of the snowstorm, at least; but if someone was behind me, he—or she—could see me now. I turned around, detecting no one; and edged sideways, holding my breath until my chest hurt. I aimed the light from my phone at the floor and exhaled slowly, trying to stop the jitters, the panicky trembling, and the intense desire just to lose my mind.

There were no lights on in the reading room. I peeked around the doorway, listening. Nothing.

A thump overhead made me jerk; I clutched the phone and flattened myself against the wall. My heart beat so hard I could hear it in my ears.

"I wish I had a rock *now*," I muttered, but I didn't really mean it.

Yes, I did. I so did.

My pulse beating at thrash-metal speed, I walked back down the way I had come, stinging with fear, aching with cold. I knew the stairs were to my right, but I couldn't make myself walk past the open doorway. It was dark, and unless I turned my cell phone light back on, no one would see me. But I was paralyzed.

"H-hello?" I called. But my voice was a dry whisper. I tried again, waiting for a blast of courage from Celia. Nothing.

I pictured Mandy. Happy, smiling. Then I saw her as a drowning victim, with an ashen face and shiny eyes. And then as a *dybbuk*, haunting the world because of her horrible murder.

That last image give me a push, and I broke free of my frozen state and dashed to my right, shoe tip colliding with a bottle; it went skittering. I braced myself for whoever was upstairs to call out; still there was silence. My hand smacked the banister and I started up, shining the light down again, glancing into the blackness behind me. Chills popped off the top of my skull, like static, as I climbed in slow motion, as if I were wearing leg weights.

I reached the landing, standing in darkness, listening for telltale creaks, for breathing, for someone else. The room with the window was behind me; I had to turn around to see it. Sucking in another breath, I pivoted, waiting for it, waiting...

The pitted, dark wood door was shut, but a slice of flickering yellow light ran along the bottom, giving me something to see by. There was a rusty latch chipped with white paint in place of a knob.

I tried to exhale, but I couldn't; with my chest about to explode, I walked to the door and raised my fist, hesitating, trying to make myself move again; and I knocked.

No answer.

My eyes fluttered back in my head as I forced the air out of my lungs; and I put my hand on the latch and pushed down. The door began to swing open.

As the hinges creaked, Celia seemed to activate. Cold on cold, fear churning inside me like a gasping fish. I could feel her thrashing, trying to force me away from the door. I tried to respond but the door vanished, and I was staring at the blurry, translucent image of a twenty-something heavyset guy sitting at an oak roll-top desk. He wore a long-sleeved white shirt and over that, a thick white apron, like a butcher's. His hair was parted down the center, and he was crying, his voice echoing as if we were both underwater.

I was stunned.

That's not David Abernathy. Not from what I could remember from the pictures I'd seen. I realized suddenly that I never asked Shayna what her ghost actually looked like. So who was this?

I took a step forward. He didn't notice me; he just kept sobbing. I saw the glint of a brass chain in his palm, smeary and unfocused.

Shayna's piece of jewelry, I thought.

I licked my lips and tried to speak. No good. I tried again, and said, "Hello?"

Ignoring me—or not hearing me—he lifted up the chain, sending beams of light all over flocked wallpapered walls. There was a large brass skeleton key attached to the end, and a book similar to the one Troy had shown me. The writing swirled like smoke, and then the elaborate, thin letters came into focus.

"*Leave,*" Celia said.

And the man gasped. He turned his head to the left and stared straight at me. I stared back at him.

"Is someone there?" he said.

He couldn't see me, but he had heard Celia. I waited; then he opened the center drawer of the desk, at his waist, and coiled the key inside. He began to cry again, burying his face in his hands.

I looked back down at the page of the open journal.

13 February

Tomorrow they will move my darling Belle and the other young ladies into the cells within the operating theater. I have seen the instruments laid out—the cloths for the chloroform, the pick, the hammer. She will be the first.

No, no I cannot let it happen. I must free her from this fate!

But I am watched. I have protested the conditions of this wretched place; it is believed that the mad can feel neither heat nor cold night and so they dispense with comforts for those chosen by Marlwood for the procedure. Thus they suffer in thin shifts with no heat, though the snow piles up around their prison doors while Marlwood warms his fat butcher's hands in his stately mansion on the hill. Last Tuesday, Leticia Dunwoody froze to death, although they wrote her parents and explained that it was "a strange malady" that took her.

I have tried to give Belle such warmth and comfort as I can. I have brought her coffee and blankets and so the others hate her, for I cannot do it for them all. But could they but draw hope that one of them, at least, lives like a human being?

And I watch my love, suffering, and I see, oh, God, I see it all. I see Abernathy go into her cell and I see her quiet and anxious after, gazing at me, begging for my help. Evil, evil. Like Marlwood he is, a scoundrel and a rogue and if I could dash his brains in, I would.

I will help her escape, though it may mean my job and livelihood. This I swear. I shall do it, or die trying.

—Edward Truscott, Orderly, Marlwood Reformatory

THIRTY

A SCOUNDREL AND A ROGUE.

That's what he'd called David Abernathy.

I left the haunted library and its weeping ghost, searching for a few seconds for some rags or piece of newspaper, anything to wrap around my flimsy parka and my tiny black dress. Anything to keep me warmer in the draining cold. There was nothing handy, and I wasn't about to go back into the reading room, even if there was a fur coat to be found in there.

I crept outside; the snow was falling more steadily, and when I felt severe cold against the back of my neck, I had no idea if it was Celia or the elements. Orienting myself, I knew I should head left. I tried to keep my eyes open, scanning for a stalker. I felt in my pocket for Marica's high heels, my only weapon.

I started moving, afraid I was about to become a Marlwood statistic—Lindsay Cavanaugh, the scholarship student who froze to death on Valentine's Day. Why was she staggering around, inappropriately dressed? Because the boy she was crushing on already had a girlfriend. Poor, crazy, pathetic Lindsay. No one would know the real reason.

Maybe not even me.

I blinked; I had started to daydream, and I knew I was lost. Trees rose around me. I was in the forest. I thought I heard something moving through the brush and I grabbed onto a branch and held tightly, just to keep myself from screaming. Were mountain lions nocturnal? Were psycho brothers and/or possessed boyfriends?

Then the coldness intensified, giving me a brain freeze, and I doubled over because it *hurt*; it hurt like brain surgery; it hurt like my heart breaking; like all the air forced out of my lungs; like my skin peeling off my face in the flames. It was a searing, horrible *hurt* and I knew that if I could see myself, my eyes would be black and empty.

My love is like a red, red rose.

I will come to thee by midnight, though hell should bar the way.

I must pretend to love Belle, Celia, because she has money; she is an heiress with a fortune and Marlwood has his hooks into her family. And there must be a way for me to dip into it. Once that is done, we shall leave together, you and I—

—you and I—

I WAS STANDING inside the operating theater. Flickering lanterns—*kerosene*—were set on folding chairs, casting yellow light over the drifting snowflakes, cascading blue through the hole in the roof, past the ruined balcony where the eager young men had once watched helpless young women lose their minds.

Below, a few yards in front of me in the center of the room, a girl was lying on a surgical table draped with a white cloth blotched with blood, and Troy, in a white doctor's coat, was bending over her.

"Here's the pick," he said, and his voice was not his voice as he raised up something metallic; the light glinted off it and I screamed, hard.

Then Marica—not Mandy—bolted upright, knocking Troy backward. They both looked at me and Marica waved her hands in front of her face: *no harm, no foul.*

"Get away from her!" I shouted, barreling into him. "Marica, run!"

"No, no, it's all in fun," Marica said, laughing, as Troy grunted and staggered backward, grabbing me around the waist.

"Whoa, whoa," he said. "It's okay."

I pulled away from Troy. "What is this?" I asked shrilly.

"I didn't think you'd come," he said. "I thought you *believed* that. It wasn't me. Listen, please—"

"What are you doing?" I yelled, as Marica slid off the table. The white cloth was a thick, fuzzy white blanket, and the blotches were scarlet Valentine's Day hearts. A shiny silver serving tray ornately decorated with a floral pattern and large Ms—for Marlwood—contained a hammer and a single long-stemmed red rose.

"I recreated the lobotomy surgery," Troy said, gesturing with the ice pick. "I thought if we went through the steps . . . "

"Are you insane?" I asked, and I hoped he was.

He looked at me, really looked. "You have to know I would never hurt Julie. I forgot that I'd given my ID bracelet to Mandy. After we left the dance, she confessed that she gave it to Miles." He raised his brows, hopeful that I was following him. "And so, you see . . . "

"I-I remembered that, too," I said, but my voice was quaking. "But why are you here?" I looked at Marica. "Why are you doing this?"

Wrapping herself in the blanket, Marica walked over to us. She opened one arm like a mother hen and cuddled me up, giving me a kiss on my cheek. I was so cold I couldn't feel anything, and Marica winced. Meanwhile, Troy walked over to the tray and laid down the pick. His hand hovered over the rose; then he dropped his arm down to his side, facing me. His face was shrouded in darkness.

I was drowning in iciness, shivering so hard my head hurt. The center of my forehead burned as if someone were dripping hot wax onto it. I saw Troy jerk, and I stiffened.

Marica whispered in my ear, "I helped him plan this. He wants you, *chica*. He broke up with her, really, he did. Tonight." Then she frowned at me. "Are you okay? Troy, I think she's got hypothermia. Like before, when she was in the infirmary. She looks so *white*."

"I could start a fire," Troy suggested. "There's a lot of trash and—"

"No!" I yelled, making them both jump. I tilted my head, straining to see him in the darkness. "No fires."

"Are you . . . feverish?" Marica asked. She touched my forehead, then my cheeks. "Ay, she's burning up."

"Get help," I whispered urgently. "Marica, *run*."

She blinked at me, then looked over at Troy as if to say, *Are you hearing this?* He was still standing in the shadows. Why? Why didn't he come over to us, unless he had something to hide? He didn't want her to see, to *know* . . .

"Help," I begged. Icy sweat was pouring down my forehead. "Marica—"

Marica took my hand and began to rub it.

They tie you down. They take the hammer—

A clang echoed through the cavernous room. Neither one of them heard it.

There was a scream. It shot around the room like a tangible object—like a bullet, ricocheting off the walls, the floor, the table, the ice pick.

The ice pick.

I smelled smoke.

"*My love is like a red, red rose,*" Troy sang, as Marica walked me toward the table.

"Oh, God," I gasped. "It really is you." I tried to move away, but I was suddenly so tired, and dizzy. I could feel myself sinking down, down, somewhere deep and frozen, somewhere where I couldn't move my own legs or arms . . .

. . . Couldn't talk . . .

. . . Couldn't warn her . . .

"*Oh, Dios mío,* I think she's fainted," Marica said. Troy came forward then, and scooped me up into his arms. My head lolled as he carried me toward the table; I saw my reflection in the silver tray.

Only it was Celia I saw. And her skin was rosy; her brown

eyes were framed with dark lashes, and her black hair tumbled down onto her shoulders.

"Troy!" someone called. It was *Mandy*. "Okay, listen, Miles says that he has proof he was in San Covino that night."

"Linz?" Troy said ignoring her and brushing my hair away from my forehead. *From my forehead.*

"Are you listening to me?" Mandy shrieked at him. "Y-you cheating bastard!"

He ignored her. "Linz, are you sick?"

He leaned over me like this, and over her like this, promising love; and then he murdered—

The smoke thickened, making my eyes water; or I was crying. Heat rose from the floor. The rush and roar of the flames drowned out his voice.

I sat up, flung out my hand, grabbed the hammer, and hit him as hard as I could. With a shout, he fell forward. I gathered up his tux jacket and hit him again; where, I didn't know; he slumped forward, against me. Then I threw down the hammer and got the pick. My hand was shaking but I held it against his neck. I got ready to jab. He groaned.

"Linz," he said, gasping, "what . . . ?"

"Mandy, he's going to kill us!" I bellowed.

"Oh my God!" Mandy shouted. I ticked my glance toward her. In his overcoat, Miles came up behind her.

"Don't come any closer. He's possessed!" I cried. "He's David Abernathy."

"*My love*," Troy said, only it wasn't Troy, it was David. My David, my own.

"Did you hear that?" I cried.

"Troy," Mandy said, her eyes ticking from me to Troy and back again, "Troy, be careful."

"Mandy, get help," Miles said through his teeth, his gaze fastened on me. "*Go.*"

"Marica, come with me," Mandy said. "She's out of her mind. Lindsay, we're going to get someone for you—"

"No one moves," I said, holding the pick against Troy's neck. And then I thought about what I was doing. This was *Troy.*

"*David Abernathy,*" Celia insisted. "*He locked—*"

And then I saw it, as clearly as I had seen the ghost of Edward Truscott:

He gave a locket to me, and then he gave one to Belle. Belle, always the favorite. Belle, who seduced Mr. Truscott, the orderly. Who had coffee and blankets, while I froze. The heiress, the rich girl, while Leticia died of exposure and I would be next.

And David—Belle didn't love him; she only wanted to escape and so she hated me because I was in the way. I took him from her because he loved me.

So I got the rags, and I set the fire . . . and I pounded on the door shouting, "Who locked it? Who locked it?"

But it wasn't locked.

I only pretended that it was, and I couldn't help but laugh as the flames caught Belle's gown; but as Lydia died, I was a bit sad—

—And then I pulled the door open—

—And then David appeared on the threshold. He was shouting, "Belle! Belle!" And when I tried to run out of the blazing room, he pushed me back in!

He pushed me back in!

He pushed me back in!

He pushed me out of the way so that he could save her, *precious, rich* Belle, *but I swung at him, and I knocked him to his knees. Then I ran through the door—*

—Too late! The flames had caught me then! My hair was on fire! My shift, on fire, as I ran through the snow, across and into the forest; on fire as I burst down the lane, fire streaming behind me, running, ablaze!

"I killed them! I killed them all and I would do it again! Because he was mine!" I shrieked.

Troy pushed himself away from me, stumbling backwards, and I felt for the hammer. Clutching it in one hand and the pick in the other, I whirled in a circle so they would all stay away. I was burning up. Sweat poured down my face.

"Linz, stop," Mandy said, as they surrounded me. And something glinted against her coat. She was wearing . . .

She was wearing—

"My locket!" I screamed, holding my weapons over my as I ran at her. "Mine! That is mine!" I came at her and as she backed away, she tripped and fell.

I was back at the shore, by the lake house, when her eyes were black—

—And her eyes were black now, blazing with hatred, and fear—

"*Fear of me*," Celia crowed. "*At last.*"

And I got ready to hit her.

"*Kill her kill her kill her*," Celia commanded me. But she wasn't afraid; she was gleeful; she wanted this not to save herself, or me, or anyone. She wanted it because she was . . .

One by one, I killed them all. First it was the birds. And then it was the cats. And then it was Leticia.

"*I smothered her to keep her from the cold.*

"*And then it was—*

"Oh my God, no!" I wailed, dropping the pick and the hammer. *Celia* was the crazy one; *Celia* was the evil one. My *dybbuk*, her unfinished business—murder.

I kept screaming. I got the high heels and threw them at someone, at everyone, as I screamed.

As my world burned away, into cinders.

AFTERMATH

No man chooses evil because it is evil; he only mistakes it for happiness, the good he seeks.

—Mary Wollstonecraft

A thing is not necessarily true because a man dies for it.

—Oscar Wilde

THIRTY-ONE

February 18
possessions: me
>how can I live with myself? how can I stand this guilt?

possessions: them
>ignorance. and, oh, God, how i envy them

possessions: mandy
>"there are different kinds of love, but they all have the same
>aim: possession."
>—*unknown*

possessions: troy
>his backbone
>my heart

Take care of the worst ones, the ones who will try to escape. . . .

———

I WAS BACK in the infirmary, and everyone was waiting for my high fever to break. I thought it had happened, but I was pretending to be asleep, because I just couldn't face them. What did I say? What did I do?

What did I *really* see?

All my insanity had been excused—Dr. Steinberg, our campus physician, said I'd been delirious, raving, due to exposure. Running around in the snowstorm that night, I really did get very sick. My fever spiked so high they talked about life-flighting me out.

They life-flighted Kiyoko's body out, after she drowned.

I couldn't accept that I might have pushed her in. But I was the one who found her. Or that I hurt those birds, or the cats . . .

I still didn't believe that I'd done it, even when Celia was in control of me. Crazy, evil Celia, more evil by far than Mandy and her sick clique. . . .

I'm possessed by a madwoman.

When Troy and Miles carried me out of the operating theater, I heard myself "raving." After they brought me to the infirmary, I felt Dr. Steinberg and Ms. Simonet taking care of me. Swaddling me; there were drugs. I was so cold. I was on fire.

Troy came, with Julie. His arm was in a sling from when I'd hit him with the hammer. And even though they both assumed that I was unconscious, Troy sat beside me, holding my hand,

and told me that he had gone back to the lake house that night to see Mandy, to break up with her. But as usual, he had lost his nerve, which was why nobody saw him.

When we'd come back from break, Mandy had asked to wear his ID bracelet, and he'd given it to her. He'd thought she wanted it to reassure herself that he was still hers.

Now he wondered if Mandy herself had found Julie's skirt after Julie's attack. Maybe she'd planted the bracelet on it—for reasons he couldn't understand—to have power over me—but he swore to me that he had not touched Julie.

Julie backed him up, saying that she thought she must have seen him wandering on the shore after he didn't go back to the party. She apologized, both to him, and to me, adding that Spider had also made friends with Troy again. She was earnest, contrite, and so very sweet. No one was sure *what* had truly happened the night of her attack. I wondered if we'd ever know. I was so tired and drifting so badly by then that I held onto the sound of their voices—loving me, wanting to spare me any pain. I heard their sincerity, and their innocence.

The Grose clan came for a group visit, but Ms. Simonet told them they had to wait to see me, because I was too sick. Marica felt especially bad, assuming responsibility for my wandering all over campus in the snow. They left flowers and balloons--and belated birthday cards, since they'd found out they'd missed my birthday, and Marica kissed my forehead.

Miles made an appearance, discussing the sordid history of Marlwood with Dr. Steinberg. He knew about the lobotomies—after all, he had been researching the history of his family's new investment. Miles had tracked down Dr. David Abernathy, who'd survived the fire, gone on to perform many more lobotomies, and had died in Boulder, Colorado, at the age of seventy.

But the seven "last" girls—the last Marlwood inmates scheduled for the brain-destroying procedure—died the night of the fire—six in the operating theater; while the charred bones of Celia Reaves were found on the road, exactly where Troy had seen her burning ghost the night we drove back to Marlwood.

As Miles lingered beside my bed, I smelled his clove scent. I felt him wrap something around my wrist. Thread. Heard him say softly, "You can come out now. I know you're there."

It was the same thing he'd said when I hid from him in the shadows outside my dorm. I wasn't sure what he meant . . . or whom he meant it for.

Dr. Ehrlenbach and Dr. Melton came, discussing my prognosis with Dr. Steinberg. They left conferring about how to catch me back up, since I'd probably be out for the rest of the week. There was much to be done to get their little barracuda ready for Harvard, or Yale, or Brown.

"Oberlin. Maybe Vassar," Dr. Melton said.

Mandy didn't come. She stayed well away.

But in the night, in the dark, Troy came again, by himself.

"Get better soon," he whispered in my ear. "I . . . I love you." And then, he laid his head down beside mine, and dozed.

I still didn't know why he had sung that horrible song, but his warm breath melted a few of the layers of the ice around my heart.

Eventually, Ms. Simonet shooed Troy out and I was alone, with Julie's stuffed Corgi, Panda, tucked in beside me, with nightmares, memories, and questions.

If I wake up now, I thought, *will Celia be gone? Will I be free? How can I ever be free?*

A line from somewhere kept playing in my mind: *Hell hath no fury like a woman scorned*. Was Celia in hell? Reunited at last with David Abernathy?

I felt the sun on my face as the day began; and a warm tear slid across my temple.

"Hey, sweetie."

It was Julie, squeezing my hand.

"Welcome back."

I began to open my eyes.

ACKNOWLEDGMENTS:

Sincere thanks to my Razorbill team: my fantastic editor, Lexa Hillyer; publisher, Ben Shrank; and publicist, Casey McIntyre. My gratitude to my agent and friend, Howard Morhaim, and Katie Menick, his assistant. To my Facebook nation and tweeps, I truly appreciate your collective wit and support, especially on those dark nights of the soul. Hugz to friends and family, most especially the awesome Chumash Woman, a.k.a. my daughter, Belle.